KU-260-198

UNLUCKY
13

JAMES PATTERSON is one of the best-known and biggest-selling writers of all time. He is the author of some of the most popular series of the past decade – the Alex Cross, Women's Murder Club and Detective Michael Bennett novels – and he has written many other number one best-sellers including romance novels and stand-alone thrillers. He lives in Florida with his wife and son.

James is passionate about encouraging children to read. Inspired by his own son who was a reluctant reader, he also writes a range of books specifically for young readers. James is a founding partner of Booktrust's Children's Reading Fund in the UK. James Patterson has been the most borrowed author in UK libraries for the past seven years in a row.

Why everyone loves James Patterson and the Women's Murder Club

'It's no mystery why James Patterson is the world's most popular thriller writer. Simply put: **nobody does it better**.'
Jeffery Deaver

'**Boxer steals the show** as the tough cop with a good heart.'
Mirror

'A **fast-paced romp** of a read.'
Best

'James Patterson is the **gold standard** by which all others are judged.'
Steve Berry

'Master writer James Patterson conjures up more **literary magic**.'
Star magazine

'A compelling read with great set pieces and, most of all, that **charismatic cast of characters**.'
Sun

'Patterson boils a scene down to the single, telling detail, the element that **defines a character** or moves a plot along. It's what fires off the movie projector in the reader's mind.'
Michael Connelly

'James Patterson is **The Boss**. End of.'
Ian Rankin

Have You Read Them All?

1ST TO DIE

Four friends come together to form the Women's Murder Club. Their job? To find a killer who is brutally slaughtering newly-wed couples on their wedding night.

2ND CHANCE
(with Andrew Gross)

The Women's Murder Club tracks a mystifying serial killer, but things get dangerous when he turns his pursuers into prey.

3RD DEGREE
(with Andrew Gross)

A wave of violence sweeps the city, and whoever is behind it is intent on killing someone every three days. Now he has targeted one of the Women's Murder Club . . .

4TH OF JULY
(with Maxine Paetro)

In a deadly shoot-out, Detective Lindsay Boxer makes a split-second decision that threatens everything she's ever worked for.

THE 5TH HORSEMAN
(with Maxine Paetro)

Recovering patients are dying inexplicably in hospital. Nobody is claiming responsibility. Could these deaths be tragic coincidences, or something more sinister?

THE 6TH TARGET
(with Maxine Paetro)

Children from rich families are being abducted off the streets – but the kidnappers aren't demanding a ransom. Can Lindsay Boxer find the children before it's too late?

7TH HEAVEN
(with Maxine Paetro)

The hunt for a deranged murderer with a taste for fire and the disappearance of the governor's son have pushed Lindsay to the limit. The trails have gone cold. But a raging fire is getting ever closer, and somebody will get burned.

8TH CONFESSION
(with Maxine Paetro)

Four celebrities are found killed and there are no clues: the perfect crime. Few people are as interested when a lowly preacher is murdered. But could he have been hiding a dark secret?

9TH JUDGEMENT
(with Maxine Paetro)

A psychopathic killer targets San Francisco's most innocent and vulnerable, while a burglary gone horribly wrong leads to a high-profile murder.

A list of more titles by James Patterson is printed at
the back of this book

UNLUCKY 13

JAMES PATTERSON

AND MAXINE PAETRO

arrow books

Published by Arrow Books in 2014

1 3 5 7 9 10 8 6 4 2

Copyright © James Patterson, 2014

James Patterson has asserted his right under the Copyright, Designs and
Patents Act, 1988 to be identified as the author of this work

This novel is a work of fiction. Names and characters are the product of the
author's imagination and any resemblance to actual persons,
living or dead, is entirely coincidental

This book is sold subject to the condition that it shall not,
by way of trade or otherwise, be lent, resold, hired out,
or otherwise circulated without the publisher's prior
consent in any form of binding or cover other than that
in which it is published and without a similar condition,
including this condition, being imposed on the
subsequent purchaser

First published in Great Britain in 2014 by Century

Arrow Books
Random House, 20 Vauxhall Bridge Road,
London SW1V 2SA

www.randomhouse.co.uk

Addresses for companies within The Random House Group Limited can
be found at: www.randomhouse.co.uk/offices.htm

The Random House Group Limited Reg. No. 954009

A CIP catalogue record for this book
is available from the British Library

Typeset by SX Composing DTP, Rayleigh Essex

Penguin Random House is committed to a sustainable future for
our business, our readers and our planet. This book is made from
Forest Stewardship Council® certified paper.

Printed and bound in Great Britain by Clays Ltd, Elcograf S.p.A.

For Suzie and John, Brendan, Alex, and Jack

PROLOGUE

KA-BOOM

ONE

IT WAS AN ugly Monday just after noon. There had been no sign of sun so far, just a thick fog that had put the blocks to traffic around the Golden Gate. I was behind the wheel of the squad car, and Inspector Rich Conklin, my partner of many years, was in the seat beside me when Claire called my cell phone.

Claire Washburn is my closest friend, and also San Francisco's Chief Medical Examiner. This call was strictly business.

"Lindsay," Claire shouted over the braying of car horns. "I've got two DBs in a single-car smash-up and I don't know what the hell I'm looking at. If you and Richie are in the neighborhood, I could use another opinion."

3

She gave me her location, and I told her we'd be there as soon as weather and traffic permitted. I repeated to Rich what Claire had said and turned the car around.

My partner is smart, steady, a glass-full type of guy, and on this particular day, he was pretty happy with himself.

He said, "Claire wants us to look at a traffic fatality?"

"She doubts it's an accident."

I followed Lincoln through the Presidio and past the Crissy Field Overlook toward the bridge as Conklin called Brady and told him we were answering Claire's call. He phoned Claire and said we were about eight minutes out, then picked up where he left off, asking my advice on his romantic dilemma.

"It's Tina's birthday. We've been together for two months," he said. "So what do I get her that means 'I like you a lot *so far*'?"

This line of conversation was tricky. Rich is like a younger brother to me. We're tight. We talk about everything. But, his ex-girlfriend Cindy is my home girl. And Cindy was still suffering from their breakup six months ago. She hadn't given up hope that she and Richie could get back together.

To tell the truth, I was hoping for that, too.

I kept my eyes on the road, staying on Lincoln, a two-laner flanked by historic buildings on the left and a parking lot on the right for visitors to the bridge. We drove slowly past the nifty old houses on Pilots' Row and then hit a wall of traffic.

"Looks like we're walking," I said.

I braked on the shoulder, turned on the flashers, grabbed my Windbreaker, and locked up. Then my partner and I started up the incline. Richie didn't miss a beat.

"So I was thinking I'd get her a pair of earrings. Or does the *ring* in *earring* send too much of a message?"

"Not unless they're diamonds," I said.

"Hah," said Conklin.

I said, "Rich, in my humble opinion, you and Tina are at flowers and dinner. That's safe, sweet, and her mother won't send out invitations."

"Okay. And do I sign the card *love* or not?"

I couldn't help it. I rolled my eyes and threw a sigh.

"Richie, do you love her? Or don't you? *You* have to figure that one out."

He laughed.

"Could you stop giggling?" I said.

He gave me a salute and said, "Yes, ma'am, Sergeant Boxer, ma'am. And could you put in for a sense of humor?"

"You're asking for it," I said.

I gave him a little shove, and he laughed some more, and we kept walking up the incline, passing cars that were inching forward and passengers who were getting out, shouting curses into the fog.

My cell phone rang again.

Claire said, "Hurry up, okay? I can't hold off the damned Bridge Authority much longer. The tow truck is here."

TWO

THE SCENE WAS surreal, and I don't use the term lightly.

From what I could see, a late-model red Jeep had lost control in the outside northbound lane and then careered across five lanes before hitting the walkway barrier and slamming into the railing, which was bulging to accommodate the Jeep's front end.

All but one lane had been closed, and a narrow ribbon of traffic was open to alternating northbound and southbound traffic that crawled past the Jeep, which was swallowed by fog up to its taillights.

Law enforcement vehicles were haphazardly parked on the roadway: Bridge Authority SUVs,

Fire Department, CHP vehicles, black-and-whites, and personnel to match were all clumped up around the Jeep. I saw people I knew from the ME's Office shooting pictures of the accident. A traffic cop heaved over the railing.

At the same time, a tow truck was pulling into position to remove the Jeep, in prep for reopening the road, the only thoroughfare between San Francisco and Sausalito.

A Bridge Authority uni checked out our badges and called out, "Dr. Washburn, you got company."

Claire came out from behind her van, shaking her head, and said, "Hey, you guys. Welcome to some kind of crazy. Let me give you the tour."

She looked worried, and as we closed in on the Jeep, I saw why. The windshield had exploded outward, the front end was crushed accordion-style, and as I peered into the passenger compartment, my scalp actually crawled.

I've seen a lot of gruesome scenes in my fourteen years in Homicide, and this one vaulted to the top of the "most gruesome" list. I mean, number one.

Two adults, white male in the driver's seat, white female in the passenger seat, both looked to be in their late teens or early twenties. Their arms were akimbo and their heads thrown back, mouths open in silent screams.

But what drew my attention directly were the victims' midsections, which were gaping, bloody holes. And I could see where the blood and guts had gone.

The driver's side was plastered with bits of human debris mixed with fragments of clothing and other detritus I couldn't identify. One air bag was draped over the steering wheel. The other covered the passenger from the thighs down.

Claire said, "We've got blood and particles of human tissue stuck all over everywhere. We've got damage to the seat belts and the dashboard and the instrument panel, and that's a button projectile stuck in the visor. Also, we've got a dusting of particulate from the air bags sugaring everything.

"These areas right here," she said, pointing to the blown-out abdomens of the deceased, "this is what I'm calling explosive points of origin."

"Aw, Christ," Rich said. "They had bombs on their laps? What a desperate way to kill yourself."

"I'm not ready to call manner of death, but I'm getting a handle on cause. Look at this," Claire said. She got an arm around the passenger and leaned the young woman's body forward. I saw spinal tissue, bone, and blood against the back of the seat.

My morning coffee was now threatening to climb out of my throat, and the air around me seemed to get very bright. I turned away, took a couple of deep breaths, and when I turned back, I had the presence of mind to say, "So, this bomb, or should I say *bombs* plural, blew all the way through the bodies?"

Claire said, "Correct, Lindsay. That's why my premature but still educated opinion is that we're looking at a bomb that exploded from inside the abdomen. Abdomens, plural.

"I'm thinking belly bombs."

THREE

THE LUNCH-HOUR RUSH had escalated from peeved to highly outraged. Traffic cops were taking crap from irate drivers, and TV choppers buzzed overhead like houseflies circling a warm apple pie.

The tow truck operator called out in my direction, "Hey. Like, can someone extract the victims? We gotta open the bridge."

Here's what I knew for sure: I was the ranking homicide cop on the scene, the primary investigator until the case was permanently assigned. Right now, my job was to protect the scene from contamination, and, no joke, the scene was a six-lane highway.

I marched over to the tow-truck driver and told

11

him, "Thanks, but the wreck is staying here and please extract your truck from my bridge."

As the tow truck moved out, I addressed my fellow law enforcement officers, saying, "Whatever this is, it's *not* an accident. I'm locking the bridge down."

"Bravo," Claire said. "We agree."

I dismissed nonessential personnel and phoned Charlie Clapper, head of CSU. I told him to drop whatever he might be doing and hustle over.

"Jam on the gas and jack up the sirens," I said.

I reported in to Brady, told him what I knew. He said he would get hold of the chief and the mayor, and would be on scene ASAP.

Yellow tape was unspooled and a perimeter was set up with a wide margin around the Jeep. Roadblocks were placed at both ends of the bridge. Conklin and I documented the scene with our cell-phone cameras and notepads and chewed over some theories.

I was enormously relieved when Clapper's van came through with a flatbed truck behind it. Both vehicles parked outside the cordon, and the unflappable Clapper and half a dozen criminalists disembarked.

Clapper is a crisply turned-out man in his late forties, a former homicide cop, and a very fine CSI. I went over to him and said, "I don't think you've ever seen anything like this."

After I briefed him on what I was calling a crime scene, we walked over to the wreck and Clapper poked his head into the vehicle.

He took a long look, then backed out and said, "It's an explosion, all right. But the way I understand belly bombs, they're mechanical devices, surgically implanted. Powder. Cap. Detonator. I don't see wires. I don't smell explosive powder. And this is strange," Clapper continued. "The blast was restricted to the front compartment. Bombs of this type are meant to blow up not just the vehicle, but everything around it. You're right, though. This is a new one on me."

I said, "We've run the plates, but I want the bodies ID'd before *Eyewitness News* notifies next of kin."

I pointed to a red nylon backpack in the rear foot well. After a tech shot photos of the bag and the fairly untouched rear compartment, I gloved up and unzipped the bag. Inside was a toy dog, a bunch of CDs, cell-phone charger, and a blue spangled wallet.

Inside the wallet was a driver's license.

"Our female victim is Lara Trimble, twenty-one, lives in Oakland," I said.

There was a mess of paper litter in the rear compartment foot well and I found myself staring at something that might be important.

"Can you shoot that?" I asked.

Once forensics had photos, I lifted out a hamburger bag that hadn't been damaged in the blast.

"Hello," I said out loud. "Is this where they had their last meal?"

Clapper said, "Thank you," and then deftly took the bag from my fingers and sealed it in a glassine envelope. "This is what we like to call evidence."

Claire joined us and said, "Charles, what are you thinking?"

"I'm thinking that this scene is going to be on the national news in a wink. The FBI, Homeland Security, ATF, as many Feds as can fit on the deck will be here in a half hour and the bridge will be closed until next Christmas. For twenty-four hours, anyway."

The Golden Gate Bridge was a high-quality target, an American icon. Bombs on this bridge would scare everyone in San Francisco. It was scaring the crap out of *me*.

I called Brady's cell and said that we were looking at possible terrorist activity.

He said, "Shit. Of course we are."

Then we all stood around in the swirling fog and waited for the Feds to arrive.

PART ONE

SAVE THE LAST DANCE FOR ME

Chapter 1

A WEEK AFTER belly bombs exploded inside two graduate students in a red Jeep, and because nonmetal bombs were of major concern to federal law enforcement, the Feds were working the terrorist implications. And they'd pretty much shut the SFPD out of the case.

While the FBI huddled and labored at our local FBI offices, the tide of worldwide headlines about a mysterious one-car crash that tied up the Golden Gate Bridge for an afternoon receded and were replaced by breaking news of a movie star's divorce, political shenanigans, and a significant freeway pile-up in south LA.

Meanwhile, the SFPD was treating the belly bombs as an unsolved crime, very likely a double homicide, and by SFPD, I mean Claire, Clapper, Conklin, and me.

It was just after 6:00 p.m. on a Monday night, and Conklin and I were at our desks in the Hall of Justice, home to the criminal courts, the DA's Office, and the Southern Station of the SFPD. Homicide is on the fourth floor.

My partner and I work at facing desks in the bullpen, a windowless, twenty-by-twenty-foot square of fluorescent-lit gray linoleum floors and dingy walls of unknown color. There are twelve desks in this room. At the moment, we had the room to ourselves and were reviewing the sparse facts of our belly bomb case.

Over the past couple of days, we'd interviewed the victims' families. Lara Trimble's grief-stricken loved ones swore that Lara had no enemies and that she was a music student, not a political activist.

David Katz, the young man who had driven the Jeep, had been doing postgrad work in psychology. Besides being shattered, his parents were completely dumbfounded by their son's unexplained and tragic death. They hadn't even the slimmest guess as to why David and Lara had been killed.

Our week of thorough investigation into Trimble and Katz's backgrounds and associates bore out the opinion of their family circle. These kids were not radical anything. They were victims.

Claire was still working with Clapper on what could have been the explosive element and its delivery system, but for now, all we had was comprehensive documentation of the demolished car and a Whitman's Sampler of trace evidence courtesy of the FBI.

Essentially we had zip, zero, nothing to go on that hadn't been evident when we stood on the bridge a week ago.

I looked at the scene photos for the hundredth time, scrutinizing them for something, anything, I may have missed. But when the night shift began filtering into our humble squad room, I was ready to close the book on the day.

I got my gear together and waved hello to cop friends and goodnight to Richie, leaving him on the phone cooing to Tina. My seven-year-old Explorer was waiting for me in the lot on Harriet Street, and when I turned the key, she started right up.

Twenty minutes later, I came through the front

door of the roomy apartment I share with my husband, Joe, our six-month-old baby girl, Julie, and Martha, my border collie sidekick and Julie's best doggy friend.

I called out, "Sergeant Mommy is home," but there was no clicking of doggy toenails on hardwood, no "Hey, sweetie."

It was way too quiet. Where *was* everyone?

I had my hand on the butt of my nine as I went from room to room and back around to the foyer, the little hairs on the back of my neck standing up as I checked reference points: keys missing from the console, baby bottle in the sink, Joe's slippers by his chair, empty crib—when the front door swung open.

Martha shot through the opening and jumped up on me. My gorgeous and wonderful husband was right behind her, wheeling our child's stroller into the foyer.

"Hey, Julie," Joe said, "Look who's home."

I threw my arms around his neck, gave him a kiss, picked up my darling girl, and danced her around. I have to say, Julie is the most gorgeous baby on the planet—and I'm not just saying that because she's ours. She's got her daddy's dark hair and both of our blue eyes, and actually, I can't take her out without people rushing over to her and saying, "Oh, you're so cute. Do you want to come home with me?"

And Julie will smile and put her arms out for them to take her! It's kind of a riot—and it kind of scares me, too. I can't turn my back on Julie for an instant, because she might go with *anyone*.

"We played a little softball in the park," Joe told me.

"Oh, right. Good idea."

"She said she's going to sleep through the night."

"Ha-ha. I want that in writing."

"Why don't you take off your piece and your shoes and stay awhile," said my husband, clicking on the evening news. "Soup's on in ten minutes."

Love, love, love coming home. Just love it.

Chapter 2

I SPENT HALF the night talking to Joe about the belly bombs. And it wasn't just pillow talk. Joe Molinari was former FBI, also former deputy director of Homeland Security, and now a highly regarded consultant who was content to be Mr. Mom while I fulfilled my calling in Homicide.

Joe had been over the case with me a few dozen times already, and he said, when we were under the covers in the dark, "Sooner or later, the bomber is going to take credit for this."

I said, "Huh," and rooted around in the creases of my mind, thinking that for certain bombers, that was true. But not all of them.

I remember that Joe got up for the baby twice. I

did it three times, and suddenly it was eight and I was late.

At nine-ish, I parked my car in my favorite spot in the shade of the overpass and went directly to the ME's Office. The reception area was full of cops and plainclothes guys standing around, wishing for cigarettes and hoping for autopsy reports.

There was a new girl at the front desk—very cute, wearing her blond hair in a low ponytail. She introduced herself: "I'm Debbie Day. The new intern."

I congratulated the young woman and told her that Claire was expecting me, which was a lie that Claire always backed up.

I found Claire in the autopsy suite, stripping off her gloves as her assistant rolled a corpse out of the room toward the cooler.

She said, "I love how I think about you and you just materialize."

"You got something?" I asked.

"Yeah. If I hadn't had my hands full of internal organs, I would've texted you."

Claire unsnapped her gown and hung it on a hook and peeled off her cap. I followed her through to her office, dying every second to know what kind of news she had.

She settled in behind her desk, rolled her chair until she was in just the right place, and said, "I got something from Clapper that he got from the Feds. What the belly bombs consist of."

"Holy crap. Tell me."

"Here's the nutshell version. Trace of some kind of magnesium compound was found in stomach contents that were sprayed around the Jeep. The compound was ingested—you with me so far?"

"If I was any more with you, I'd be sitting in your lap."

"Stay where you are. I've got no room on my lap."

"Fine."

"Okay, so, this compound interacts with stomach acid."

I blinked a few times, then said, "You're saying that those kids *ate* something and when it got to their stomachs—*ka-boom*."

"Exactly," said Claire.

Until new or contrary evidence challenged our theory, I was calling the belly bomb case a double homicide.

Chapter 3

I WAS STILL wrapping my mind around bombs you can eat when Claire picked up her ringing phone and got into something long and windy with a lawyer who wanted her as an expert witness.

While I waited for Claire's attention, I stared at the picture on her desk of the four of us in what we cheerfully call the Women's Murder Club. The four members are Claire, Cindy, Yuki, and me.

Claire was the bosomy African-American stalwart in the middle of our group, a mom three times over, my best buddy for the past dozen years, a woman with a heart big enough to move into and set up housekeeping.

To her right was Cindy, a sweet-looking bulldog of a reporter, working the crime desk at the

Chronicle, who'd helped me bust a few criminals in her search for an exclusive story. Cindy and I have fought at times. Lots of times. She doesn't back down until she's tried every possible way around me and a few impossible ones. But I know her well and love her fiercely.

To Claire's left was Yuki Castellano, who had given up private law to prosecute bad guys for the DA's Office. She's a bird-size beauty, a high-speed talker, a brilliant woman who has caught some bad breaks and still never says die.

I was the tall blonde on the end of the line, wearing my working-cop clothes and a sour expression. Bah. I don't know what was bothering me the day that picture was taken. Well, taking a guess, maybe our new lieutenant, Jackson Brady, had stepped on my toes.

In front of me in real life, Claire picked up her intercom line and yelled into her phone, "Debbie, tell Inspector Orson to cool his giant heels and I'll be with him in ten minutes. Hey, tell him to get coffee. I like mine with a lot of sugar."

Claire slammed the phone down and said, "No peace for the weary."

"I think you mean 'No rest for the wicked.' "

"That, too."

The phone on her desk rang.

"Don't take that, okay?" I said. "What do you make of this ingestible bomb?"

"Well," said Claire. She uncapped a bottle of water and took a really long pull. Then she said, "Since you ask, I believe this belly bomb was as personal as a knife."

"Meaning?"

"It was a micro-bomb so it was easy to disguise. Limited impact because it was only meant to kill one person at a time."

"So these kids were targeted?"

"Not necessarily. Could have been random. Remember the psycho who put cyanide inside Tylenol capsules."

"So those one-person bombs were a kind of message?"

"My thoughts exactly," said Claire. "Both of us go to the head of the class."

Chapter 4

DEBBIE CAST A slim shadow through the doorway to Claire's office and changed the subject big time.

She said, "Yuki Castellano is on line five. Wants to speak to both of you. She said, and I quote: 'If you don't put them on the phone, you'll be sorry you came to work today.' Unquote. She was kidding, right, Dr. Washburn?"

"Was she laughing?" Claire asked.

"Well, yeah. The cutest laugh I ever heard."

Although Yuki was our resident bad news bear, she'd been quite merry lately. She'd won a couple of cases and was getting along well with her big hunk of burning love boyfriend.

Debbie gave me a knowing look. "Doctor, all of your friends try to walk right over me."

Claire said, "That's them teaching you to push back. Thank you, Debbie." Then she stabbed a button, putting Yuki on speaker.

Yuki chirped, "I knew you two were together, goofing off, eating doughnuts, drinking coffee, livin' la vida loca."

"Are you high, sweetie?" Claire asked.

"You bet I am. Love makes me a little goofy."

"Tell us something we don't know," I said.

"Okay, how's this? Brady and I are getting married."

Yuki let loose one of her trademark delightful merry-bells chortles. There was a long pause as Claire and I stared at each other across Claire's desk, just trying to comprehend what Yuki had said.

Claire recovered first.

"Did I hear you right, Yuki?" she said. "You're not fooling with us, are you?"

"I'm at the bridal shop. Right this minute."

I had just gotten used to Yuki dating my boss—now she was marrying him? Well, never mind the kink their relationship had put in the chain of command. Yuki was getting married.

"Oh. My. God," I said, "Did you expect this? Or

were you surprised by what could be the best news of the year?"

"Sur-prised!" she shrieked. "Brady's divorce came through. So he just hangs up with his lawyer, rolls over in bed, and he says to me, 'Nothing to stop us now.' "

Yuki treated us to another round of happy-over-the-moon laughter, then took a breath and chirped, "We're saying the I do's on Saturday."

I said into the speaker phone, "Saturday? What Saturday? This Saturday?"

"Yes. So listen, I hired this great wedding planner, and all you girls have to do is put on the dresses and show up. Details to follow."

"We're wearing bridesmaids' dresses?" I asked, totally horrified.

"Of course. Pink ones. Off the shoulder. Big skirt."

Well, Cindy and Claire would look good in pink. I would look like a half-baked ham.

"Don't worry, Linds," Yuki said. "You can use it after the wedding. It's a nice little cocktail dress."

"And I was just sitting here wishing I had an off-the-shoulder pink cocktail dress," I said, laughing in order to keep the terror out of my voice. "Can I get a tiara to go with that?"

Yuki laughed and said, "I'm kidding about the dresses, girls. I'm not having any maids of honor, none of that. Having a judge. Having vows. Having food. Having dancing. Sound okay?"

"Brilliant," Claire said. "We're throwing your engagement party. For four. Tonight."

Right after we said good-bye to Yuki, I left Claire's office, jogged through the breezeway, and entered the back door to the lobby of the Hall of Justice, with its super-size ceilings and garnet-colored marble walls. I took the stairs to Homicide and after passing through the squad's outer office went through the little swinging gate and into the bullpen.

I said, "Yo," to our PA, Brenda, and then made my way around the desks in the bullpen. I found Brady in his hundred-square-foot glass cubicle at the far end.

He looked just like always—delts and biceps pulling the fabric of his blue shirt, white-blond hair pulled back and banded in a short pony, head bent over his computer.

I'd had a few issues with Brady since he'd taken over my old job as squad boss. From the first, I bucked at Brady's impersonal management style. But lately, I hate to admit, I've become a fan. He's impartial. He's decisive. And he has a track record as a really good cop.

I knocked on Brady's glass door. He said, "Come in, Boxer."

I did and kept coming, all four steps to his desk. Then I grabbed his shoulders and kissed him.

"Congrats, boss."

The look on Brady's face was priceless.

"Thanks."

I was grinning my face off as I crossed the squad room to my desk and Conklin's. My partner looked up from his computer and said to me, "I saw you kissing up to the boss."

"He and Yuki are getting married. Swear to God. And we've got a hot lead. So, let's get to work."

Chapter 5

I SWUNG DOWN into my desk chair and said to my partner, "The explosive material in the belly bomb is a magnesium compound and the victims ingested it."

"They ate it? And it exploded? That's not possible."

"I'm quoting Claire, who got that from the FBI lab. They found a trace of the compound in the stomach contents. Seems that stomach acid activates the explosion."

"Damn," Conklin said, rocking back in his chair. "Do the Feds have any theories as to who put this stuff into the food?"

"Not yet. I'm way open to anything you come up with."

I pulled up the scene pictures again, this time focusing on the hamburger bag and waxed-paper wrappers among the pile of litter on the floor. The hamburger bag had come from Chuck's Prime, a chain of fast-food restaurants that had made a name for themselves for hamburgers of superior grass-fed, made-in-America beef.

I turned my computer so Conklin could see the photo and said, "Look here. I think Trimble and Katz had a couple of Chuckburgers—and sometime not long after that, they blew up."

Conklin said, "There's a Chuck's in Hayes Valley, about fifteen minutes south of the bridge."

We signed out a squad car and Conklin drove. I listened to the car radio with half an ear while Conklin said, "I should tell you, Linds. I eat at Chuck's twice a week. Maybe more."

"I've had a Chuck's bacon burger a few times and have to say, they're pretty tasty."

"Yeah," Conklin said. "Might be time for a change."

Twenty minutes later, we parked at the corner of Hayes and Octavia near the park known as Patricia's Green and in the heart of the Hayes Valley commercial district, a strip with trendy shops, boutiques, restaurants, and cafés.

In the middle of the block was a big parking lot, and beside the lot, like a sunny seaside trattoria, was Chuck's.

The outside tables were shaded by market umbrellas, and inside, a counter wrapped around two walls, and square wooden tabletops formed neat lines. Few people were eating burgers at this time of morning, but the serving folks were ready for the lunch crowd, smartly dressed as they were in aqua cowboy shirts with pearl buttons and tight white jeans.

I badged the girl at the cash register and asked to speak to the manager. Mr. Kent Sacco was paged and about thirty seconds later, a pudgy man in his early thirties came from an office at the back and greeted us with a sweaty handshake and a business card.

We took a table by the front windows and I told Mr. Sacco that the victims on the bridge last week may have eaten their last meal at Chuck's.

I said, "We need to see your security tapes."

"Sure. Whatever I can do for you."

"We need contact information for your kitchen and serving staff."

Sacco took us back to his office, where he printed out a list of personnel with copies of their photo IDs. He left us briefly and returned with security DVDs from the four cameras, two positioned inside and two outside the restaurant.

On the way out, Conklin bought burgers and fixings to go. In the interest of full disclosure, when we got back to our desks, I offered to take one of those sandwiches off Conklin's hands. I was nearly starving. Still, I scrutinized the meat very thoroughly. Then I closed the sandwich and ate it all up. It was delicious.

Conklin and I watched videotape for the rest of the day, jumping a little when we found the gritty images of David Katz and Lara Trimble ordering hamburgers, sodas, and fries to take out. A young cowgirl behind the counter took their order and their cash, then handed them the bag of food. The victims took the bag and left with their arms around each other.

We looked at the footage forward and back, enlarged it, sharpened it, focused on every area in the frame.

No one but the girl behind the counter had

spoken to Trimble and Katz, and there was no altercation of any kind.

I called Clapper and brought him into the loop. He asked me to forward the employee contact material to him and said he'd call his FBI contact.

"They're gonna tear Chuck's apart," he said.

Chapter 6

IT WAS THE end of the day. We were nowhere on belly bombs and I was hungry. I was pulling on my jacket when Brady dropped by the double desk I share with Conklin.

"I just got a call from the FBI," he said.

"Belly bomb bulletin?"

"Just open the mail I sent the two of you."

Conklin and I both did that and saw a grainy black-and-white photo of a woman leaving a post office on a rural street. I almost recognized her, but not quite. Conklin, however, looked frozen. He looked shocked.

Brady said, "That's our old friend Mackie Morales, in a one-stoplight town in Wisconsin."

I got it now. Mackie had clipped her long, curly

hair, a standout feature of her natural beauty. Now her dark curls were very short and she was wearing a canvas jacket to midthigh. Mackie was angular and thin. She could dress like a man and get away with it.

Along with recognition came images and chilling memories of Randy Fish, a savage serial killer who had fixated on me. Fish should be on death row, but instead he was serving out his eight consecutive life sentences in some extra-toasty corner of Hell.

Fish's lady love was this woman, Mackenzie, aka Mackie, Morales, midtwenties, who had spent the summer right here at the Southern Station of the SFPD. Posing as an intern while working her way to her PhD in psychology, she had worked her way into Conklin's heart and used information she gleaned from interning with us to commit some murders of her own.

Her plan had been to distract us, impress her lover, and set him free.

Her plan had backfired.

She, too, should be languishing on death row, but she had escaped from a hospital bed and hadn't been heard of again—until now.

I looked over at Conklin, who was staring at the image of Morales. I knew that he was still ashamed that this criminal nut job had conned him. Actually, she'd conned both of us.

I flashed on Morales's three months in our house, a proficient and slippery killer convincingly disguised as our cheerful back-office summer temp. No one was safe while Morales was free.

"So is she in custody?" Conklin asked Brady.

"Afraid not. This was a random video from a security cam across the street from the post office in Two Rivers, Wisconsin. That's about a half hour from Cleveland. Someone who had been in the post office recognized Morales from the wanted poster, and after a few days, this video ended up at the FBI.

"She could be anywhere by now," Brady said. "So keep your eyes open. And have fun tonight, Boxer. Take good care of my baby."

Chapter 7

CLAIRE HAD PUT Yuki's all-girl engagement party together in a flash. Instead of going to Susie's Café, our customary watering hole, we met at Rickhouse, a restaurant bar in the financial district known for its sophisticated cocktails and its cozy brick and bourbon-barrel-stave decor.

I was late, but with a little help from the maître d', I found Claire, Yuki, and Cindy in the mezzanine level overlooking the bar below.

Yuki was radiant in office wear: vintage I. Magnin, 1960s black silk chiffon with rhinestones, and she was wearing her open-toed silver pumps that she never gets to wear.

She also had her mom's diamond ring, a four-carat solitaire the size of a cocktail onion, on the ring finger of her left hand. That thing almost lit up our little table in the dark.

Claire stood to let me slide in next to Yuki, saying, "We're drinking something called 'Corpse Reviver Number Five.' Should be our signature Club cocktail."

"What's in that potion, if I may ask?"

Cindy said, "It's the reverse of embalming fluid," and lifted her glass to show me her sunny-looking drink. Like me, Cindy is blond, but unlike me, she's got corkscrew curls and adorable, slightly overlapping front teeth, and she's a graceful size six.

"The key ingredient is tequila," she said. "We've got Yuki on pass-out alert. Brady's going to pick her up when we call."

Yuki grinned and said, "Thanks for having faith in me."

We said, "You're welcome," in unison. It was no secret that Yuki was an easy drunk with a weakness for margaritas, and this Corpse Reviver was close enough to her favorite drink.

I ordered what they were having, and when my drink arrived, we toasted the bride-to-be in turn. We'd given her a lot of crap over the years for her go-nowhere relationships. One of her former frogs had actually set out to kill her.

"To Yuki, with thanks for putting an end to the frog parade."

"I'll drink to that," she said.

"To you and Brady," said Cindy. "Perfect together."

"I'll drink to that, too," said Yuki, already slurring softly. She guzzled her drink down to the bottom of the glass.

Claire said, "Darlin', here's to the best sex, best friends, and best times, for the whole of your lives."

"Hear, hear," I said.

We clinked glasses of lemony-pineapple-y tequila, and Yuki put down her empty glass and dipped her head. I saw a couple of tears gathering in her eyelashes. I put an arm around her shoulder.

"Hey. Don't cry. What's wrong, for Pete's sake?"

"Happy tears," she said. "How much I love the three of you. And I miss my daffy mom."

"She would've loved this," Claire said. "You getting married to that big, brave, blondy-haired man."

Yuki smiled. She cocked her head and in her

mother's voice she said, " 'Yuki-eh, be good wife. Cook what he likes. Say yes alla time. Keep yourself up.' "

We all laughed. And then asked Yuki a hundred questions, which she answered in full—about the wedding plans and the honeymoon, and she told us that she and Brady were going to live in her apartment, which had been her mother's, once they came home from their cruise.

Claire grabbed the check and Cindy leaned toward me and said, "I may be too sloshed to drive."

"Then I'm your designated driver," I told her.

Once Cindy was strapped into my passenger seat, I buzzed down the windows and fired up my trustworthy Explorer. As I drove, I told her about the belly bombs—off the record. And when I finished with that, I told her about the Mackie Morales sighting in Wisconsin.

Cindy sighed, then said, "She was bound to turn up sometime, but I guess I thought maybe she'd stayed off the FBI's radar by crossing the border."

I knew Cindy was thinking about Mackie and Richie.

I was thinking about Mackie, too. The last time I saw her, she was bloodied from the crash that killed Randy and narrowly missed killing their baby. I had seen Richie getting into the ambulance with Mackie cuffed to the stretcher. And that was the last of Mackie until Brady's news of her today.

Mackie shouldn't have escaped. It was a crime that she was on her own two feet with nothing to stop her from killing again.

I was just about to go on a rant about Morales being a textbook psycho when the phone in my pocket rang with Joe's ringtone.

I filled my husband in on my location and ETA and by the time we hung up, I was parking in front of Cindy's apartment, the place where she and Richie had lived together.

I wanted to tell Cindy again that she needed to move into a new apartment, start fresh where she wouldn't see Rich in every room, but before I could open my mouth, Cindy leaned over, gave me a big hug, and said, "Don't worry about me, Linds."

"I can't help it," I said hugging her back.

"I'll be fine, okay?"

"Okay."

Of course I worried about her. Cindy was tough

but not invincible. I watched her until she disappeared behind her front door. Then I pulled my car out onto Lake Street. I thought of the four of us Cindy had jokingly dubbed the Women's Murder Club.

Claire and I were in good, happy marriages, and Yuki was about to tie the knot with a demonstrably good man. As I drove home to my dear husband waiting up for me and my little girl asleep in her crib, I felt grateful and very lucky.

I fiercely wanted good luck for Cindy, too.

Chapter 8

CINDY WENT THROUGH her ground-floor apartment, switching on lights, thinking about how just about every time she was with the girls and something interesting came up in conversation, one or all three of them would turn to her and shout, "That's off the record, Cindy."

It was a recurring joke, and actually not all that funny. So here was the thing. If she was going to be preemptively accused of running off with private tidbits for public consumption, she might as well do it.

Tonight, when Lindsay told her about the Mackie Morales sighting in Wisconsin, she had neglected to post the usual warning. So if Morales wasn't off the record, she was on. And Morales was *huge*.

Morales had killed three people. She was a fugitive. And she'd never been interviewed. An in-depth Mackie Morales story was a crime reporter's dream.

Cindy had worked the crime desk at the *San Francisco Chronicle* for five years and according to the publisher, she was a rising star. She'd gotten regular pay bumps and a coveted office with a door, and her byline had been on the front page regularly, top of the fold, on the home page of the website.

But by Cindy's own admittedly high standards, she hadn't blown the lid off the cooker.

Cindy went directly to the bay window niche in the front room, which she used as an office. She booted up her laptop, and while it loaded, she went to the kitchen and put on the kettle. After that, she washed her face and changed into plaid pajama bottoms and one of Richie's SFPD T-shirts with the slogan, Oro en Paz, Fierro en Guerra. ENGLISH TRANSLATION: "GOLD IN PEACE, IRON IN WAR."

Cindy was well aware that wearing Richie's shirts, living in these rooms, sleeping in the bed they'd shared together, made it harder to get over him. But she wasn't ready to get over him.

She loved him. He loved her. He'd proposed and she'd said yes. Then she'd blown it.

She vividly remembered the night they'd broken their engagement, on Jackson Street in the rain, after a fight about having kids, a fight they'd had many times before.

Here was the headline:

He wants kids. She wants a career. First.

They both insisted that it had always been so.

But the imminent lifetime commitment had caused them to polarize their individual needs. At least that's how she saw it. She hadn't said that she'd never be ready to have children, but that's how he'd taken it.

By then, Mackie Morales had faked her way into the SFPD and manipulated Richie perfectly, even using her adorable fatherless little boy in a scheme to use Richie for her own purposes.

Richie was far from stupid, but he'd gone for it. That's how good Morales was. And when she was exposed as a stone-cold killer, Richie's heart and faith were shattered again.

File the whole mess under Humpty Dumpty.

Tonight, when Lindsay mentioned that Mackie Morales had been sighted, an idea with the size and brilliance of a four-carat white-diamond solitaire had burst into her mind.

She was an excellent investigative reporter.

She could track Morales down, trade information for exclusive access. A first-person interview with Mackenzie Morales would be a stunning career move.

By the way, Rich Conklin would know what she'd done, and he'd be moved.

Actually, she was pretty sure that he'd welcome an opportunity to see her again.

Chapter 9

CINDY TOOK HER mug of Earl Grey into her home office, facing Mission Street, and got settled in her hydraulic chair with the memory foam seat. She checked her e-mail and returned all work-related messages.

Then she opened her original files on the Mackenzie Morales/Randolph Fish story.

She reacquainted herself with Morales: She was born in Chicago, and although unmarried, she had had a child with the infamous convicted serial killer Randy Fish, a boy named Ben, now age four.

Cindy read up on the three murder charges against Morales, and she reread her own interview with Lindsay, who had witnessed Fish's last mortal moments and death.

And there was the quote she'd gotten from the SFPD press liaison: "Mackenzie Morales had confessed to three homicides and was in police custody at Metropolitan Hospital when she escaped. She is an extremely intelligent individual and may be armed and dangerous.

"If you see Mackenzie Morales, don't approach her. Contact the SFPD."

Duly noted.

She went out to the Web and typed "Mackenzie Morales" into her browser. A second and a half later, a list of Morales-related stories filled her screen.

She opened the most recent articles first and saw pictures of Morales being wheeled into the ambulance bay four months ago. The familiar figure walking alongside the gurney was Richie. Rich had been in some kind of hell.

She stared for a moment, then clicked through.

After reading all the publicly available information on Morales and Fish, she signed on to LexisNexis, the by-subscription electronic database for legal files and public records.

The legal files on Fish were extensive. The FBI had linked him to the bodies of eight young women who had been brutally murdered. Fish was a sexual sadist, a type of killer that got off on torturing his victims. The pathology had been documented and studied for hundreds of years.

Fish had never given a press interview, but as Cindy paged through court transcripts, she found one bit of information that had gotten little, if any, attention. Randy Fish's father had owned a small house on Lake Michigan in a town called Cleveland, Wisconsin.

When Cindy went through the tax records, she found that the property was still in William Fish's name. It was not in arrears and it had never been sold.

This was significant. Morales had been seen within thirty miles of William Fish's lake house.

Cindy grabbed her mug and held it in both hands. She was getting a rush from linking two facts that had never been linked before.

She imagined interviewing Morales. She could see the small gray room, gray table, Morales in orange with handcuffs and chains. She would sympathize with the woman, get her to open up about Randy Fish. Cindy would write a double exposé of Fish and Morales that could very well become a crime classic, like the interviews of Bundy, Gacy, BTK, and Dahmer.

Fish and Morales put Bonnie and Clyde in the shade.

First, she had to get a go-ahead from her boss, *Chronicle* publisher Henry Tyler. Tyler liked her, but this story would take her out of state and away from her regular assignments.

She would have to be damned convincing.

Cindy put her laptop into sleep mode, then went to bed. She hugged the king-size body pillow that used to be Richie's.

She lay awake for more than an hour, organizing her pitch, refining it. When she woke up in the morning, she was invigorated—fired up and ready to go.

Chapter 10

CINDY WAS READY for her 8:15 a.m. meeting with Henry Tyler when she entered the old Gothic Revival-style *Chronicle* Building at the intersection of Mission and 5th. She went directly to her office and put down her bags, then took the elevator to the executive floor.

When the doors opened, she said "Hey" to the receptionist, who buzzed her in through the double glass doors.

She walked down the carpeted corridor to Tyler's office. She was five minutes early. Which was perfect.

Tyler was behind his enormous glass desk in his many-windowed corner space, furnished in pewter-colored leather with enormous abstract canvases on three walls.

He was a handsome man in his fifties, a Harvard graduate and former reporter for the *New York Times*, former war correspondent for Reuters, and now corporate honcho.

Tyler put down the phone and beckoned to Cindy to come in, saying, "I haven't seen you in a while. Is everything okay?"

Cindy's pitch had to be both comprehensive and concise, and she had probably two minutes to sell Tyler on her idea.

She took a seat across from his desk and said, "I'm fine, Henry, thanks. Listen, I've kept an open file on Mackie Morales. You remember her—"

"Sure. She was attached to the SFPD—and to Randy Fish. His love interest, right? She shot three people dead."

Cindy nodded and said, "Morales is a pretty spectacular killer, Henry. She's beautiful and cold. Killed three people that we know about—and she's only twenty-six. Her relationship with Fish was symbiotic. I think he was her mentor and she inspired him. But there was love and sex involved, highly unusual for a sexual sadist like Fish to love someone who fit his victimology. And they have a child."

"Huh," said Tyler. "Interesting. So you want to do some kind of Sunday-magazine piece on this killer couple?"

"I want to get an interview with Morales."

"You've lost me."

"Well, I saved the kicker. I've got a hot lead, an authenticated sighting of Morales that I'd like to follow up. I connected that lead to a location—and I think I'm the first and only person to have done so.

"If I'm right, and I find Morales, I'll turn the cops onto her, provided I'm in at the takedown. I'll negotiate with them for access beforehand. And then, as long as that falls into place . . ."

"A lot of big *ifs*."

Cindy laughed.

"You know I love to turn big ifs and cold maybes into 'git 'er done.' "

Henry treated her to a generous smile.

"Keep going," he said. "I'm enjoying this."

"Morales has never been interviewed," Cindy went on. "Even the SFPD didn't get to interrogate her before she escaped. I know a ton about Morales. I know people she knows. I think I can flatter her into a tell-all about her love affair of the century with Randolph Fish."

"You're saying you're that good."

Cindy grinned. "Exactly."

Tyler said, "Do I need to remind you that on a danger scale of one to ten, ten being psychopathic killer—"

"She's a fifteen. I know, Henry. I'm just scared enough to be smart about this."

Tyler nodded thoughtfully.

"Don't get me wrong. You had me at 'Morales.' I'm just saying I don't want to be delivering your eulogy, you understand, Cindy?"

Cindy smiled. "This will make you feel better. I have a carry permit. I have a gun."

Clearly impressed, Tyler said, "You're a surprise a minute, Cindy. And you've been practicing?"

"You bet. Target practice every weekend for two years. I was living with a cop, you know."

Tyler pushed his chair away from the desk, swiveled it, and looked out the window.

"How long do you need?"

"I'll keep you posted on that."

At nine, Cindy went to Human Resources, signed a release, and arranged for a cash advance. Her overnight bag was in her office and her small but efficient gun was in its case in an inside pocket.

Three hours later, Cindy flew out of SFO— destination, the city of Cleveland, Wisconsin.

Chapter 11

THE NEXT MORNING, having spent a restless night on a sprung motel mattress, Cindy dressed in brown trousers, a Fair Isle sweater with pastel colors around the neck, and brown leather boots with flat heels. She pulled her blond curls into a ponytail with bangs, put on her camel hair coat, and tucked her snub-nosed Smith & Wesson .38 Special into the pocket.

She checked out of the Red Moon Motel using her corporate card and headed due west in her rented Ford Focus. Her computer bag was on the seat next to her, milky coffee was in the cup holder, and she had programmed the GPS with the address of William Fish's lake house in the woods.

She couldn't know for sure if Mackie Morales

had been staying at the Fish house, but it was a good bet. Morales had been seen in a town only thirty minutes from this lightly populated area on the ragged fringe of nowhere.

Cindy's instincts rarely let her down, and right now they were swearing that she was on the right track.

Driving north, Cindy easily found Lakeshore Drive, which hugged Lake Michigan's shoreline. She passed blocks of nice older homes on wooded lots on her left, the lake just visible through thinner clumps of trees on her right.

She continued on, and as she drove farther away from the town, the homes became more spaced out, then sparse, sunlight flashing through gaps in the woodland like strobe lights.

Ten miles out, the GPS spoke and Cindy took the car right onto a dirt road toward the lake. The road was more like a rut, bumpy and potholed, winding between walls of trees crowding in on both sides.

The road branched into a narrower dirt rut, and as the GPS announced, "You have reached your destination," Cindy saw a green chalet-style house at the edge of a clearing. The white trim and the lines of the house were crisp against the dark woods behind it, making the house look almost like a paper cutout. The lake wasn't visible from here.

Cindy drove past the house and stopped her car on the road to the lake. From where she had parked, she could see the house through a break in the woods.

Cindy cut her engine and took her binoculars from her bag. From what she could see, the house was in good repair. There was no mailbox and no car, and the only sign that the house was occupied was a small tricycle on the sun-deprived patch of grass that served as a lawn.

Was someone living here?

Or was the place abandoned?

Cindy thought about getting out of the car and approaching the house with a story of being lost, in case someone was there. She wanted to take a look through the windows, listen, and maybe even ring the bell.

But since her cloak of invisibility was at the dry cleaners, she couldn't take the chance that Morales might open the door with a loaded gun in hand.

The tricycle wasn't proof, but it was a definite

maybe that Morales was here, seeing her boy.

Cindy had done what she'd come to do. She'd checked out her lead, and now she needed help with the next step.

It was time to see what kind of deal she could cut with the local authorities.

Chapter 12

CINDY WAS WITH Captain Patrick Lawrence in his office on West Washington Avenue, the Village of Cleveland PD.

The captain was a big, stocky man, about forty, with thick brown hair and florid skin. He was wearing a sling, recovering from a gunshot wound to the right arm from an accident at a gun show, where a one-chambered bullet went off.

Lawrence was on the phone with someone called Reilly, saying he couldn't use a phone or his computer or even a pen, for Christ's sake, and don't even think of pulling a gun. He listened to Reilly for a few seconds, then laughed and said, "Yeah, my left hand works okay."

Cindy looked around the office. She saw the

shelf of Green Bay Packers bobble-heads, the marksman plaques on the wall, the photos of the captain with a twelve-point buck, and a family photo with a good-looking wife and four boys who looked like their dad.

Lawrence was saying, "I gotta go, Reilly, but thanks for your support."

He hung up the phone and turned to face Cindy.

"Sorry about that," he said. "My brother-in-law was worried about me. Now, do I have this right? You're a reporter from San Francisco and you have a line on a fugitive who was seen in my district?"

"She's wanted for murder," Cindy said. "Multiple murders."

Lawrence said, "And the name of this fugitive?"

"Not so fast, Captain," Cindy said. She smiled, showing that despite the ponytail and the pastels, she was a pro. "I want to help you catch this person, but I need something in return."

"Christ, yeah. You want me to go out with you on a fishing expedition, and if we hook something you want an exclusive story. Something like that, Ms. Thomas?"

"Exactly like that, Captain. And if this is a

fishing trip, we're trawling for a Great White that's been spotted in these waters."

The captain grinned at her. Nice grin, actually.

"I can tell you're a writer," he said. "What's the nature of your lead, Ms.—"

"Please call me Cindy."

"Okay, Cindy. Explain what you know and spare me the bull, please. I got a limited number of people on my force and none of us are going anywhere until I verify this killer you say is around here."

Cindy told the captain that the fugitive was wanted by the FBI and had been captured on videotape within thirty miles of Cleveland.

"I'm not going to name my source—not now, not ever. But I scoped out the location this morning, Captain. This fugitive has a small child. I saw a trike on the lawn.

"Maybe that's nothing," Cindy said, "but this house would make an excellent hiding place for this individual."

The captain tapped his fingers on the desk and said, "Cindy, that's just not enough. We can't go out to some location where there might be a dangerous felon without doing our own scoping.

Give me the address and let me do this right.

"I'll send out some guys in unmarked cars, vans, whatever, see who is coming and going, do our due diligence, before we show up with guns blazing. You follow me?"

"I understand. And now I have to be clear, Captain. You want to catch this fugitive before she runs. You really do."

"I hear you. Now give me the name. If there are warrants out, I'll work something out with you. Do we have a deal?"

Cindy stuck out her hand and the Captain shook it with his good one. Cindy was spelling out "Mackenzie" when Captain Lawrence's good hand paused over the keyboard.

"Mackie Morales. That's Randy Fish's woman."

"Right. You know about Fish?"

"Went to school with him. He was always a little shit, but I underestimated him. He turned out to be one of the biggest turds to come out of this state in a hundred years."

"He was ruthless and cunning," Cindy said. "So is Morales."

Captain Lawrence said, "I'm on board with you, Cindy. Tell me what you know."

Chapter 13

AN HOUR AFTER meeting with Captain Lawrence in his office, Cindy was sitting in the passenger seat beside him in a cruiser, parked on the same section of dirt road beyond the green house where she had parked earlier this morning.

The captain's terms had been good enough for Cindy.

She could ride to the location in his car. She had to stay back from any action. Anything he said was off the record unless he said she could quote him. She couldn't take pictures. She couldn't hotdog or in any way go off on her own, or the deal was null and void.

In exchange for giving him the lead, Captain Lawrence would give Cindy credit for the tip, and he'd give her whatever advantage he could in protecting her exclusive on the story.

It was a great deal, and Cindy liked the captain and felt sure that he wouldn't go back on his word.

And the operation was seriously in play.

Minutes after she and the captain were in place, a second cruiser had blocked off the long dirt drive where it branched off toward the Fish house. There was a boat on the lake and two teams of armed men were hidden in the woods.

Now a white van marked Zimmer Construction came up the drive to the house. The radio in the captain's car came to life, Sergeant Bob Morrison reporting that he and Officer Barton were going to go to the door.

Captain Lawrence told them to go ahead, then said to Cindy, "I looked you up. That story you wrote about Randy Fish. I read it at the time. I'm sorry I didn't recognize your name."

"That happens. Like all the time."

"It was a good story, and you wrote it well. I keep going back in my mind, trying to picture Randy, asking myself when he turned into such a monster. He was brought up in a good family. Bill Fish was a dentist—"

The radio crackled and Lawrence grabbed the mic and said, "Morrison, what's happening?"

"No answer to the doorbell, Captain. We're going to take a look around back."

The two cops dressed as construction workers disappeared from view. A couple minutes later, they returned to the front door of the house. The one named Morrison cupped his hands at the front window and looked in.

After that, Morrison gestured to his partner, who also peered through the glass. Lawrence opened the mic and said, "What have you got, Morrison?"

"The house appears wired, Captain. Booby-trapped."

"Get out of there now," said Lawrence.

Cindy listened to the rapid-fire radio communications between the captain, the men in the woods, and the undercover cops, who got back into their construction van.

Cindy's mind was on fire. She saw how this story was going to start: right here, with Morrison telling Lawrence that the house was rigged to blow. This was a beautiful lede. A movie-style fricking opening.

Lawrence released the brake and headed the car south toward the main road with the construction van following right behind.

He said, "Cindy, we have to talk."

"Absolutely," she said to the captain. "The house is wired. Booby-trapped. This means that she set up explosives so that if the law came in through the door—"

"I *mean*," said Captain Lawrence, "we have to talk about our deal. If Morales is staying here, we can't let on. She may come back if she thinks her safe house is still *safe*. That's what we want.

"Now I have to call the FBI. You can thank me later for keeping you out of *that*. They will not make a deal with you, but you *will* have to give up your source. Count on that.

"Also, Morales may have had nothing to do with wiring that house. And as I understand journalism, if you can't verify it, you can't write it. Am I right?"

"You're right as to the kind of journalism I do."

"Okay, then. Bottom line, Cindy," Lawrence said, turning to her as he negotiated the rutted road. "You cannot write a single word until or unless I say so. Not one single word."

Chapter 14

MY PHONE RANG on the table next to the bed, cracking my deep sleep wide open.

I was pretty sure it was Saturday. I looked at the clock. 10:30 a.m. I had slept at least six hours straight and—hey, the baby wasn't crying. Cause for celebration!

The phone was still ringing.

Joe groaned beside me. He said, "I'll get her. My turn."

I said to Joe, "It's Brady," and I reached for the phone.

I asked myself, why was Brady calling me? He and Yuki were getting married today. I clicked to answer the call, hoping he just needed me to pick up something for the wedding and Yuki hadn't gotten cold feet or there'd been a quadruple homicide and he was handing off the case to me.

I said my name into the phone.

"Boxer, someone just called in something that sounds like a belly bomb. You want it? Or you want me to give it to Paul Chi? It's your call."

I said, "You know me too well."

I took the address and said I'd be on scene in twenty minutes. I didn't see how I could do that, but belly bombs were mine. I called Conklin, who said his car was in the shop. And he was at Tina's house.

"Get dressed," I said. "I mean now."

I had fallen into bed last night thinking that Joe and I were going to make love in the morning. Pretty sure that he'd been having similar thoughts.

I got out of bed and opened the closet. Pulled out a pair of jeans and a man-tailored white cotton, no-iron shirt. My usual.

"No fair," Joe said.

"I'll make it up to you, Joe. I swear I will."

"I think I've heard that before. A few thousand times."

I laughed. I got dressed, strapped on my shoulder holster, and put on a jacket. My blue one. One of my three almost identical blue blazers.

Then, I took the dress I was going to wear to the wedding out of the closet—a gorgeous deep blue, almost-black dress with a swishy taffeta skirt, a cinched-in waist, and a pleated matte jersey bodice. My sapphire pendant on a chain would look good with this. Oh, my.

I hung my dress on the back of the door, then rooted around the closet shelf and found the box with my barely-ever-worn black Stuart Weitzman shoes. I put the box on the floor under the dress. I just couldn't wait to put on some glam.

I said to my husband, "I'll check out the scene, and with luck, I'll be back in a few hours."

"Right," said Joe. "I'm not feeling lucky."

"Will you make sure Maria Teresa is on to babysit for Julie?"

"You bet."

"Are you mad?" I asked.

"Hell, no," Joe said. "What makes you happy, makes me, uh, happy enough."

I told Joe that I loved him "this much" and spread my arms.

He laughed, and I kissed him, then looked in

on the baby and blew her a kiss so that I didn't wake her. Martha followed me out to the door and yipped. She also gave me the big, pleading eyes.

I nipped back into the kitchen and filled her bowl. "Okay, Boo?"

Christ.

I was still at home and the crime scene was waiting.

Chapter 15

CONKLIN GOT INTO my car, combed back his brown forelock with his fingers, and said, "Brady said it's a belly bomb?"

"That's what it sounds like."

We drove to Scott Street near O'Farrell and parked in front of a brown-shingled, two-story house, one of a dozen just like it that squatted under a tangle of overhead lines on a tree-lined street in the Western Addition.

Officer Shelly Adler, one of the cops at the door, ran the scene for us, saying that the victim was a white female, dead on the kitchen floor in a world of blood. There were no signs of a break-in or any kind of altercation between the single mom and the son who lived with her.

"As for belly bombs, Sergeant," Adler said, "I've got no idea. She's still warm, so she hasn't been dead long. Her name is Belinda Beadle. Her son, Wesley, is upstairs in his room with my partner. The kid is sixteen."

Conklin and I signed the log and had just walked through the door, when a brown-haired teenage boy burst down the stairs and came toward us. Adler's partner called from the top floor, too late.

"Wes. You can't go down there."

The boy looked bad: pale, wide-eyed, maybe in shock. There was blood on his hands and smeared on his cheeks, and his T-shirt was soaked with it.

He grabbed my arm. Hard.

"It's my *mom*," he said. "She *exploded*. Like those people on the *bridge*."

"Tell me what happened, Wes," I said.

His chest heaved, and he put his hands to his eyes and cried. After a minute, he used the hem of his T-shirt to wipe his eyes and said, "I came home late last night or this morning, and was sleeping in my room. I heard a sound, like *boom*. And so I got up and ran down and found my mom on the floor with blood pouring out of her, from here."

Wes Beadle grabbed his stomach with his hands.

"I tried to get her to speak to me. I tried to wake her up, but she was *dead*. She was *dead*."

He looked horrified. Devastated. And it hurt me to think that he would never be able to forget what he'd seen this morning. That he'd relive the sight of his dead mother for the rest of his life.

Conklin and I left Wes with Officer Adler and, after clearing the barrier tape between the front room and the rest of the house, found Belinda Beadle on the kitchen floor near the sink, lying in an odd position. She was sitting on her left side but leaning about thirty degrees toward the floor. Her light brown hair had been brushed. She was barefoot and wearing makeup and a navy-blue bathrobe.

As Adler had said, there was a lot of blood. It had soaked through the front of her robe and made a wide pool on the floor. The blood appeared to have come from her midsection, but the way her body was leaning, I couldn't see where she'd been wounded. But I did see that her robe was intact. Unlike the clothing of the belly bomb victims in the Jeep, the garment hadn't been shredded.

I conferred with Conklin and then called Clapper and the weekend ME, Dr. Massimo. I reported in to Brady, and my partner and I returned to the front room.

I had more questions for Wesley, who was sitting in a chair flanked by two uniformed police officers.

I asked him, "Do you know of anyone who wanted to hurt your mom? Did she have a boy-friend? Did you or your mom bring home hamburgers? Or any takeout food?"

He answered: No, no, no, and no.

When the Crime Lab van pulled up, I asked Officer Adler to take Wes out to her cruiser and keep him company for a while.

Crime scene analysts streamed into the small house. Conklin and I stood off to the side as they took photos of the body and everything that surrounded it. I asked them to open the kitchen trash bin. I saw no hamburger wrappers. No fast-food packaging of any kind.

The ME arrived and the body was turned and lifted onto a sheet.

That's when one of Clapper's techs found the Glock under Ms. Beadle's body.

I said to the tech, "Do an instant GSR, will you?"

As the tech swabbed the back of Ms. Beadle's hand, Dr. Massimo opened the woman's robe.

He said, "Don't hold me to it, but at first look, death was caused by a bullet to the heart at close range."

If the wound was self-inflicted, as it appeared to be, Belinda Beadle wanted to have an open-casket funeral. And maybe she thought her teenage son wasn't home when she took her life.

"Her right hand is positive for GSR," said the tech, showing me the test vial.

Conklin and I took Wes Beadle down to the Hall and gave him a clean SFPD sweatshirt. Then we interviewed him with tape rolling. He told us, yes, his mom had a gun. Yes, that was her gun. Yes, she'd been sad lately. But he didn't know she was *so* sad. And, no, he didn't always come home on Friday nights.

Wes was crying, blaming himself for being a bad kid, and I just had to do it. I got up and opened my arms to him, and he fell into me, hugged me hard.

Child Protective Services came about then. Wes

had an Uncle Robert who lived up the coast, and I promised I would keep calling him until I reached him.

I was speaking with Robert Beadle and had just told him about the morning's events, when my phone alarm beeped an alert I had programmed into my phone. What was it?

I could hardly believe it. The wedding was starting in forty-five minutes—and Conklin and I were both in work clothes.

Speaking for myself, I could not miss Yuki's wedding.

I just couldn't let that happen.

Chapter 16

I GAVE CONKLIN the keys to my car and called my husband. "This is an emergency, Joe. SOS."

It took Joe almost a half hour to get to the Hall. He was wearing a two-thousand-dollar suit that he hardly got to wear anymore, and my hot designer dress was hanging from the hook in the backseat of his Mercedes.

He'd even remembered to bring my shoes.

And my makeup kit.

I love my husband. *Love* him.

I got into the backseat, and Joe took the famous rollercoaster streets of San Francisco at pretty close to the speed of sound.

I struggled in back with undergarments, snaps, and fasteners as the car climbed and swooped. It was almost a riot. The makeup, well, that was an *actual* riot. I viewed my face in a two-inch-square mirror and did my best to color within the lines. I sprayed myself with fragrance and got a little on Joe.

"Hey," he said. "Watch out, Blondie."

We arrived at City Hall and parked in the underground lot with two or three seconds to spare. It was so perfect that Yuki was getting married in City Hall, a stunning building, so familiar to all of us in law enforcement, who passed through constantly.

And she was getting married in the Ceremonial Rotunda.

Joe grabbed my hand and we ran upstairs to the beautiful round hall laid entirely in Tennessee pink marble. About fifty people were clustered at the foot of the staircase waiting for the wedding ceremony to begin.

I saw Brady, taller than almost everyone there, his pale blond hair hanging loose to his shoulders. He was wearing a slate-blue suit that made him look like a movie star.

Brady turned toward me, and I saw Yuki, out-rageously beautiful in a white satin sheath, her hair swept up and held with pearl combs. Her bouquet was a great bunch of creamy peonies with trailing pink ribbons. Oh, my.

Together, Brady and Yuki looked like they should be in the Style section of the *Chronicle* as the most beautiful couple of the year.

Yuki called out, "Okay, we can start now. Lindsay is here." And then her laughter echoed in the round, and Yuki did a little dance of her own devising. Brady doesn't laugh out loud too much. In fact, this might have been the first time I'd ever heard his hearty "Ahahaha."

Judge James Devine wore a black suit and a yellow bow tie. He cleared his throat, and as the wedding guests grouped at the foot of the stairs, Yuki and Brady climbed them in tandem. They stood opposite the judge under the grand 24-karat gold dome like figures on the top tier of an extraordinary pink wedding cake.

The vows were simple, time-honored.

"Dearly beloved, friends and family, we are gathered today to witness the joining of this man and this woman in matrimony."

I thought of my own wedding, not so long ago, and my heart was there with Yuki and Brady when they exchanged vows and rings.

Judge Devine said, "On the east wall, there is a wonderful engraving of Father Time. The inscription reads: 'San Francisco, O glorious City of our hearts that has been tried and found not wanting. Go through with like spirit to make the future thine.'

"That is what I wish for the two of you.

"And now I pronounce you, Jackson, and you, Yuki, husband and wife. Jackson, you may kiss your bride."

Brady took Yuki's face in both his hands and kissed her and then he lifted her into his arms. To a wonderful echoing cheer, Brady carried our dear friend down the stairs.

My husband kissed me and said, "I love you, Blondie. That much."

I told him that I loved him that much, too.

We all ran out onto the street in our wedding finery, like a flock of tropical birds.

I was ready to dance.

Chapter 17

I DON'T KNOW how Yuki's wedding planner managed to get a private room at Epic Roasthouse with so little notice, but she did it. This great restaurant was wall-to-wall glass panels with a full-on billion-dollar view of the Bay Bridge and the San Francisco Bay. It doesn't matter how many times you see this wonder of wonders, it never gets old.

We had cocktails and I found myself standing with Brady. He said, "I can't believe what a miracle it is that I found Yuki. And you introduced us, Lindsay. You did that."

"Yeah. Well, she was visiting me, and you came over to my desk. So, okay, I guess I introduced you."

"You deserve all the credit. My brother will tell you. She saved my ass from a life of grouchiness and solitude."

"Your brother Doug? He already told me."

Another great laugh from Brady. "Yep, I'm so lucky to have found Yuki."

He went on in that vein a few more times. It was funny to hear him sounding like a young kid.

And then someone clinked a fork against a glass, and dinner was served. Our private room had its own dedicated chef, and the tables were arranged in a horseshoe so that we could all see the lights of the bridge and the glittering moonlit waters.

Joe and I sat at a table with Brady and Yuki, Brady's two enormous blond brothers, Greg and Doug, and Yuki's uncle Jack, her only relative in San Francisco.

Cindy, Claire, and her husband, Edmund, who plays bass with the San Francisco Symphony, completed the guest list at the head table.

The first course, spicy citrus ceviche, arrived, and during the next five courses, there were toasts to the bride and groom. Brady was roasted by his brothers, making everyone laugh helplessly. And Yuki's coworkers and Murder Club friends offered warm anecdotes and best wishes that made our eyes water with sentiment.

Once the dishes were taken away, the lights were dimmed, and Judge Devine, who was a weekend disc jockey, cranked up the CD player and started with Bobby Darin's up-tempo classic "More."

Yuki and Brady took to the floor and soon the space between the tables was packed with couples, backlit by the Bay Bridge.

Rich and his athletic-looking, hot new girl-friend were stunningly good dancers. They had their moves down, as if they'd been dancing together for years. I wanted to be mad at him for bringing Tina to Yuki's wedding, where Cindy could see how good they looked together, but realistically, a lot of time had passed since he and Cindy had broken off their engagement.

It was okay for Richie to be moving on.

I took a few turns around the floor with Joe, then switched off with Claire and danced with Edmund Washburn, who was very smooth.

When I needed a break, I left the floor and

found Cindy, pretty in baby blue, sitting alone at the table. She hadn't said anything more than hi to me all evening.

I could see it all in her face: the love and the pain.

Judge Devine put on something slow, Nat King Cole's "Unforgettable," which was just divine.

I put my hand on Cindy's shoulder and said, "May I have this dance?"

"You don't have to do that, Linds. I mean really. No."

"Come on. Just one dance. No strings attached."

"And *why* do you want to dance with me?"

"Uh. Because you look so fetching sitting here, clutching your wineglass?"

"Okay, that's not it."

"Because I love you?"

Cindy flashed me a smile and got to her feet, and I walked her a couple of yards to the dance floor.

I took her in my arms, turned her so she was facing away from Conklin and Tina. I said, "Relax. Let me lead."

She laughed.

Then she said, "I'm fine, Lindsay . . ."

"And what?"

"And I love you, too."

Chapter 18

CINDY PAID THE cabdriver and stepped unsteadily up the walk to her front door. She fiddled with the key, went inside her dark apartment, and locked the door behind her. She bounced off the hallway walls a couple of times on her way to the bedroom, where she undressed, dropping her clothes on the floor.

Images of Rich and Tina flooded her, and she had no defense. They looked good together. They were having fun. It was pretty clear from the way they danced, and from the fact that Tina was Richie's plus-one at Yuki's wedding, that this date wasn't their first or their last.

Lindsay was right when she assumed that watching Rich and Tina dancing together was agony for her. And Lindsay didn't know the rest of it. She didn't know about her trip to Wisconsin.

Cindy turned on the shower, sat down in the corner of the tub under the hot spray, and sobbed over what a total loser she was. She'd blown the best relationship she'd ever had, and she'd gone to Henry Tyler and basically told him she was teeing up her Pulitzer Prize. Now what was she going to tell him?

Henry, Morales wasn't there.

When she was all cried out, Cindy dressed in striped-pink flannel, top and bottom, no T-shirt with SFPD slogans or attached memories of her Richie.

She wanted another drink, but she made coffee, turned on the gooseneck lamp in her home office, and booted up her Mac. After her mailbox loaded, she opened an e-mail from her new friend Captain Patrick Lawrence of the Cleveland, Wisconsin, PD.

Hey, Cindy,

Just to let you know, the FBI bomb squad defused the explosives in case some knucklehead campers come up from the lake and break in. There were three trigger points. Good thing Morrison saw a wire. The milk in the fridge had a sell-by date of two weeks ago. That's all I know. The Feds are keeping sharp eyes on the place and we can always hope Morales drops by. Thanks again and take care.

Pat.

Cindy leaned back in her chair and stared at the ceiling. She was going to have to tell Henry Tyler what happened to her glorious mission and she would have to come up with another plan. Somehow, she didn't know how, she was going to have to "git 'er done" or die trying.

Cindy wrote back to Captain Lawrence and then got to work researching every place Morales had been in her entire twenty-six years on earth. Morales was no Randolph Fish. She was no genius, just a merciless killer bitch.

Where could that bitch have gone?

Chapter 19

MACKIE MORALES WALKED quickly along West Washington Street in the Loop, Chicago's central business district. It was a Monday morning, and pathetic office workers were marching into ugly gray office buildings. Cars and taxis sped past like they were actually going somewhere. The streets were gray, the people were gray, and the very atmosphere was gray.

It was a day when coats and hoods were everywhere and, therefore, unremarkable.

Mackie had been born in a hospital only a short jog from here. She knew every street in this city—every alley and every building and where it fit into the cityscape. She didn't even have to look up as she crossed LaSalle and continued on toward the bank in the middle of the next block.

Randy began speaking to her from inside her head, where he was forever safe. He was saying she should put up her hood to foil the security cameras and to slow her pace.

Hug the shadows, sweetheart. Be a shadow. You know?

"Gotcha, lover."

Sometimes she could see his face. That was the best, but even when she couldn't see him, he was with her. Talking to her. Keeping her company. Watching her back.

Bury yourself in pedestrians.

"I wasn't born yesterday, baby."

He laughed and she smiled, pulled up her hood, and jammed her hands deep in the pockets of her gray three-quarter-length waterproof coat. Her right hand fitted the grip of her Ruger quite naturally.

Mackie saw her reflection in the windows of the shops she passed: the boutique with silly girly clothes on display, and the AT&T store, murky inside with a crowd of customers; then the dark glass of the bus shelter, where four people clustered together, staring out at the street.

Now she was at the entrance to the Citibank branch, her destination. She walked through the open doors as two women were coming out, passing between her and the armed security guard. The guard was in his twenties, out of shape, and carrying a lot of excess gear in the heavy leather belt around his waist.

He didn't seem to notice her.

Still moving forward, Mackie passed the ATMs on her left and, keeping her head down, entered the main part of the bank. It was warm inside and lit with bluish light from the overhead fixtures, making the space evenly bright. No shadows here at all.

Randy was humming a lilting, wordless tune in her mind. He did that sometimes, and she found the melody sweet and comforting.

She looked around the bank, assessing the customers and the bank employees, sweeping her gaze across the circular customer-service station to her right, where a large customer rep with purple bangs and her middle-aged paunchy colleague attempted to calm an irate man with a big battered briefcase.

Directly ahead, to the back of the bank, were

the teller windows. A line of three customers waited to conduct their transactions, and Mackie joined the queue.

The woman in front of her was maybe twenty-five, wearing a full-length yellow raincoat. She had a heavy handbag over her shoulder and black rubber boots. She was reading something on her tablet and seemed lost in it.

Mackie figured it would take about four minutes to get to one of the three tellers, and Randy agreed, suggesting that Mackie use the time to read their body language.

Mackie observed the nearest teller, a gray-haired white woman in a blue silk blouse, speaking in brief rehearsed sentences to her customer. Next to her, a white male teller was counting out money, paying close attention to the count, then counting again.

The teller to his right was a black woman, pretty, wearing a tight floral-print blouse and a gold chain around her neck. She was laughing at something the customer had said.

Mackie thought the old woman would probably take directions best.

The line advanced and then the black teller

flipped on the light at her station to show that her window was open. She looked at the woman in the yellow slicker standing in front of Mackie and said, "Miss? You're next."

Mackie walked right up to the woman in yellow, close enough to see the chipped red polish on her fingernails. Mackie said, "Gee, I think you dropped this."

The woman turned her head and looked at Mackie, who had taken her Ruger out of her pocket and now pressed it hard into the woman's side.

She didn't need Randy to feed her her lines.

"This is a gun," Mackie said quietly. "You want to live? Do exactly as I say."

Chapter 20

THE WOMAN IN yellow said, "What?" and stiffened her back.

Mackie hissed, "Keep your eyes front. What's your name?"

"J-J-Jill."

"Jill, we're going up to the window. Be good or be dead. Understand? Let's go, now. Move."

Randy's voice inside her head: *You're doing fine, baby doll. Wake her up.*

Mackie said, "Jill. I. Said. Move."

"Please don't shoot. *Please.*"

Mackie gave the woman a hard poke and they crossed the eight feet of granite floor between the rope line and the teller's window. The teller wore a name tag on her blouse. SANDRA CARNAHAN.

Sandra said, "And how may I help you ladies today?"

Mackie leaned in and speaking over Jill's shoulder said, "I have a gun. Act normal."

"I understand," the teller said. Her eyes were huge and fixed on her.

"Don't hit the alarm, or I *will* shoot."

"I have a baby," the teller said.

"Good for you, Sandra. Your baby wants you to clean out your drawer and give the cash to me. No dye packs. No alarm. Screw with me and your baby loses her mom."

"I'm doing it. Don't worry." Sandra sniffed.

She opened her drawer, piled three stacks of bills into the metal transom, then flipped it so that it opened on the customer side.

Mackie reached around Jill and had just wrapped her hand around the money, when Jill lost it. She *screamed*.

Sandra was hyperventilating, looking like she was going to scream, run, or both. All the eyes in the bank went to Mackie and the woman in yellow.

Inside Mackie's head, Randy said, *Sandra stepped on the button.*

Really? Big mistake, Sandra. This is on you.

Mackie raised her gun, aimed, and fired. The bullet punctured the plexiglass window, but Sandra had ducked under the counter. Mackie turned to see everything going crazy. People dove behind pillars, got under desks, pressed against walls.

Jill dropped to the floor, covered her head, and began keening, "Nooooo, nooooo, noooooo."

Mackie spoke in a cold monotone, saying to Jill, "Look what you made me do."

She fired twice, bullets punching neat holes in the yellow vinyl. Then Mackie turned to face the audience from her place on the stage.

Chapter 21

MACKIE FELT A surge of adrenaline, the good kind that made her fearless and able to do anything. She had killed before but only in a crowd.

Blending in was her strength.

This was something different.

She held her gun in front of her and yelled out into the open areas of the bank, "Everyone get down on the floor. *Down*. I'll shoot anyone who moves."

People scrambled, dropped, covered their faces. Briefcases, phones, and umbrellas clattered to the floor and echoed in the new silence.

It was as if time had frozen, and Mackie used that solid moment to take stock.

She saw everything in sharp detail: the paralyzed faces of customers and bankers, the fat girl with the purple bangs, an office girl with big black glasses, a white-haired man with a red face that was turning blue.

She noted the clock on the south wall reading 10:03, the vid-cams on the pillars, the shock on the guard's young face.

She could make it. She would.

She had the money, a loaded gun, and a clear path to the front doors thirty yards away.

Time resumed. The guard came to life and took a stance in front of Mackie, holding his gun with both hands. He looked young. Green. Terrified.

The guard shouted, "Drop it, miss. Cops are coming. You can't get away, miss. Now, lower your gun. Slowly."

Randy was speaking: *Go ahead, Mackie. Make my day.*

Mackie wanted to laugh. Firing her gun, she landed three shots in a tight pattern around the guard's neck and chest. He grabbed his throat and, looking stupefied, collapsed to the floor. Blood spilled. He wheezed and exhaled his last breath.

Mackie scampered toward the guard's body and

scooped up his gun, and when she turned back to face the crowd, she was holding a gun in each hand.

That should give any heroes pause before rushing me.

She was on camera. She knew that. Cops were coming. But not very fast.

She backed toward the doors and pushed one open with her shoulder. She shouted into the bank, saying, "First person out the door after me gets a shot to the head. Have a nice day."

And she was back outside in the gray morning.

Mackie drafted along behind a group of three white-collar tools on North Dearborn, unbuttoning her coat as she walked. Ten yards ahead was a trash can next to the bus stop. Mackie blended with the passengers getting off the bus. She emptied the pockets of her gray hooded raincoat and transferred the cash and her Ruger to the navy-blue coat she wore underneath the gray one.

She dropped her gray coat into the trash and kept moving, plumbing her pockets as she walked, smoothly putting on sunglasses and slicking on bright lipstick. She fluffed her hair. She had changed her appearance in maybe thirty seconds.

Mackie felt exhilarated as she continued on, walking north at a moderate pace, crossing West Randolph against the light.

She guessed she had about a couple thousand dollars, which would be enough to get the hell out of Chicago.

But the real plan, the one that included making an actual home for Randy and Ben in a new place, with new names—that plan had been destroyed when Randy died.

She had Sergeant Lindsay Boxer to thank for that.

She would thank her in person, though.

She could hardly wait.

Chapter 22

AT THREE IN the afternoon, the bustling Seattle waterfront was swarming with passenger arrivals, food and luggage transport, and other commercial vehicles bringing fuel and cargo into the Port of Seattle. A cruise ship was moored along the waterfront at Pier 66.

Yuki and Brady were in the backseat of their hired car, holding hands as the car nosed through traffic into a sliver of a parking spot outside the pier. The driver got out and opened the car door for Yuki. Brady exited on the other side and signed for the ride.

Their luggage had been sent on ahead, and Yuki took in the salty marine air and thought about the future. She was married! She was Jackson Brady's *wife*. She loved her husband, loved him so much.

And there was no other way to say it: her job wasn't the center of her life anymore.

"There she is," Brady called to her.

"She" was the *FinStar*, the flagship of the Finlandia Line, dead ahead, moored on the far side of the terminal. This grand ship would be taking her and Brady and about six hundred other people on a ten-day luxury tour of Alaska.

Even from here, the *FinStar* looked entirely awesome. The car pulled away, and Yuki's husband called out, "You okay?"

"No."

"What's wrong?" he asked, his face full of concern.

"I'm not okay. I passed 'okay' about six months ago. I'm over the *moon,* Brady. I'm over *Pluto.*"

He grinned at her, put his arm around her waist, and walked her toward the terminal doors.

"I hope we can handle this, sweetie. Ten days with nothing to do but enjoy ourselves. It's been about twenty years since I had ten days off."

"I plan to spend a lot of time in bed," Yuki said.

"Oh, no, not that," he said.

They grinned at each other and kissed. And then, over the next two hours, they checked into their awesome, shipshape honeymoon hotel. They visited their cabin, bounced and wrestled on the bed, and at 5:00 p.m. they were on deck.

From this windswept point of view, they could see all of the Seattle shoreline to the north and south, Elliott Bay and Puget Sound extending out to the west. Seabirds dove into the waves and then Yuki covered her ears as four long horn pulls signaled that their ship was ready to depart. Harbor Police and Coast Guard boats scurried to escort the cruise ship out of the port.

All along the dockside railing, passengers waved goodbye, took pictures, and shared the moment with other guests around them as the ship pulled slowly away from the moorings.

Yuki touched the little card in her pocket.

It had been on the tray with the bottle of champagne that had been waiting for them in the cabin. It said, *Dear Mr. and Mrs. Brady. Thank you for spending your honeymoon with us. I look forward very much to meeting you over dinner this week.*

And the captain had signed his name, George Berlinghoff.

"I've got something here," Brady said. "It's, uh,

a wedding present." He took a longish black box out of his Windbreaker pocket.

"I saw this," Brady said, "and it looked like you, and I don't know what the hell to do in a jewelry store, so I hope you like it."

Yuki said, "I do."

"Open the box, smarty."

She smiled, then opened the long clamshell box. She sucked in her breath when she saw the strand of pink coral beads the size of marbles.

"How absolutely perfect."

"It's called 'angel skin coral.' "

"These are *beautiful,* Brady. I can't believe how *beautiful* they are."

Yuki stood on her toes and kissed her brand-new husband, kissed him again, thanked him, and then handed him the necklace. She turned so that he could fasten it around her neck.

He swore at the clasp, apologized, then managed to close the necklace on the third try. He leaned down and pressed his cheek to Yuki's.

"Happy honeymoon, Mrs. Brady."

Yuki was too moved to speak, but she knew this. She was both happier than she'd ever been, and confident that she and Brady were meant to be together.

PART TWO

LOOK OUT.
OL' MACKIE'S BACK.

Chapter 23

I WAS ALREADY awake when Clapper called.

He said into my ear, "Glad I got you, Boxer. We've got breaking news on the belly bombs."

At 7:15 or so, I texted Claire, and within an hour she and I were high on caffeine and optimism, on our way out to San Francisco's Police Department Crime Lab at Hunters Point.

We met Clapper on the ground floor of the 13,500-square-foot lab. In answer to our questions, he said, "Keep your lids on. You'll hear all about it in another couple minutes. And better from her than from me."

Clapper walked us through the lab's labyrinthine corridors and between rows of cubicles until we reached a corner office at the back of the building that was pretty much crammed with lab furniture and shiny high-tech equipment.

At the center of it all was Dr. Damaris Cortes, lab manager and point person working with the FBI on the belly bomb case. Cortes was a radiant forty, with short blue hair, large diamond studs, and a tattoo of an atom in the cleft between thumb and forefinger of her right hand.

She almost shimmered with energy.

Cortes offered us small chairs in her cramped office, while Clapper stood in the doorway, saying, "I'm pretty sure the three of you could speed up the rotation of the earth."

Cortes said, "Fasten your seat belt, Clapper. Buckle up."

Clapper laughed and said, "Copy that," then disappeared down the hallway.

Cortes fixed her big gray eyes on us and said, "Claire, Lindsay, you understand this belly bomb is impossible, right? And yet—it was done. The FBI gave me a few cc's of stomach contents—about one tablespoon. And, guess what? I found something."

Cortes spun her chair around and began clicking open files on her computer.

"Nope, nope, nope—there you are, you little

stinker," she said. "Come look at this."

Claire and I peered over the doctor's shoulders and looked at the screen, but I had no idea *what* I was supposed to be looking at within this splotchy pinkish smear.

"Is that it?" Claire said. "That little oblong shape there?"

I squinted and said, "Why don't you tell us ordinary folks what you've got?"

Cortes had a wild, untethered laugh that totally suited her mad-scientist personality.

"That, my friends, is your smoking gun."

Chapter 24

DR. DAMARIS CORTES looked luminous and had a pleased *ta-dah* look on her face, as though she'd just discovered the eighth wonder of the world.

"Smoking gun?" I said. "How so?"

She was happy to explain—at length—which only told me how much work had gone into finding what was revealed to be a miniature gel cap. And, most important, it was *intact*.

Dr. Cortes's explanation, translated into everyday English, came down to this.

A small soluble capsule had been filled with three ingredients: magnesium, which we'd already known about; RDX, which we had known *nothing* about; and oil to keep the two ingredients apart until stomach acid dissolved the capsule.

Cortes refreshed my understanding of RDX, a stable explosive in granular form that was developed for the military. RDX packs a huge bang more powerful than TNT, and to this moment, had only been detonated in conventional ways.

Now there was a new method.

Cortes theorized that when the capsule dissolved, stomach acid activated the magnesium, which created a *flare*. That flare ignited the RDX, causing a secondary explosion with enough power to blow through muscle tissue and seat belts and windshield glass.

Cortes went on, "The execution was brilliant. The capsule was evidently folded into top-grade hamburger meat, which could be preformed into patties, frozen, and cooked whenever."

I asked, "And the person eating the encapsulated explosive wouldn't notice it?"

"Not really," said Cortes. "The gel cap is flexible and small. And now it's embedded in this thick meat sandwich, maybe accompanied by cheese, bacon, and bread. The way most people tuck into hamburgers, they hardly chew, am I right?"

Cortes shrugged expansively.

I thought about recently wolfing down a

Chuckburger at my desk and gave myself a belated scolding for taking a chance like that.

Cortes went on.

"Odds are your killer didn't get it right the first time. I can imagine some trial runs before there was liftoff. But to conceive of this bomb at all, well, you're dealing with some kind of genius. You see that, don't you?"

Claire said, "What they used to call in the comic books an *evil* genius."

Cortes said, "I ran a simple comparison between the beef in my sample and what's available locally, and I've concluded that my sample of mush is consistent with the beef at Chuck's Prime."

We thanked Cortes, and Claire and I back-tracked through the maze of offices out to the parking lot.

I said to Claire, "You know what I'm thinking?"

"Hold on." She put her thumbs to her temples. "Let me tune in to your frequency."

"I'm thinking maybe the Jeep victims' belly bombs were the test run. If that's so, if that was the first—"

Claire said, "So you're thinking there could be another belly bomb?"

"I think so. We still don't get the message."

Chapter 25

CONKLIN WAS IN the break room, washing out the coffee pot, when I found him.

I got a fresh can of coffee from the cupboard and popped the top. "I've got a belly bomb update," I said.

"Hit me with it."

I filled him in on the two-stage explosive that had been packaged in a gel cap and disguised inside ground beef consistent with Chuck's Prime Beef blend.

"The FBI is locking down Chuck's meat-processing plant. We should go to Emeryville," I said.

"Let's do it."

Conklin put on his good tie. I refreshed my

lipstick and then drove us across the Bay Bridge to Emeryville, which sits along the east side of the bay.

The morning sun filtered through the fog and put a flattering glow on the streets of Emeryville. Gentrification had bred lots of modern structures in this former industrial flatland—new shops and restaurants and, near the marina, film production companies and office parks with some historical buildings thrown into the mix.

Chuck's corporate headquarters was on 65th Street in the Emery Tech Building, a streamlined, block-long, brick-and-glass building that had once been a valve-and-regulator plant.

I parked right out front and placed a card on the dash that identified our gray Crown Vic as a cop car. Then Conklin and I entered the building.

We sat in a reception area appointed with gears and parts from the old plant and waited to meet the chief executive officer, Michael Jansing, the son-in-law of Charles "Chuck" Andersen, the original Chuck.

After about twenty minutes of thumb twiddling, we were shown to a conference room where we met CEO Jansing, a sandy-haired man of fifty with narrow, closely spaced blue eyes.

Jansing in turn introduced us to six other people sitting around the sturdy redwood table: the marketing director, the heads of PR, HR, and Security, two lawyers, and the head of the product-development team, who was attending the meeting by teleconference.

It was a diverse group with one thing in common: they weren't glad to see representatives of the SFPD. Their body language and facial expressions told me they were wary, angry, defensive, and suspicious. It was obvious that they thought we weren't friends of the Chuck's family and that we could have a bad, or even a fatal, effect on their reputation.

Accordingly, Jansing was putting on an extraordinary show of force for a preliminary meeting with two midlevel cops.

I can't say that he was crazy to do so.

After we took seats at the table, Jansing said, "The FBI tore apart our Hayes Valley store and found nothing. Frankly, I was a little surprised to hear from you, Sergeant Boxer."

"We're working with the FBI," I told the executives, "but we're running our own investigation on what may have been a double homicide. We have new evidence that places high explosives inside hamburger meat that originated at Chuck's."

Jansing's eyebrows shot up.

"You can prove that?"

It was a bit of a stretch, but I said, "Yes, we can. Mr. Jansing, two people ate Chuck's hamburgers and died as a result. It doesn't mean that someone who works for you planted those explosives, but it does mean that Chuck's is square one."

What followed was like a freestyle Ping Pong tournament, in which balls could go to any table and anyone could return them. There came a point when so many aggressive questions were being fired at us that Conklin stood up and said, "Hey. That's enough. We're willing to talk to everyone in this office and keep it out of the Justice Department. Or we'll get subpoenas and interview each of you down at the Hall. Up to you."

Donna Timko, the product-development manager connected to the meeting by way of the two-way video screen, was the only person who expressed concern or humanity.

Timko said, "Sergeant Boxer, I can't tell you how distressed we all are at any implication that

Chuck's could be involved in any way."

Her voice broke, but Timko pushed on.

"We have already questioned everyone in the production division, and I can assure you, this random act of violence . . . it was not caused by someone who works at Chuck's."

And with that, Donna Timko started to cry.

Jansing said, "Donna, calm yourself, dear. It's all right. We have nothing to hide from the police."

And then he looked back at us.

"Do what you have to do, Inspectors. But do it fast so that *we* don't have to take legal action for harassment by *you*."

Chapter 26

WHILE THE FBI shut down Chuck's central meat-processing plant in Petaluma and began sifting through I don't know how many tons of beef, Conklin and I spent the next day at Chuck's Prime's HQ, taking statements from executives and office staff.

Here's what we learned.

Michael Jansing had vision and high standards. His people liked and trusted him. He paid fairly. The product was good. Employees took pride in their jobs.

No one reported hate mail or knew of current or former employees who exhibited erratic behavior, insanity, or aggression.

Net/net: we did not have one stinking lead on

who might have spiked a hamburger with military-grade explosives. And that meant we had no idea how to head off future belly bombs.

I handed the car keys to Conklin, who said, "Well, there went two days of my life that I can't get back."

"I'm never eating hamburger again," I said. "I mean it. I'm off ground beef forever."

I strapped into the passenger seat, and as Conklin drove us back to the Hall, I took out my phone and opened some mail. I got caught up in one e-mail in particular. I started laughing to myself.

"Okay. What's so funny?" Conklin asked me.

"I want what Yuki's having."

"Hot sex with Brady? Really?"

"No. Shut up. Listen to this.

" *Dear Girlfriends.*

" *I don't even know where to start talking about the awesomeness of Alaska. But let me try.*

" *Crack a dawn this morning, we went out on a tender with an onboard naturalist, and OMG, we saw a pod of Orca whales. Yes! A family pod of them, breaching or "spyhopping," where they point their* heads straight out of the water as if they're standing on their toes. Guys, this was amazing.

" 'Then a bald eagle swooped down right in front of us and grabbed a salmon with his talons. It was a big fish, almost the size of the eagle and it was no sure thing he was going to be able to carry it off—but he kept holding that fish and beating his wings and he achieved lift-off!

" 'We climbed a glacier. Me! I did it! This is a stunning experience, my buds. Walking on a world of ice the color of Brady's eyes. In between the jagged blue and white boulders as far as I could see, a river of ice ran through it.

" 'I knelt down and drank from a glassy well of blue water that had just melted for the first time in millions of years.

" 'It was dazzling. Just incredible.

" 'And get this.

" 'I was climbing down off the glacier and had just about reached the boat. Brady reached out to me and I slipped, guys. My feet went outward and I skidded asswise and dropped my booty right into the water.

" 'Brady saved me, pulled me out of the drink, gave me a hard time, and promised he had a nude *cure for hypothermia. Geez, I almost laughed my chilly butt off.* ☺

"'I'm writing to you from our outstanding cabin on the FinStar and now Brady is calling me to go to the spa. Think of me having the best time of my entire life.

"'What Claire said; best friends, best times, best sex—or something like that!

"'Sending you all my love.

"'Yuki C. BRADY' "

I finished reading and turned to Conklin. "Isn't she hilarious?"

He shouted at a car in front of us that was switching lanes without signaling. "Hey, buddy, make up your mind, will you?"

Then, to me: "So, what now, Sherlock?"

"Really. I wouldn't mind taking a slow boat to Alaska."

"Who wouldn't? So we should talk to that Timko woman. The boss of the product-development office?"

"Tomorrow. First thing. Just drop in on her. You know, Richie, I never got to have a honeymoon," I said as the sun slipped down behind the city of San Francisco.

Richie was back to verbally negotiating rush-hour traffic.

I thought about my friend and realized that I'd never said these two words before. But, I said them now.

"Lucky Yuki."

Chapter 27

WE WERE THIS close to Conklin's apartment when a radio call came in that had our name on it. There had been a shooting that had likely stemmed from a domestic dispute. A crying child had called 911. The address was about four miles away.

I grabbed the mic and said that we were on our way, then asked Richie to stop the car.

He pulled into a handy driveway, and we got out, took our vests from the trunk, and put them on. We headed out and I snapped on every flasher we had, the grille lights, the visor lights, and the one on the roof of the car.

Richie stepped on the gas and eight short minutes later, we braked in front of a tan wood-frame semi-detached condo, one of dozens just like it on Jerrold Avenue.

The front door was open. We entered with our guns drawn, Richie calling out, "This is the SFPD."

We came to a full stop in the living room, where a woman sitting in a crouch position with her back to a wall was holding a shotgun pointed at us. Blood and tissue fragments were sprayed on the wall, and there was a body—it looked like a man's—ten feet to the north of the woman.

His heart was pumping blood onto the wooden floor.

Conklin said, "Ma'am, we need you to lower your weapon."

The woman was white, about thirty, and wearing a torn T-shirt and jeans. There was blood spatter on her face, telling me that she had been very close to the victim when the gun fired. It looked to me like half his face had been shot away, but I thought he was still breathing.

I heard children crying somewhere down the hall.

This was a volatile situation, and I flashed on what could happen if we didn't shut it down fast. I imagined the woman unloading that shotgun on us. Reloading. Taking out the kids. Reloading. Turning the gun on herself.

She wasn't responding to Conklin, so I shouted, *"Lady. Drop the damned gun."*

"I can't," she said in a small, almost little-girl voice. She looked at us with crazy eyes, shaking her head and trembling at the same time. "He'll kill me."

"We're here now," Conklin said, coming forward. "He's not going to hurt you. We're here now, ma'am. We're here for you. So put the gun down, okay? You have to do it so we can go to your children, make sure they're okay."

"My kids? You know my kids?"

Her eyes flashed back and forth between me and Conklin and skipped right over the downed man on the floor.

Conklin holstered his gun. I covered him as he walked slowly toward the woman, showing her his empty hands.

"I'm just coming to help you. What's your name?"

"Holly."

"Okay, Holly. I'm Richie."

One of Conklin's many strengths is that he has

a terrific way with women. It's a real gift, that's for sure.

I said, "I'm just going to walk behind you, Holly."

She looked at me as I edged around her, and Conklin saw his chance. He stepped forward and, grabbing the gun, cracked it open and knocked out the remaining shell and threw the gun onto the couch.

"There we go," he said. "Now we can talk. Holly, tell me what happened here."

Chapter 28

ONCE HOLLY WAS disarmed, my breathing and my heartbeat returned to something like normal. I was not just relieved that no guns had gone off. I also wanted Holly to be all right.

I already had a pretty good idea what had happened in this house. Holly's husband had been abusing her and had introduced a loaded shotgun into the fight. He'd been pointing that gun at her when she surprised him, grabbed the weapon, and got off a shot.

Very likely Holly had saved her own life.

But that didn't mean that she wouldn't have to prove self-defense in court. Her crappy life wouldn't get better for some time, if ever.

I retraced my steps and bent to the man bleeding

out on the floor. He was stocky, maybe in his thirties, and had tattoos on his arms and neck. A mixture of blood and air bubbled through what remained of his nose and lower jaw. He was alive. But he might not want to survive what he was facing—surgery, pain, food through a straw—while in jail.

I called dispatch and was told the ambulance was only three minutes out. I said that the situation was under control, that the EMTs could come directly into the house, and I asked for Child Protective Services.

Conklin led Holly to a plaid tub chair and sat on the couch across from her. She was babbling incoherently when I went down the hall in search of children.

I found two youngsters in the smaller of the two bedrooms, hiding between a bed and the wall. They popped up when I called, "Hey there."

I thought the little girl was about four. The boy looked eight. The little girl looked me in the eye, then sucked in a deep breath and screamed before crawling under the bed.

The boy dried his face with his T-shirt and sputtered, "Are you the police?"

"You called us, right?"

I showed him the badge hanging from a chain around my neck.

"I'm Sergeant Boxer, but you can call me Lindsay. What's your name?"

"Leon. Leon Restrepo. That's Cissy."

"Do you know how many people are in the house?"

"Yes."

"Can you tell me?" I asked.

He pointed out to the living room. "Her. Him. Me and Cissy."

"Is Holly your mother?"

Leon nodded his head. Tears started flowing down his cheeks.

"Okay, Leon. Okay. Can you tell me what happened here?"

"She's always hating on him," the little boy said. "She's always threatening to shoot him, and my dad, he always says, 'She's just talking.' But she killed him, didn't she?"

"No, no, your dad is alive, but he's hurt."

"Oh, man, this is so bad."

Leon fell across the bed and cried like he would never stop. Between his sobs, he cried, "I love my dad," he said. "I love my dad so much. Please don't let him die."

Chapter 29

I OPENED THE front door to our apartment on Lake Street, and Martha came tearing around the corner from the living room. She threw her front feet hard against my solar plexus and sang her special welcome-home anthem.

I stooped, kissed her, ruffled her coat, and followed her back to the room where my husband was rising from his big chair, coming toward me, arms open.

"Maria Teresa just left. Julie's had her bottle and her bath and she's sleeping," he said, giving me the biggest hug. "She made chocolate pudding for us, and, yes, I took Martha for a good long stroll."

"Thank you, Joe. What a day I've had."

"Did you eat?"

"Hah. No."

"Come on, my sweetheart. I'll heat up some meat loaf and you can tell me all about it."

I looked in on Julie, who was sleeping like a lamb. Without warning, I flashed on her first months, when Joe and I were afraid that she might die—a memory that was too, too awful. I shook the thought away.

I straightened Julie's blanket, kissed my fingers, and touched her cheek. I whispered, "Sweet dreams, baby girl."

I turned to see Joe waiting for me outside her door.

"I turned off my phone," he said. "And I unplugged the landline."

"I should turn off *my* phone, too, right?"

"How about it, Linds? Go off duty. We need some quality time, you and me."

Turning off my phone was the easiest thing I'd done all day.

Joe served up meat loaf and green beans on a blue-and-white plate at the dining table, and he joined me in having a glass of Merlot. I asked for a refill, then attacked a bowl of pudding.

I took a long bath while Joe sat on the toilet

seat and we talked together about my day of corporate go-nowhere interrogations, Yuki and Brady's magical honeymoon, and a scene of bloody awful domestic violence. He told me some good news. He'd been tapped for a consulting job, home-based, laptop variety.

We went to bed early in our blue bedroom with soft city lights glowing through our windows. It was a blessing to make love and not think about the phone ringing.

And throughout it all, little Julie slept.

Chapter 30

I WAS IN the gym, huffing and puffing on the elliptical, when a hulking guy in a tan overcoat clumped across the red carpeting and approached me. I knew the elephant in the room. Knew him as well as I know myself.

"Boxer, hate to interrupt." He grinned. He leered.

"This is a no-shoes zone, Jacobi."

Warren Jacobi is my long-term friend and former partner. We spent about ten years of day, night, and overtime shifts catching gang shootings and homicides by various means, including bathtub electrocutions and angel-of-mercy-spree executions, to name but a few.

When I was promoted to lieutenant, Jacobi teamed up with Conklin. Later I demoted myself out of the bureaucratic nightmare of squad management, and Jacobi took the lieutenant's chair. Not too long after that, Brady became lieutenant, and Jacobi, who had more street experience than all of us together, and who was suffering from old gunshot injuries and was also closing in on retirement, was bumped up to chief of detectives.

As chief, Jacobi was the go-to guy while Brady was on his honeymoon. I didn't think the gym visit was a social call, but I got off the elliptical and gave him a sweaty hug anyway.

"What brings you here, bud?"

"I'm just a messenger, Boxer."

What the hell? What kind of message got the chief of detectives out of the office? I pulled back from the hug and scanned the creases in his face, his hooded gray eyes. Had Joe called him? Had something happened to Julie?

"Spit it out, Jacobi. What's wrong?"

"Take it easy, Boxer. It's nothing personal. You didn't answer your phone."

I said, "So, okay. What brings you to Body Beautiful?"

He laughed. "I'm signing up so I can gawk at the spandex girls review."

"Funny."

"Okay. I'm running an errand for the FBI."

"Oh. I guess my workout is over."

"Yeah, good guess. Get dressed so we can talk in private."

I took a quick shower, dressed PDQ, and met Jacobi in the lobby of the health club. We went out onto Folsom Street and leaned up against the building.

Jacobi said, "There was a fatality in LA about an hour ago. A guy was having a breakfast burger in his car in the parking lot of a fast-food joint when his stomach exploded. He was killed instantly. The glass blew out, blinding a pedestrian. There were other injuries, but only the one fatality."

"This happened at a Chuck's?"

"Correct. Chuck's, Marina del Rey. Here's the phone number of the FBI agent who called me. Jay Beskin. We'll get along with them better if we play nice. You want to work this case right, okay, Boxer?"

I told Jacobi that motherhood had brought out the sweetheart in me. He smirked, like *yeah, right*. We said good-bye and I called my current partner.

"Saddle up," I said. "I'll meet you at the Harriet Street lot, ASAP."

Chapter 31

CONKLIN AND I took seats opposite Michael Jansing in his office/Chuck's Prime museum of ads and artifacts.

Jansing, Chuck's chief executive officer with the hay-colored hair and narrow blue eyes, glared at us over engraved plexiglass cubes, slabs, and obelisks on his desk, all trophies awarded for fast-food advertising.

I said, "Do you understand me, Mr. Jansing? The FBI is investigating another death by Chuck's as we speak. Do you want to help your company and cooperate with us, or should we just back off and let the Feds take you in and treat you to enhanced interrogation?"

Jansing got up from behind his desk and went to the doorway.

He said to his assistant, "Caroline, get Louis, would you?"

Jansing returned to his desk.

"My lawyer."

"That's fine," said Conklin. "If that makes you more comfortable."

"Listen, I'm sorry."

"Sorry?" I asked.

"I'm sorry. Our head of legal has something to tell you," Jansing said.

A stooped man came through the doorway. He wore a corporate gray suit and a comb-over with a dark metallic sheen, and he had nicotine stains on the fingers of his right hand. I recognized him as one of the players at the executive Ping Pong meeting we'd attended.

He came toward us and introduced himself again.

"Louis Frye," he said and shook our hands before taking the chair next to Conklin.

Jansing said, "Lou, please tell these officers about the text messages."

What was this? We hadn't heard about any

texts relating to the belly bombs. If Jansing had withheld information, he'd better have a damned fine reason or he was going to be charged with obstruction.

"This text came from a prepaid boost phone," Frye said. "I printed it out for you."

He passed over a plain sheet of copy paper with a smattering of words: "Time to pay up."

"When did you get this?" I asked.

"After the bridge bombs. It came to me," said Jansing. "I thought it was spam. It meant nothing to me. We didn't know that the bridge incident was related to us," said the lawyer, "until the FBI descended on our Hayes Valley store."

Frye said, "Then Michael got another text. Identical message, but they followed up the text with a phone call naming the amount. We decided to pay."

Of course they paid. Chuck's Prime only cared about keeping the company name off the record and out of the news.

"How much?" Conklin asked.

"Fifty thousand," said Frye. He was slapping at his pockets, looking for his smokes. He found a worn pack of an unfiltered brand, opened it, closed it, and put it back in his jacket pocket.

He said, "We bundled the bills in a Chuck's Big Lunch Box and left the box in a garbage can at our Monterey location."

Conklin said to the head cheese, "You're telling us you believed that would be the end of it?"

"Yes. Of course. And we agreed, Lou and I," said Jansing. "Rather than let someone else die, we forked over the money. It seemed like the best course."

I wanted to shout at the two suits, "You morons."

Instead I said, "So rather than call the cops, have them monitor the transfer, you trusted a bomber, a murderer, an extortionist, when he *said* that there would be no more bombs."

Jansing had gone pale around his eyes and mouth. I didn't think he was feeling remorse. More like he was realizing how much shit was about to hit the fan.

"We employ thousands of people, all of whom would be negatively impacted if the public—"

"The FBI contacted us two hours ago," I said, cutting his self-serving spiel off at the knees. "A Chuck's customer exploded from inside out.

Happened in one of your parking lots in LA."

I passed the name of the FBI guy across the desk to Jansing and said, "I spoke with this gentleman, Special Agent Beskin, and he's about to call you. I advise you to tell him everything you know. Any questions?"

Chapter 32

CINDY WAS AT her desk at the *Chron,* rereading her old Randy Fish files, straining them for any missed morsel of information that could lead to Morales. By 10:00 a.m. she had put down three cups of coffee and two churros, the only food groups that appealed to her in her current mood.

Apparently her body was telling her what she needed.

Henry Tyler was in Washington today, meaning Cindy had a reprieve from a humiliating meeting where she would have to inform him that her story had gotten away from her and she wouldn't be nominated for the Pulitzer anytime soon.

It was a conversation she *really* didn't want to have.

Just then, a gaggle of her coworkers who were raving about a new reality dating show parked themselves in the hallway outside her office. Cindy got up and shut the door, and when she returned to her desk, an e-mail had arrived from Capt. Lawrence@CWPD.com.

Hope sprang, leapt around, did a pirouette and a curtsy.

Hi Cindy,

Morales's prints were found in the house, but they were dusty. So give yourself a gold star for figuring that out, anyway. Fyi, if you don't know, there was a bank robbery in Chicago on Monday and the perp was tentatively id'd as our friend Mac. According to what I got from our cop network, she shot and killed two people and got away with about a thousand dollars. Disappeared in plain sight, right outside of the bank. So maybe Morales was last seen in Chicago. Or maybe it was someone who looked like her.

All the best,
Pat

The few short lines felt to Cindy like bright sunshine breaking through the cloud cover after forty days and nights of torrential rain. She'd been *right* that Morales had used the Fish house as a hideout.

And now here came a fresh lead.

Morales had staged a bank holdup and she had killed two people—both a measure of her psychopathy and of her desperation.

No question in Cindy's mind, Morales was going to need money again soon and she would resurface.

Cindy went online, searched for "bank robbery, Chicago" and spent the next hour reading about it in the Chicago papers. Mackie Morales wasn't mentioned by name. Law enforcement was no doubt working according to the same principle as when Cindy had found out that the Fish house was wired with explosives.

Namely, they had to keep Morales out of the press so that she wouldn't know that she'd been exposed.

Cindy located the videos from the Chicago news broadcasts. Customers who had fled the bank right after the shootings had been interviewed by the local press.

Cindy noted the names, and she sent out an e-mail to the staff writers at the *Chron*, asking if anyone had contacts in the Chicago PD.

Then Cindy wrote to Henry Tyler:

> To: H. Tyler
> From: C. Thomas
> Subject: Update Morales
> Henry, Morales may have held up a bank in Chicago and killed two people. Her name has not been released. I'm following up, digging in. More TK as I get info. Cindy.

Then Cindy wrote to Captain Lawrence, thanking him for the lead. Next, she booked a flight to Chicago.

Chapter 33

MACKIE MORALES WAS behind the wheel of the silver Acura she'd boosted from a parking space on State Street, a high-end shopping street in Chicago's Loop. Well, she'd seen the keys in the trunk lock, so the Acura's owner was definitely a dummy, probably still wondering where she'd parked the car, and would take her time to report the theft.

Meanwhile, as Mackie set out due west, she and Randy had had some laughs. He said, *Sometimes life hands you dummies.*

"Good one, lover."

When Mackie stopped for gas in Bettendorf, Iowa, two and a half hours west of Chicago, she found the dummy's peacoat in the trunk. She transferred her gun from her blue trench to the dummy's felt coat and stuffed her own coat into the trash bin near the pumps.

About that time, she also found a pair of leather gloves in the pocket of the peacoat, very handy, and about sixteen dollars in ones and coins. It would have been great if the dummy had had some real cash in the car, but there had been a package of Oreos in the console and Mackie had been glad for those.

Now, after several cash purchases—gas and snack and dinner in a truck stop outside Cheyenne—Mackie was keeping to the speed limit on the interstate, cutting through the barren plains of southern Wyoming. She was looking for a good radio signal and a clear road with no cops. Instead, she saw a figure on the side of the road near the Laramie on-ramp.

As she drew closer, she saw that the figure was a young woman wearing jeans and a denim jacket. She had long dark hair and held a piece of cardboard with a sign written in marker, reading ROCK SPRINGS.

Randy's type. To a T.

Mackie slowed the Acura to a stop, and the girl

picked up her backpack and ran toward the car.

Mackie buzzed down the window.

The girl said, "Hi, wow, thanks for stopping. How far can you take me?"

"I'm driving to Portland," Mackie said. "I can take you all the way."

"Oh, that would be great. Thanks."

The long-haired girl took a bottle of water from her backpack. Mackie saw the finger marks on her wrists just before the girl pulled her jacket sleeves down to hide the bruises.

"I'm Leila," she said.

"I'm Hannah," said Mackie, picking a name out of the air. "Leila, sorry to be nosy, but why are you hitching this late at night?"

"Oh, boyfriend trouble. I was visiting my, well, I guess he's my ex now, at the University of Wyoming."

Leila used her thumb to point behind her to Laramie.

"We had a fight. About another girl he's been seeing, of course. Now I have to get back home on my own, but I sure don't ever have to see that shit again."

"And you're not afraid to hitchhike?"

"Not at all. I would only get into a car with a woman. Do you live in Portland?"

"My mom. I'm going to spend a little time with her. She's a million laughs and she cooks, too."

"Cool. Hannah, I didn't get any sleep last night. Would you mind if I nap for a few minutes?"

Mackie dialed around and found a light-music station. By the time Leila was asleep, Mackie was thinking about Lindsay Boxer. It was good to be going back to San Francisco. Richie and Lindsay wouldn't even be thinking about her.

Surprise. We're ba-a-ack.

Beside her, Leila stirred.

Between now and San Francisco, she had to deal with the girl.

Chapter 34

YUKI STOOD WITH Brady and gangs of light-hearted after-dinner guests who were filling the *FinStar*'s world-class Ocean Bar to the walls. Inside, the bar was all gold trim and rusty autumn colors. Beyond the curving floor-to-ceiling windows, the night was ink-black, lit only by the foam breaking, leaping around the bow as the glorious ship steamed toward Sitka.

Yuki wore a sexy black dress, her new pale coral necklace, and strappy heels. She nursed her first margarita, hoping to see the aurora borealis, an amazing natural light show that often appeared at night in this part of the world.

Brady looked savagely handsome. He, too, was wearing black: turtleneck, blazer, and trousers. His dark clothes contrasted wonderfully with his flashing blond hair. He held out his hand.

"Come with me, sweetie. Let's go to the Veranda Deck."

Back home, Yuki was up at six, organized and overworked, always moving, doing whatever she could to prosecute criminals and put them away.

She felt different with Brady. With him it was okay to show her softer, more vulnerable side, to let him take the lead and take care of her. It was the first time she'd ever trusted a man this way, both emotionally and practically. She trusted him that much. But she didn't like heights.

Yuki put down her glass and, taking her husband's hand, said, "Lead the way."

Together she and Brady climbed the three winding flights of tawny carpeted staircase that coiled below the huge illuminated art work of stars suspended above the staircase. Arriving at the Veranda Lounge, Brady put his hand to the small of her back and steered her through the crowd to the glass right at the front of the ship.

Just then, the room filled with awed murmurs.

There, off the starboard side, Yuki saw a pale aqua feathering in the sky. The color gathered depth and motion, forming a swath of light that ran from east to west, curling back on itself in a loose swirl.

Brady stood behind her and wrapped her in his arms as they watched the effect of atomic particles colliding, discharging energy some sixty miles overhead, creating an ethereal watercolor that bled through the velvet night.

"I *must* get pictures," Yuki said.

"That can be arranged," said her husband.

He took her hand, led her to the door, and made sure she safely cleared the high threshold.

The cold wind on the deck brought tears to Yuki's eyes, but she shot a dozen pictures, each with her blowing hair across the lens. Then she saw Lyle, their cabin steward, who volunteered to point and shoot.

"How long will this last?" she asked him.

"Maybe hours, or—the way I heard it—it could disappear if you *sneeze*."

"Quick," she said, shoving her camera into his hand.

She and Brady stood with arms around each other, their backs to the blackness below and above, lit now with the magical northern lights.

Yuki thanked Lyle and took back her camera. She turned to Brady, stood on her toes, and pressed her body against him. He pulled her in even closer.

She shouted above the wind, "You should take me to bed."

"How did we ever get so lucky?" said Brady.

Chapter 35

MY DAY STARTED in Jacobi's big office with its view of the bail-bond storefronts and All Day Parking on Bryant.

Jacobi had new information from our contact at the FBI. He said, "The evidence from our bridge victims and the one in the LA parking lot matches. Same type of injuries, and they found a granule of RDX."

"Nice of the FBI to keep us posted. But I'm still working a double homicide by hamburger bomb."

"You know what, Boxer? Leave it with the Feds. It's their case. They've got the mega-lab and the manpower. We've got plenty to do in our own backyard."

"Is that an order?"

"Yeah, right. Would that work?"

No. It wouldn't.

"I'm working the case, Jacobi."

I called Donna Timko, head of Chuck's Prime product development, but after learning that she was out of town for the day, Conklin and I got Holly Restrepo out of holding.

We gave the woman an intensive six-hour, three-way chat, and she entirely, adamantly stuck to her story. Namely, her bastard husband had been threatening her. She didn't remember anything until we arrived and she was holding the shotgun and Rudolfo was bleeding out on the floor.

My sweetheart of a partner said, "Holly, time is flying. If you tell us you shot Rudolfo in self-defense, you might be able to work out a deal. If he dies, you're looking at capital murder. You'll never touch your children again."

Holly Restrepo rolled her crazy-twitchy eyes and said, "Do I seem like I'm in my right mind?"

Yes, she did.

She was practicing her insanity defense on us.

It was that kind of day. Frustrating and haunted by belly bombs yet to explode. I was ready for it to be over.

I'd been home for about ten minutes and had just hung up my jacket and unpacked my gun when Cindy's ID came up on my home phone.

"Linds, may I come over?"

"Of *course*. Joe's making veggie lasagna. Get your skinny butt over here."

A half hour later, Cindy bounced in, looking cute in jeans and a pink cardigan, with a rhinestone barrette in her hair. She also looked wired.

"I need some baby love," she said.

"Sit yourself down."

Cindy reached out her arms, and Joe handed Julie over. For a woman who didn't want kids—not now!—she took to holding our little one like she held babies every day.

She made intense small talk with Julie, nothing deep or personal apart from asking her if she preferred Leno or Letterman, causing Julie to burble, which made me laugh out loud. I had to tear Julie away from Cindy so I could put her down before dinner.

Cindy picked at her lasagna, and she asked Joe the kinds of questions that come easily to a reporter. She even asked follow-up questions. I continued to feel that something was bothering her, though—and she didn't care to discuss it in front of Joe.

Whatever was stuck in her shoe, she softened it with a couple of glasses of wine, then turned down coffee and dessert in favor of a third glass, effectively killing the bottle. About then, Joe said he had some calls to make. He kissed the top of Cindy's curly-haired head and left the room.

I said to Cindy in my best film noir cop growl, "Okay, sister. Start talking."

Chapter 36

CINDY CAREFULLY SET her wineglass down on the coffee table, kicked off her ballet flats, and curled up in a corner of the couch. I sat across from her in Joe's big leather chair.

"What's going on?" I asked her.

"You're going to kill me," said Cindy, "but I wish you wouldn't."

I read her face and saw something that looked like guilt in her eyes. I felt a stinging shock of alarm. What the hell could Cindy have done to tick me off?

I said, "Only one way to find out."

And then she told me.

"When you said Morales had been seen in

Wisconsin? In a town near Lake Michigan? I tracked her there."

"You're joking. You didn't do that, Cindy."

"Randy Fish's father had a house on the lake that still belongs to his estate. I thought Morales might be there. I brought cops with me when I went. I wanted to be in on the takedown and write about her, you know. Get an exclusive. But—she was already gone."

"You took something I said to you as a friend—"

"I know, I know. But *you weren't working the case*, Lindsay. She was in *Wisconsin*. Not on your patch."

"And so you went out on this, this story, using my private information without asking me? Do you realize how that could come back on me?"

Cindy picked up her glass, drained it, and said, "You know, I figured I'd turn the information over to you and Richie and you'd nail her and she would be prosecuted here and we'd all win. Look, I don't blame you for whatever you think of me. I was wrong. I'm really sorry. Thanks for dinner, Linds."

She put down her glass and toed around for her shoes. I didn't think Cindy was actually steady enough to make it through the front door. And there was no way she could drive.

"I'm not going to beg you, Cindy. But if you don't spit it out, I will come over there and smother you with a throw pillow."

She laughed and said, "Please don't hurt me."

"We'll see."

She grinned, sat back on the couch, and said, "Okay. So when we got to the house, Morales was gone. But she had wired the house with explosives. Yeah! To blow up. I have that on excellent authority."

"How do you know it was Morales who did that?"

"*Off the record*—her prints were found under a layer of dust. Anyway, the FBI is watching the house. Hoping she'll go back to it so they can nail her. Personally? What do I think? I think she's out of that house for good."

"Because?"

Cindy took a deep breath and let it out as a long sigh.

"Earlier this week, a female fitting Mackie's description robbed a bank in Chicago. She killed two people—a guard and a bystander. I just flew out there and talked to two customers who had fled before the cops locked them down. The way they described her, Linds, get this: five foot six to five foot eight. Athletic. Could be Hispanic."

I said, "That's a *description*? I call that a vague generality that could fit too many people to be useful at all. But listen, Cindy. Please look at me. Let's say you're actually onto Morales. Thank God you didn't confront her. Are you kidding me? She's on the FBI's top-ten most-wanted list. Number *five*. You know better than almost anyone how dangerous she is."

Cindy said, "I'm a *crime* journalist, Linds. A damned good one, as it turns out."

That was indisputable. Cindy had helped me solve more than one case with her doggedness, and she had some kind of intuition that couldn't be put down to luck. She had told me once that she was one killer story short of national acclaim. I understood what Morales meant to her.

But that didn't mean she should be trying to get close to her. I nodded my head in agreement and said, "I know how good you are. I know."

Cindy said, "So—may I have some coffee now? I'm not done telling you what's going on."

Chapter 37

I KEPT MY eyes on Cindy while I brewed the coffee. She was tapping on her phone, looking as distracted as she had seemed over dinner.

Joe came into the kitchen and I whispered to him, "She's tracking Morales."

His eyebrows shot up to his hairline.

"By herself? You gotta love her," he said.

"And—why?" I said dubiously.

"She's a lot like you."

"Come *on*," I said. "You really think that?"

He grinned, gave me a swat on the behind, poured coffee for himself, and went back to his office.

I called out, "Cindy, come get your mug."

She sugared and milked her java, after which

we took our mugs to the living room and assumed our former positions. She swiped at her cell phone with her thumb, and just when I was ready to scream, she got up and brought her phone over to me.

"I just got an e-mail with these attachments about three hours ago," Cindy said. "Sometimes a picture is actually worth a thousand blah-blah-blahs."

"What am I looking at?" I asked her.

The first photo was of three State of Wyoming Highway Patrol cars, flashers on, clumped up along the side of a highway.

The second shot showed traffic cones across the lane and a half-dozen khaki-uniformed troopers standing around what looked like a female body lying in the ditch off the shoulder of the road.

"You're saying that's Mackie?"

"No," said Cindy. "Keep flipping through."

The next photo was a tighter shot of the corpse. I thought that I was looking at a hit-and-run, but by the fourth photo, it was clear that the victim had been shot through the left temple.

"Who sent these to you?" I asked.

"Off the record," Cindy said, "they're from a

cop friend of mine who got the pictures from an undisclosed source. There's no ID yet on the victim. I don't know her, Linds," Cindy said, "but she looks familiar."

I looked at the close-ups of the victim. She was pretty, in her twenties, long dark hair, pale skin, slender build.

The gunshot wound to the temple made me think that if she had been a passenger, the driver could have shot her and dumped her out of the vehicle.

Or, if she had been driving and stopped her car for someone and rolled down her window, the person standing outside the car could have popped her, dragged her out, and stolen her car.

Then I came to the close-ups of the victim's hands. All of her fingers had been cut off at the first joint—and that changed everything.

Cindy said, "Remind you of something?"

Yes. It reminded me of Randy Fish, a sexual sadist who had used different methods to kill and torture his victims. He had cut the fingers off one of his last kills with a pair of pruning shears—while the girl was alive. He'd told me all about that.

Randy Fish was dead. I was a witness to that.

But his soul mate was still alive.

Cindy said, "How could this be a coincidence? This murder looks to me like an homage to Randy Fish. And that makes me think Mackie did it."

Might. Could be. Definite maybe. But there was no evidence that Mackie Morales was connected to this crime at all.

I asked Cindy a lot of questions: Had any ID been found on or near the victim? Were there any witnesses? Any missing persons report leading to the victim? Any anything?

Cindy said, "Linds, I've told you everything I know *and* everything I'm thinking."

I wasn't buying it.

Cindy was looking straight at me with her big round baby blues, but I wasn't sure she was seeing me. Maybe she was inside her head, working on her killer story about a Mackie Morales murder spree.

Or maybe it was something else.

I said, "What is it, Cindy? What aren't you saying?"

Chapter 38

CONKLIN SHOWED UP at our work space at half past nine, which was late for him. He hadn't shaved or combed his hair, and he'd missed a couple of shirt buttons. Either he'd taken a tumble in the clothes dryer or I was looking at the hallmark of new love: late nights, morning delight.

"I just made coffee," I said, tipping my chin toward the break room.

Conklin said, "Thank God."

"You're welcome."

He headed out and then came back a minute later with a cup of Mocha Java, wrestled his chair out from under the desk, threw himself into it, and raked back his thick brown hair with the fingers of both hands.

He said, "Coffee without doughnuts is like a day without sunshine."

"Sorry to disappoint," I said.

I opened my pencil drawer, took out a packet of peanut butter crackers, and chucked them over to my partner. He caught them on the fly and opened the packet with his teeth.

"Tina and I."

"Uh-huh."

"She doesn't like my politics. I never thought something like that would matter."

"You had a *fight?*"

"I guess you always think that someone you like shares your values. I keep getting this wrong."

"Are you two going to be all right?"

He shrugged, chewing his crackers, and with his mouth full he asked what was new with me.

I found myself telling him that Cindy had come over to my house for dinner last night. I held back that she had wanted to play with the baby.

Conklin said, "How is Cindy? She didn't look good at the wedding. She's lost weight. She hardly spoke to me. Is she all right?"

I said, "Men are so clueless."

"What's that supposed to mean?"

"Anyway. A few days ago, I stupidly mentioned to her what Brady told us—that Morales might have been seen in Wisconsin. Cindy decided to follow up in person."

Conklin choked on his coffee, and when he'd stopped sputtering, he stared at me and said, "You're saying she went to Wisconsin to find Mackie Morales? By herself? Then what was she going to do?"

I filled my partner in on Cindy's search for our former summer intern with a taste for murder—that she was working on a career move. "What she is calling a once-in-a-lifetime story."

Conklin's face bent through several gradations of shocked disbelief as I told him what Cindy had uncovered in the past few days, a trail of incidents that spelled out that Mackie Morales had resurfaced.

"Cindy wasn't telling me everything," I said to Rich. "When I prodded her, she said, and I quote, 'I'll tell you if and when I know more.' "

Conklin crumpled his empty cup and tossed it into the trash. He said, "You tried to talk her out of this? Never mind. I know what she's like. I hope to God Mackie doesn't find out that Cindy is dogging her."

My desk phone rang too many times before I finally punched the button.

A man's voice said, "Sergeant, this is Lou Frye. From Chuck's Prime."

I signaled to Richie to pick up on line four, and I told Frye that Conklin was on the line.

Frye coughed and wheezed, then got enough wind to say, "Jansing got a text from the extortionist saying he's going to call today with a demand. I guess you want to be here."

After Cindy and Conklin broke up, my partner lived in his car for a couple of weeks and used the office facilities until he found a new place to live. Now he opened his desk drawer and took out his toiletry kit, which still lived in his desk. He rooted around and pulled out a razor, then headed toward the men's room.

"We're on our way," I said to Louis Frye.

Chapter 39

I COULD MAKE the drive to Chuck's HQ in Emeryville while handcuffed, blindfolded, and in my sleep, but still, there was no getting there *fast*. We were handicapped by morning rush from the west end of the Bay Bridge, and after we cleared the tunnel at Treasure Island, a panicky driver up ahead braked into a turn and fishtailed across all lanes, forcing me to skin a guard rail. I regained the road on two wheels.

Conklin, to his credit, didn't puke. When we got to the straightaway of 580 East, I shut down the sound and fury in case the bomber had eyes on the Emery Tech Building.

It was almost 10:30 when I nosed our car into a spot in Chuck's executive lot. Therese Stanford, a pretty, bespectacled young woman from our crime lab's electronic trace division, was waiting for us in a souped-up red Mustang, probably a recent confiscation by Narcotics. She got out of the car with a laptop case slung over her shoulder.

Lou Frye, Chuck's Prime's attorney, was smoking a cigarette just outside the back door. He stubbed his butt out against the brick wall, and once Conklin and I had feet on the ground, we introduced him to CSI Stanford and he let us into the building by the back way.

"No phone call, yet," Frye said, pressing the elevator button. "Jansing is a wreck. I've never seen him this way before, but he's got a big conflict. He wants to do the right thing, but he has to protect the company. He loves Chuck's. He *is* Chuck's."

Michael Jansing was in his office, rocking his desk chair, staring out the window. He dropped the chair into its upright position when we walked in. He stood up, said hello to the three of us, shook our hands with his sweaty one, and offered us coffee.

As his assistant brought in a coffee tray, Stanford set up her laptop on Jansing's desk.

"What if the bastard doesn't call?" Jansing asked Stanford.

"If he wants his money, he will."

"And what do I do?"

"Try to buy us some time to get a bead on him. Ask his name. Ask, 'What's your beef?'—no, no," Stanford said, laughing nervously. "I didn't mean that."

Conklin took over. "Fumble a little, Mr. Jansing, but don't overdo it. Get the time and address of the drop and Sergeant Boxer and I will take it from there."

Everyone took seats and settled in for a wait. The silence was thick and then thicker. I can't speak for what was going on in the minds of those around me, but I knew how much could go wrong.

If the guy called from his cell phone, we'd own him, but would he call? Would he direct us to the drop, or was he the kind of sadist who could race Jansing around from place to place until he was sure that his pigeon had flown alone? Then take the money and split?

And by the way, while Stanford had worded her question indelicately, she was on the right track. What *was* the killer's beef? What did he have against Jansing? What did he have against Chuck's Prime? Or was planting explosives in hamburger meat a crime of opportunity?

Jansing's office was as quiet as a morgue during a blackout. We'd exhausted our Q and A the last two times we visited Jansing, and he was silent and tense and had no further questions of us. We drank coffee and watched Jansing rock in his executive chair for forty-seven excruciating minutes.

And then a phone rang. Jansing grabbed at his breast pocket. He took out his cell and showed the caller ID number to Stanford.

She tapped the number into a cell phone attached to her computer, and her tracking software almost instantly pinpointed the base station the bomber was calling from.

Stanford said, "He's in Emeryville."

She disconnected the line, then, redialing the caller's number, nabbed the exact location. By then Jansing's phone had rung four times.

"He's going to hang up," I said.

"Go ahead and answer it," Stanford said to Jansing.

Chapter 40

JANSING PUT HIS phone on speaker and said his name.

The voice that came back over the phone was electronically modulated, giving the speaker a high-pitched robotic quality that was sick, chilling, and crazy.

"How you doing, Jansing? I hoped I'd catch you in."

Therese Stanford was at her computer keyboard, typing in the phone number of the no-name phone. Her screen showed the location of cell towers in Emeryville and environs. With luck, she'd be able to ping the bomber's phone.

"I don't understand what you want from me," Jansing said. "I gave you the money."

"The first payment doesn't count because you brought in the cops. Now my fee has doubled."

"The cops came to *me*," Jansing protested.

"I warned you about cops," the killer said in his eerie, uninflected voice. "You really should've listened to me. There are serious consequences, you know, like *ka-boom*."

Jansing looked at me helplessly.

I mouthed words at him, and he spoke them into the phone.

"I understand."

"I want a hundred grand. Small bills. No tracking devices."

"I-I-I have to go to the bank. I need some time."

"I'll call you in a half hour," said Robo-bomber.

"Wait. Where am I supposed to go after that?"

"I said, I'll call you."

The line went dead.

I said to Jansing, "Where is your bank?"

Jansing got up, walked six yards to the far side of the room, and, lifting a framed poster of Chuck's iconic snorting bull off the hook in the wall, revealed a wall safe. He punched numbers into the lock and pulled down on the handle. The door swung open and Jansing took out four stacks of hundred-dollar bills, each with a wrapper reading $25,000.

As Jansing returned the poster to its original position, I called Jacobi and requested cars be stationed at intervals off the main streets in Emeryville—Hollis and 65th in particular—and prepared to follow Jansing's car at a distance.

Stanford said, "The phone is on the move, traveling west to east over the bridge, crossing now to Oakland."

I relayed that information to Jacobi, and as we continued to track the bomber's phone while waiting for him to call back, Jansing's phone rang. Again I listened in as the killer told Chuck's sweating CEO to get into his car and turn left on 65th, then right on San Pablo, and to keep his phone line open for further instructions.

"Don't screw it up," said the bomber's mechanical voice, "or I will kill again. You can't imagine what a good time I'm having."

And then he laughed.

I conferred with Conklin and we made a spot decision.

He and CSI Stanford would follow Jansing in

his BMW. I would take the unmarked Ford to Oakland and await the address of the drop.

As I left the building by the back door, I thought of my daughter, as I did every hour of every day.

The job felt different since Julie was born. My love for Julie made me very careful, yet at the same time, I was aware that that love could play out as a momentary delay when I was at risk, and a split-second hesitation could prove fatal.

I put on my vest, hung my badge outside it, and shrugged into my Windbreaker with POLICE in big white letters across the back. I touched my hip, double-checking that my Glock was right there, and I dropped my phone into my jacket pocket.

Then I climbed into the unmarked car and headed out.

Chapter 41

I HAD TWO open lines of communication inside my unmarked Crown Vic. My phone was on speaker for Conklin and Stanford, who were tracking the bomber's phone and listening in on Jansing's ongoing conversation with the bomber.

I was also monitoring the staticky blare of my car radio, which was locked on a channel dedicated exclusively to the cops working this case.

I buzzed down my window as I drove through Oakland's Fruitvale area, a shopping district that had been economically up, down, and iffy for a long time. I passed a Chuck's on the corner of East 12th and 35th Avenue. The restaurant was busy, and typical of the chain's cheery bistro style, aqua-and-white market umbrellas shaded the brunch crowd at the tables outside the restaurant.

Therese Stanford's voice came over my cell phone: "The subject told Jansing to go to a vacant liquor store on San Leandro Street. The front door is open, and he's supposed to leave the package on the counter. Subject says he's watching Jansing, and he's telling him to be smart. Okay. Okay. Now Mr. Jansing says he's got dead air. Subject has shut off the cell phone and disconnected the battery."

My pulse picked up. I saw the vacant liquor store up ahead, situated between a bakery and a bike shop. The sign read BARNEY'S WINE AND LIQUOR. The plateglass window had been soaped from the inside and tagged from the outside, and rampant weeds had overtaken the pansies in the flower boxes.

I circled the block, and as I approached Barney's on the return pass, I saw that Jansing had pulled up to the curb. I slowed and saw him get out of his car with a taupe metal Zero Halliburton briefcase in his right hand.

Stanford and Conklin, who had been following Jansing two cars back, pulled past him and made a U-turn before parking on the opposite side of the street, facing Barney's.

Radio dispatch confirmed that plainclothes were covering the rear exit of Barney's and the parking areas behind the row of shops facing 45th Avenue.

We were as ready as we could be.

I didn't like the idea of Jansing going into a building that hadn't been cleared, but his open cell phone served as a wire. If Jansing was in trouble, he only had to say "I'm not armed" and the abandoned store would fill with men with guns.

I still didn't like it.

By definition, our so-called belly bomber was a psychopath. He'd killed innocent people for fun and money, and he was threatening to do so again. If he was inside the former Barney's liquor store, he might shoot Jansing and make a break with the money.

I watched as Jansing carried his metal briefcase into the store with the opaque windows. Moments later, he came out empty-handed and got into his car. Stanford reported over the radio, "Jansing is out and safe. He left the money."

All around San Leandro Street, cops in utility vans and unmarked cars watched for the belly bomber to go into Barney's to retrieve his loot.

Chapter 42

CONKLIN UNFOLDED HIS lanky body and got out of CSI Stanford's low-slung muscle car. As she took off, he walked to our unmarked and got into the passenger seat. We had a good view of Barney's from our spot in the middle of the block, and there we sat.

It was a long wait. Conklin tipped his head back and caught some of the z's he'd lost while fighting about the President's economic policies with Tina, and I scrutinized all traffic—car, foot, and skateboard. There was a plant nursery to my left, a coffee spot to my right, and an elevated BART track across the way. The whoosh and hum of the train added a sound track to the casual afternoon scene. After an hour, I felt I knew the neighborhood as well as my own.

But I didn't see what I was looking for: a man walking under the red metal Barney's sign, going through the doors into the vacant liquor store, and coming out with a package.

Three and a half hours after staking out this block, I'd had enough. I nudged Conklin awake and then, along with a half dozen cops, we surrounded the liquor store with guns in hand.

I assigned places, and when we were all ready, I opened the front door.

The interior of the store was gloomy, with just enough light coming through the soaped windows to see the walls of empty shelves and cardboard cartons and one shiny object: the Zero Halliburton case on the counter.

The case was open. The money was gone and a note had been left inside it. Block letters on lined paper.

NO POLICE, REMEMBER? KA-BOOM.

Two cops went to the basement and returned a minute later. They had found that the basement door that opened out to the parking lot was unlocked and that the basement itself was shared by the bakery next door.

Conklin and I exited Barney's by the front door and then entered the Frosted Fool Bakery next door, where a browsing crowd of shoppers checked out the glass cases and stood in line with numbers in their hands. I fetched the owner from the kitchen and invited the customers to leave. Then I turned the sign on the door to closed while Conklin gathered the salespeople together for questioning.

We interviewed the owner and the three salespeople who'd been behind the counters all morning.

All four agreed. No suspicious customers had been seen in the Frosted Fool. However, they did say that the basement door they shared with the defunct Barney's was left unlocked during the day for deliveries and garbage removal.

Undoubtedly that basement door was used by the unknown subject who had taken the four packets of cash totaling a hundred grand.

And the game was still on. As the bomber had told Michael Jansing, he was enjoying himself immensely.

That's when a soft *ka-boom* went off in my mind.

But was it already too late?

I dashed out to our car and yelled into the radio: "All units to the corner of East Twelfth and Thirty-fifth. Now!"

Three minutes later, we converged on Chuck's Prime two blocks northeast of San Leandro Street, where grass-fed Chuckburgers were being served by fresh-faced guys and gals in cowboy outfits, every one of them looking too innocent to be real.

In my mind, every employee was a suspect and every customer was a potential victim. Maybe there was a bomb under the broiler lamps now. Or maybe a ticking hamburger had just been served.

There was no time for finesse.

I stood with Conklin and a squad of armed cops at my back and yelled, "SFPD. Everybody stop eating! Put down those hamburgers! Now!"

Chapter 43

CINDY HAD LOCKED her office door at the *Chronicle* and was high on extra-sweet coffee, as she liked to be, working a newly hatched Mackie Morales angle, when Claire called her to ask, "Cin? You on tonight? Susie says that laughter and jerked pork are on the menu."

Cindy said, "Yeah, of course. Wouldn't miss it."

She signed off, but her thoughts took a sharp turn toward Susie's Café, which is where she'd met Mackie Morales in the flesh. The memory was indelible, and sometimes when it came over her, she couldn't block it.

She had been at Susie's with the girls, at their regular table in the back, where she, Claire, Lindsay, and Yuki met just about every week.

Mackie had been working her role as squad assistant at the Southern Station Homicide squad, and Lindsay had invited her to Susie's. It was nice of Lindsay to bring Mackie to their clubhouse, and Cindy had thought Mackie was upbeat, bright, a cute person. It still amazed her how wrong she and innumerable top law enforcement officers had been about her.

That time at Susie's, Mackie had been in the ladies' room when Richie showed up at their table, uninvited. He was frustrated and had made the rash decision to bring their increasingly stormy relationship issues to her girls.

He was in mid-rant about what he needed and wasn't getting when Mackie came back from the restroom. She sat down, became uncomfortable in the middle of this inappropriate conversation, and almost immediately made an excuse to leave the café, saying she had to go home to her child.

Cindy and Richie had continued squabbling at the table, and after too much of that, they'd taken their fight outside and had broken off their engagement on Jackson Street, shouting at each other in the rain.

How long had it taken Richie and Mackie to hook up after that?

Cindy didn't know and it didn't matter now.

What mattered was that she locate Morales, help bring her down, and then give Henry Tyler a story the *Chronicle* readers would never forget.

To that end, she called Captain Lawrence, her police contact in Wisconsin, to ask him about Randy Fish's father, Bill, who had owned the green house near Lake Michigan.

Captain Lawrence picked up his phone on the first ring. She could tell he liked her now, and as long as he didn't break the law, he was willing and even happy to help her.

She asked, "Pat, do you know Bill Fish's wife's name and her last known address?"

"Her name was Erica Williams before she married Fish. I think she was from Honolulu but I don't know for sure. As to where she is now? I don't even know if she's in the United States. She was so ashamed of Randy. She couldn't hold her head up. After Bill died, she had a tag sale. Sold most of her things and then just took off."

Cindy thanked the captain and stared out her window for a couple of minutes, organizing her many disparate thoughts.

She decided to take her laptop out to lunch.

Chapter 44

CHOW'S WAS A coffee shop on 3rd Street, two long blocks down Mission from the *Chronicle*. It was a popular hole in the wall, serving home-style Thai and Chinese dishes as well as classic American diner fare. The place was packed from noon until three, but at just after eleven, Cindy thought Chow's would offer the perfect change of scene she was hungering for.

She pushed open the heavy glass doors, waved at George behind the cash register, cruised past the takeout line, and slipped into a two-person booth at midpoint of the center aisle. When the waiter came to her, she ordered French fries and a chocolate milk shake.

"That's it?"

"For now," said Cindy.

She opened her MacBook and began a search for Erica Fish. Even before her fries and shake arrived, she found more than a hundred and fifty women with that name, equally distributed across the country. Between courses, she typed "Erica Williams" into her browser and found another four hundred listings, scattered from sea to shining sea.

Her search assumed that Erica Williams Fish was using some version of her actual name and that the closely guarded custody of young Ben Morales Fish had gone to the little boy's paternal grandmother.

So it was also logical to check out Mackie's mother, Deanna Mackenzie Morales, and her father, Joseph Morales. Mackie and her parents had lived in Chicago, but the thousands of listings for J. Morales totally swamped any possibility of a fine-tuned search without limitless funds and endless time.

But it took no time and cost nothing to type Mackie's mother's name in different permutations into her browser. Cindy did it—and like freakin' magic, she got a hit. D. M. Morales, the one and only person in the entire country with that name, was listed in the San Francisco white pages.

Just the name.

The number and address were unlisted—which made sense.

If Mackie's mother had lived in San Francisco prior to her daughter getting busted, she may have gotten custody of the child. If so, she would want to be way under the radar. So she'd blocked her phone and address so that people like Cindy couldn't find her.

Cindy slurped her milk shake down to the bottom, paid the check at the register, and walked back to the office. As she crossed 3rd Street, she thought about how Mackie Morales's recent past had taken her from Wisconsin to a bank in Chicago and possibly to a highway in Wyoming. She was heading west.

She might well be coming to San Francisco to visit Ben and her mother.

And here was the dark hunch she'd been harboring. Morales might have other business in San Francisco as well.

Chapter 45

TO BE HONEST, I had to force myself to go to Susie's that night. Normally, a Club meeting was like a dip in the Caribbean Sea—salty, warm, rousing, and comforting at the same time.

But tonight, as I stood in my bare feet in my bedroom, I wanted to take off all my clothes, get into bed, and pull the covers over my head.

But I knew even that wouldn't assuage my twin feelings of frustration and bone-deep exhaustion from the fruitless day in Fruitvale. And the upshot of the entire pathetic operation was that the belly bomber had the money and was planning to kill again.

Joe said, "You'll feel better if you go out with the girls. I'll wait up."

I showered and changed my clothes and drove to Susie's, hoping that Claire and Cindy would both be okay if I ate and ran. That was pretty much all I could handle.

I pulled open the big wooden door, and the calypso party spilled out. Hot Tea was working the steel drums, the rum punch and margaritas were flowing, and the whole place smelled like spiced meat on a grill.

My girls were waiting at our booth when I got there. I slid in next to Claire, who read the expression on my face and put her arm around me.

I laid my head on her shoulder and pretended to cry, and she squeezed me and said, "There, there. Whatever is wrong, it will get better with beer."

I leaned across the table and exchanged cheek kisses with Cindy, who said, "Someone had a bad day. Are you all right?"

Cindy looked kind of radiant, as did Claire, so I guessed I would be tapped to be the first to piss and moan.

"You're not still mad at me, are you?" Cindy said.

"What?" said Claire. "I didn't hear anything about a fight between the two of you."

Cindy smirked and said, "It's off the record," then called our waitress over.

Lorraine appeared, her red hair freshly permed, and wearing a new, brighter-red lipstick than ever before. She said, "Hey there, Sergeant Boxer. You look thirsty. What can I get you?"

Before I could say, "I'm just going to watch," Lorraine vanished and returned with a foamy pitcher of brew. She said, "I'll be right back with glasses and to take your order. The fish and rice is nice."

Claire said, "Have you all seen Yuki's Facebook page? Pictures of that aurora borealis? It's like something you'd see on the Discovery Channel."

"I haven't checked her page," I said, "due to a belly bomb mission of the epic fail kind. What a day this has been."

The beer glasses arrived. We all ordered the Friday-night fish-and-rice special with ripe plantains and extra-hot sauce. Cindy booted up her tablet and we perused Yuki's honeymoon pictures —and yeah, without my knowing it was happening, my mood lifted.

We cracked some off-color jokes about just-married sex rocking the boat and we toasted my boss and Yuki, our good friends who'd fallen in love. After we ordered a second pitcher of beer to cool down the hot sauce, I talked about the belly bomber and wondered out loud what the creepy killer extortionist was really after.

I said, "The ransom is so puny relative to Chuck's Prime's bottom line. And the logic is weird. 'Please stop me before I bomb again.' Well, he *got* the ransom."

Claire aimed a forefinger at her temple and rotated it in the universal hand signal for cuckoo.

She said, "This bomber. He doesn't want to be stopped. He keeps telling you. He likes to blow people up."

Claire signs in a couple thousand dead bodies a year to her fine establishment, and after we'd exhausted my story of a stakeout that got us exactly nowhere, the good Dr. Washburn told us a few gruesome tales from the crypt.

She laughed as I covered my ears and said, "La-la-la."

"Here's to dying peacefully in our sleep," Claire said, hoisting her glass. "After putting down a big bowl of ice cream."

"Cheers to a nice cerebral hemorrhage—in

our nineties," I concurred.

Cindy clinked her glass against ours, "And here's to finding Mackie Morales and piling stones on her chest until she stops breathing."

"What?" said Claire. "Mackie Morales? What did you say?"

"Lindsay didn't tell you?" Cindy said, looking genuinely surprised.

"Both of you better start talking. I want to know what's going on behind my back," said Claire.

"That would be your cue," I said to Cindy.

Chapter 46

CINDY SAID, "AW, Lindsay, you don't mean that you want me to talk about this."

"Absolutely," I said and then sat back and watched her try to figure out what to say to Claire that didn't make her sound like a lunatic.

"What is this about Mackie Morales?" Claire asked. "No, really, what is this? How come you're not talking, Cindy?"

"Because Lindsay is having fun with me."

Claire laughed. "Seriously? Well, I like to have fun, too."

She said, "Fine, Claire. This is the whole truth. Lindsay told me that Morales had been seen coming out of a post office in this small town called Two Rivers, Wisconsin."

"*What?* Mackie resurfaced, Lindsay?" Claire asked.

"That's what I was told."

"Lindsay didn't tell me why or how," said Cindy, mounting her defense. "But she told me where. That was all. And I took it from there."

"And you did *what?*" Claire asked.

"I went to Wisconsin to find her."

"No way."

Cindy looked down at the table and drummed her fingers.

Claire laughed at Cindy's expression, then started to pour herself more beer.

I put my hand on the top of her glass and said, "Who's driving you home?"

Claire twisted her head around and shouted, "Lorraine? Coffee, please. All around."

Lorraine came over with three mugs of coffee on a tray and said, "There's been a complaint, Dr. Washburn. Laughing too loud at this table. But keep it up. I like it."

We all laughed at this one, and I found that I was getting over myself. Cindy, too, was passionate about her work, and she was winning at it.

"I want pie," Cindy called out before Lorraine

had gone too far. "Anyone else?"

Lorraine returned to the table. "I've got coconut cream and key lime."

"One of each," Cindy said.

Claire stirred her coffee and said, "Okay. So did you find Morales?"

Cindy said, "Not me. Not the SFPD. And not the FBI either, but I'm still working on it."

Cindy went on to tell Claire what she told me, that she had found out that Randy Fish's father had lived in Wisconsin, that she had located the house and made friends with the local gendarme, and that they had found out the house was wired to explode three ways, and that Mackie had, in fact, been inside the house not long before.

"Are you shitting me?" said Claire. "Whoa, Cindy. That's hard-core."

Cindy was totally warmed up. She talked about the two DBs at a Citibank in Chicago, victims of a thin, dark-haired female shooter who might be Morales. And then there was the fresh corpse found in a drainage ditch off Route 80 outside Laramie, Wyoming.

"The victim was a dark-haired college girl," Cindy said with meaning.

"Randy liked dark-haired college girls," I said.

"I remember," Claire said thoughtfully. "What was the cause of death?"

Cindy said, "Gunshot to the temple. And her fingers were amputated postmortem."

"I get you. You think that was some kind of Mackie tribute to the Fish Man."

Cindy said, "Yeah, I do. But I've got no proof."

She delicately folded a forkful of pie into her mouth and managed to keep talking without looking gross doing it.

"The college girl was Randy's type. Hell, *Mackie* is Randy's type. There were no prints or shells or witnesses, but I'm getting a sense she's on a spree and she's heading this way."

"And so what are you going to do about that?" Claire asked. Now, like me, Claire was alarmed.

"I just want to write a great, great story," Cindy said. "There's nobody better to do it than me. You guys should stop thinking of me as a kid. Really."

"No one thinks of you that way," Claire said.

"No one," I said.

"Right," said Cindy. "Look."

She put her pearly-pink quilted handbag on the table and opened it so we could see inside.

I saw a snub-nosed .38 between her makeup kit and a packet of gum.

"Shut *up*," said Claire.

"Are you kidding me?" I said.

"No joke, girls. I can ride 'em, I can rope 'em, and I can shoot, too. Richie taught me. And I have a carry license to prove it."

Claire and I blinked at Cindy as she finished the last of her pie and scraped the plate with her fork.

I *knew* I was supposed to stay home tonight. My girlish merry mood was gone. And guess what?

I was scared to death for Cindy.

Chapter 47

MACKIE MORALES HAD been driving for more than seventeen hours, crawling at sixty, making pit stops in rundown gas stations off the highways, paying cash, avoiding toll booths, and keeping to service roads—whatever she had to do so that the stolen car wouldn't be tagged on camera or noticed by a state trooper.

So far, so good.

Randy was humming an uplifting tune inside her head.

He was feeling good, proud of her and looking forward to seeing Ben. That little booger.

She felt that way, too. She couldn't wait to scoop Ben up in her arms and hug him and kiss his adorable baby face. And after she'd loved up her baby, she wanted a toilet seat that she could actually sit on and a hot shower and clean towels. She wanted her mother to make her a big fattening meal. Anything Mom cooked would be the best thing she'd eaten in her life, and then a long, deep sleep in a big clean bed. Oh, wow. Just think of that.

It wouldn't be safe to stay more than a day, but if she slept and kept indoors, a twenty-four-hour layover should be okay.

After that, she had work to do and plans to execute.

"You'll have my back while I sleep, right, lover?" she said to Randy.

Right, Princess. Best Girl. Goddess of my heart.

Mackie laughed and then became more focused as she homed in on her mother's house.

It was after 11:00 p.m. when Morales entered the Anza Vista area, northeast of Golden Gate Park. The night air was clear, and the moon was really turning on the wattage, making it look like blue daylight.

Her mother's neighborhood was treeless, block upon block of what could be called modernist row homes. The houses were all different but close enough in appearance that they gave the development a bland sameness and uniformity.

Now she was driving up a deserted Anza Vista Avenue, which divided the double row of pale facades with their parking garages on street level and stairs going up to the front door.

Her mom's house was just ahead, and like the rest of them, it was tan-colored with two gable-like rooftops over square alcoves, a two-car garage on the lower level, and an ornate iron gate locking the stairway to the front door.

Mackie's eyes started to tear up. Minutes from now, she'd be in her mother's warm hug—but Randy was disturbed.

Something's wrong, he said.

"What? *What?*"

She saw a blue sedan, Japanese, parked several houses down, with a good view of her mom's front door. What was wrong was that the sedan was parked on the street *between* two of the homes and yet the driveways of those homes were empty.

Why if you had a driveway and a garage would you park a car on the street?

Maybe it belonged to a guest. Maybe, maybe

. . . or maybe a plainclothes cop was watching her mother's house.

Mackie drove slowly toward the blue car, and just before she passed it, her headlights hit the windshield. A woman was behind the wheel. She was white and blond, and Mackie had seen her before. She worked very hard at not pressing the gas pedal to the floor. Instead, Mackie drove down the avenue at the same cautious speed, took a turn at the end of the next block, and headed out of the development in the direction of the bridge.

She knew the face of the driver. It belonged to Cindy Thomas, Richie's ex-girl and Lindsay Boxer's friend.

Mackie's face flushed. She could feel her heartbeat pounding all the way out to the ends of her fingers. Randy was dead because of Lindsay Boxer. Everything that had gone wrong was because of her.

It all began and ended with Lindsay.

PART THREE

PART THREE

RED SKY IN THE MORNING

Chapter 48

FIRST THING MONDAY morning, and at DA Len Parisi's request, Conklin and I jogged down to the third floor to his offices to meet the new ADA, who would be representing *People versus Holly Restrepo*, scheduled for arraignment at ten.

The new ADA was Travis Cummings, in his first year out of law school and about to try his first case. His cuffed pants were too short, his eyeglass frames were bent, and his cuticles were torn, but to his credit he was smart and he worked fast and well.

Conklin and I took turns briefing the young attorney. We told him that we'd been the first officers on the scene and that we'd found Holly holding a smoking double-barreled shotgun and her husband bleeding out on the floor.

We told him that Ms. Restrepo told us that she did not remember the circumstances of the shooting, but gunpowder residue had been detected on her hands. And we reported that her little boy had said that she had threatened her husband, his father, and he was sure that she had killed him.

We went over all of this in detail until Cummings felt comfortable, and a half hour later, Conklin and I went with him to the small blond-wood-paneled courtroom on the third floor, where my partner and I took seats in the back row.

Holly's case was called first and she pled not guilty, of course.

Her court-appointed attorney argued that Holly had two small children whose father was severely injured and might never recover, and so they needed their mother now more than ever before. Furthermore, said Holly's attorney, she was not a flight risk because of said children and the fact that she had no available funds.

Cummings stepped up and argued that Restrepo's children had told Child Protective Services that their mother had killed their father, and he made a strong request for remand, which the judge granted.

Bail was refused and a trial date was set.

The judge told Holly that her kids, Leon and Christine Restrepo, ages eight and four, were to remain in the custody of CPS pending foster care, which, no kidding, given the option of being returned to their mother, was the best thing for them.

In my opinion he was absolutely right.

Holly screamed and cried that she was the victim here, and Conklin and I slipped out the door. Despite the importance of arraignments, the reality is that in most cases, even murder cases, arraignments take about five minutes.

We took the one flight of stairs to our squad room on the fourth floor, and as we headed for our desks, Conklin said he hadn't eaten anything for breakfast and wanted to run out for a midmorning snack.

"Go ahead," I said. "I need to check my mail."

I was waiting for a call back from Donna Timko, Chuck's Prime's product-development manager, who had seemed willing, even eager, to help us sort through names of personnel who might be the belly bomb extortionist.

I asked Conklin to hang on because there was,

in fact, an e-mail from Timko in my in-box, a brief message sent from her iPhone.

"I'm back from my business trip. Could we meet at ten-thirty this morning in my office? I can give you a half hour."

I wrote back that Conklin and I would see her then. As I relayed this to Conklin, I noticed an e-mail at the very bottom of my inbox. It was from Yuki, and it had come in many hours ago, at two a.m. this morning.

The subject heading read "Help."

She had to be kidding. What is it, Yuki? Too much love and sex? An overabundance of four-star food and five-star views of nature's wonders?

Conklin muttered, "You need something while I'm out, Boxer?"

I said, "Okay. Surprise me," and I clicked on Yuki's e-mail.

There was no text, but I watched the attached ten-second video. And I could not believe what I was seeing with my own eyes.

Rich was heading out the squad room door, but I yelled out, "Rich. Look at *this*. Come over here and look at *this*."

Chapter 49

CONKLIN WASN'T MOVING fast enough for me, so I screamed at him again, even louder.

"Come here, quick! Look at this video from Yuki."

I had seen the ten-second video Yuki had attached to her blank e-mail, but all I could comprehend for sure was that something unthinkable was happening on the *FinStar*.

"Run it again," Richie said reasonably. "And bring up the sound."

I replayed the too-short video. The phone Yuki had used as a camera whipped around and from side to side as her clip opened with an unfocused view of a bright orange lounge inside the ship. I saw streaks of tables, a sofa, and what might have been a piano. And I saw blurred groups of people in defensive postures.

Yuki's voice was recognizable, even though she spoke in a whisper that crackled like crumpling cellophane.

"Lindsay. Our ship was *attacked*. We were hit with *explosives*. The engine room is dead. Men with assault weapons boarded us. *Pirates* or terrorists. I can't talk long—some passengers were shot—"

Shit, shit, *shit*.

The camera angle shifted, and I saw blurry images of people crying into their hands, an elderly couple standing next to Yuki clutching one another in an embrace, their faces contorted in horror. A terrifying blend of shouts and muffled cries nearly overwhelmed Yuki's words.

She said, "We're in a lounge. Just women and elderly. The men are somewhere else. I don't know where Brady is—"

Yuki's voice broke up. I strained to hear her when she said, "We don't know what they *want* or what they're going to—"

A man in camo fatigues, assault weapon in hand, with a knitted black ski mask covering his face, filled the screen and was coming closer. Two seconds of that, then half the picture went dark. There was another flash of orange carpet and then the video was over.

I was screaming inside.

I replayed the video, hoping to extend the ten seconds, to see something beyond this one heart-rending window of time. But of course, the wildly whipping video repeated the frightening scene before going black.

Rich, his eyes fixed on the screen, kept saying, "Holy crap."

I said to him, "This has to be a hijacking. But in Alaska? There can't be terrorists there, right, Rich? It's not the Gulf of Aden, for God's sake. Where's the Navy?"

Richie left my side and went to his computer and typed.

"Oh, man," he said.

"What did you find?"

"This: 'Rogue pirates attack the cruise ship HM *FinStar*.' And this. 'The HM *FinStar*, flagship of the Finlandia Line, filled to capacity with approximately six hundred and fifty passengers and two hundred crew, was attacked by an unknown group of commandos as it prepared to enter Alaska's Inside Passage at Dixon Entrance near Prince Rupert.' "

"Send me the link," I barked.

He did it.

I reached for my keyboard, backhanding the coffee that Rich had left on my desk this morning and sending it spilling in every direction. I didn't even try to contain it.

Richie brought over a wad of paper towels as I read the latest breaking news.

Summarizing: Eight hours ago rocket-propelled grenades had slammed into the *FinStar*'s hull above the waterline, possibly hitting the engine room. An unknown number of gunmen boarded the ship in the small hours of the morning. The group was unidentified. The ship was damaged but afloat. There was no information about casualties. No official word of any demands made by the presumed pirates.

When Yuki had sent the video, she was well. Was she still safe? Was Brady?

I played the video again, looking for any new detail.

I felt that I was looking through Yuki's eyes.

Where was Brady?

Chapter 50

I WAS STARING at the last frames of Yuki's video when my desk phone rang. It was Joe.

I said, "Honey, turn on the TV—"

"I just saw," said Joe. "That's Yuki's ship, right?"

"Can you find out what's happening?"

"I'll try," Joe said.

I heard Julie whimpering in the background, the voice of Maria Teresa, her funny nanny, talking as the baby bawled.

"Call you back," said Joe.

When Joe was with Homeland Security, one of his areas of responsibility was port security. If anyone was connected, it was my husband.

I found a day-old jelly doughnut in the break room, took one bite, and delivered the rest of it to

Conklin. Then I maniacally hit news links while across the desk Conklin took calls from frantic cops, asking if we'd gotten any word from Brady.

When Joe called back, I grabbed my cell, fumbled it, and recovered it just before it hit the floor.

"Talk to me," I said tersely into the phone.

Joe said, "The first mate got out a distress call to the Coast Guard just before the radio room was breached. A man, self-identified as Jackhammer, warned that if anyone approached the ship, people would be shot. The crew is detained in the hold. Passengers have been rousted out of their cabins and corralled under guard to various lounges. There's a Coast Guard vessel in contact with this Jackhammer. I guess some kind of negotiation is in progress."

"That's *it*?"

"No. That's the good news. A passenger got out a phone call saying two passengers were dead, but they weren't named. I'll keep checking."

I called Jacobi to tell him what I knew.

He said, "Brady will take care of Yuki. If you were a hostage, Boxer, who would you pick to break you out? Brady, right?"

That was true. But where *was* Brady?

I forwarded Yuki's video to Jacobi, then sent it to Cindy and Claire, both of whom had e-mailed me after they'd caught bulletins about the *FinStar* on the news.

Cindy had uncut video, just in, of helicopters in the air above the beleaguered ship. It was a haunting fifteen seconds, during which time sections of the ship went dark until the entire ship had been blacked out. Then shots were fired into the air. A lot of shots. Long bursts of them. These hostage takers, whoever they were, had no shortage of ammunition.

I organized a conference call, and Cindy, Claire, and I gibbered anxiously, helplessly. We sounded panicky because we were in a three-alarm panic. We were all accustomed to making things happen, getting things done—but this time we had no moves, no action plan, nothing.

My skull felt as hollow as a drum, empty except for the bad thoughts ricocheting around inside. How could this be happening off the coast of Alaska? Where was Brady? Was Yuki okay? Was she still *alive?* Was Brady?

When I looked up, Conklin was watching me with a steady brown-eyed gaze.

He said, "Can we do anything to help them?"

"You know that we can't do one damned thing."

"Then we've got a meeting with Donna Timko."

The name rang a distant bell.

"Who?"

"Timko. Donna. Head of product development. At Chuck's," my partner said distinctly. As if he were talking to a child.

"Right. When are we supposed to see her?"

"You told her ten-thirty."

It was 10:15 right now.

"I called her. Told her an emergency came up," Conklin said. "She said, 'It's your meeting.' "

"Okay, okay," I said. "Let's hit the road."

Chapter 51

CONKLIN DROVE US northeast on Bryant Street toward the Bay Bridge and West Berkeley, a mixed-use residential/commercial area separated from the bay by the Eastshore Freeway.

As we drove, the car radio chattered, dispatch and squad cars urgently tracking the chase of a hit-and-run driver in the Financial District.

Conklin closely followed the chase and also negotiated traffic while I manhandled my phone. I jumped from news link to news link, cruising for information about the *FinStar,* a fully loaded floating ocean liner under siege.

I found snippets on YouTube—video clips like the one Yuki had sent, truncated and poorly shot, and also taped phone calls from terrified, clueless passengers who'd managed to get out calls before their phones were confiscated.

These postcards from the front were like random pieces of a table-size jigsaw puzzle, giving only ambiguous hints of the big picture.

And then there was breaking news from a passenger's cell phone. A CPA from Tucson, Charles Stone, had hidden in a storage container on the sports deck. He called his brother in Wilmington, who taped the call.

Said Stone: "These guys spoke American English. Or I guess they could be Canadian. I don't know. They've taken a bunch of hostages to the Pool Deck. I heard a burst of gunfire. Tell Mollie that I love her. I love you, too, bro."

I looked up as Conklin was backing our Crown Vic into a spot between two vehicles parked in front of a modern two-story office building with clean lines and a stucco facade. I was so preoccupied with the thoughts of the passengers on the *FinStar* that I was almost surprised to see we were still in California.

We entered the building, which had high ceilings with exposed timbers and lots of windows letting in the bright morning light. The reception area was devoid of advertising posters and other incidentals, which told me that this was a practical workplace and that the staff here had no contact with consumers. We presented our badges to security at the desk and took an elevator up one floor.

A young man with a black faux-hawk and a guarded expression was waiting for us. He said, "I'm Davo. Donna just got out of her meeting. Stick with me."

Conklin and I followed Davo, who opened a locked door and led us down a yellow-carpeted corridor to Donna Timko's sanctum, as spacious and as open as the entrance on the ground floor.

Timko stood and came forward to greet us.

She was a very large woman, obese, actually. She wore a flowing blue dress to just below her knees, an enviable diamond bracelet, and a radiant smile. She looked as kind as she'd looked when we'd seen her on the video screen at the executive meeting.

She said, "It's good to meet you in person. I am so glad you could come."

I don't know what Donna Timko saw in my face, but here's what was in my mind: I didn't want to be there at all.

Chapter 52

I DID MY level best to wrench my thoughts away
from my friends on the *FinStar* as Timko shook my
hand and asked, "Would you like to see the
facility? I'm in love with this place and have very
few opportunities to show it off. You could even
say that I have *none*."

Oh, no. Not a tour.

Timko told her assistant we'd be back in fifteen
minutes, and Conklin and I joined Timko on her
rounds. She started us off with the executive offices,
introduced us to staff, and showed us the plans for
the introduction of Baby Cakes, a new product that
would be rolling out within the next six weeks.

Next stop was the sparkling stainless-steel test
kitchens, fragrant with sugar and spice.

"We're very focused on Baby Cakes right now," Timko told us. "The promotion for this product is going to be huge, and none of our competitors have anything like it."

Baby Cakes were the size of big button mushrooms, each one a single mouthful of a premium flavor combination of cake and frosting to be packaged in six-cake variety packs with a price point of $1.99.

Conklin was like the proverbial kid in a candy shop. He taste-tested mocha cakes frosted with marshmallow and a bunch of tutti-frutti ones topped with shredded coconut and I don't know what else.

He was being affable with a purpose.

Making friends inside.

Almost unnoticed, I took up a position between a mixing station and a huge fridge and watched the cheerful elf chefs with confectioner's sugar on their gloves and noses. I wondered if one of them could be salting cake batter with micro-encapsulated belly bombs.

We returned to Timko's office and assembled in her sunny seating area, banked with potted greenery under a skylight.

"So now that I've had my fun, what can I do to help you?" the product-development chief asked us.

"We need your informed opinion on what's behind the bombs, Donna," Conklin said. "Why do you think Chuck's is being targeted?"

"I've thought of nothing else since the get-go," said Timko. She reached into her handbag for an e-cig and puffed until the end of it turned blue. She seemed to be considering how to say what was on her mind.

Finally she said, "I don't know if this is worth a dime, but last month, there was an offer to buy Chuck's. Space Dogs. You know of them?"

Sure I did. Space Dogs was a hot dog chain based in the Northeast somewhere, Philadelphia maybe, or Scranton.

"Space Dogs wants to get into hamburgers?"

"More like they wanted to take over our real estate—our stores and our plants—and also to cherry-pick our personnel. They'd be expanding the Space Dogs franchise into the West Coast in one very big move," said Timko.

"And did Chuck's management want to sell?"

"Stan Weaver, our chairman, was all for it. He

had golden parachutes ready for key executives ready to go in exchange for supporting the sale."

"How did Michael Jansing feel about selling out?" Conklin asked.

"He's as loyal to Chuck's brand and culture as I am, but there was a lot of money involved. In the end, Jansing voted in favor of the buyout. But listen. Whether the company is sold or not, I want to help you catch the maniac who is killing our customers. That's just so wrong."

I said, "There isn't much time. If the bomber isn't arrested in the next day or so, the governor is going to have to close Chuck's down, maybe permanently."

Timko's eyes watered, and then, after a moment, she said, "I don't know anyone who would want to sabotage this company. Most of us just feel damned grateful to work here."

Conklin and I left Timko to her job and went out to the car, talking about this corporate buyout wrinkle as we walked.

If Chuck's was associated with food-related fatalities, the value of the company would tank, making it a cheaper buy for Space Dogs. On the other hand, there had to be plenty of Chuck's employees who wouldn't profit from a buyout.

Conklin said, "People get fired when companies are bought out, right? Someone at Chuck's might want the deal to fall through."

I said, "Too many twisting roads. Too little time. I don't know about you, Richie, but I hear the ticking of the next belly bomb about to explode."

Chapter 53

CINDY WAS HUNCHED over her laptop at the *Chron*, crunching toward her four o'clock deadline, which was ten minutes from now, a piece about a hit-and-run that had turned into a nightmare on Fillmore Street.

Cindy checked the spelling of the victims' names, did a last polish, then forwarded the piece to her editor.

Before jumping back into her Morales obsession, Cindy checked her e-mail and was cleaning out her spam filter when a subject heading made her heart lurch to a stop.

I MADE YOU CINDY.

Cindy stared at the heading. The meaning was ambiguous, but the words radiated malevolence. She didn't recognize the sender's screen name, but her own e-mail address was posted at the end of her column every day and anyone in the whole wide world could write to her here. She had been about to delete it without opening, but those four words stopped her.

I MADE YOU CINDY.

You made me *what?*

Cindy sucked in a breath and tapped on the envelope icon. The capitalized text was aimed at her like a shotgun muzzle.

I SAW YOU WATCHING FOR ME, CINDY.

MAYBE YOU'RE STILL PISSED OFF BECAUSE RICH FELL FOR ME. HE IS SO HOT, ISN'T HE? I COULD TEACH YOU HOW TO CATCH AND LAND A MAN. BUT, AND DON'T TAKE THIS THE WRONG WAY, IT WOULD BE A WASTE OF TIME. YOU DON'T HAVE WHAT IT TAKES. SO HERE'S MY ADVICE. GO FUCK YOURSELF. AND STAY OUT OF MY WAY. MM

Cindy felt numb, absolutely frozen stiff, but her mind was flashing like a Fourth of July sparkler.

MM was Mackie Morales.

Mackie had made her. In cop jargon, it meant that she'd been seen and identified. Cindy flashed on the other night. While she was parked outside Mackie's mother's house, a dark sedan had driven toward her. It had slowed, hesitated, then sped up and kept going.

That had been Mackie.

And not only had Mackie identified her staked out on the street, she'd also made her as a broken woman, a woman she had trumped.

Cindy's nose smarted and tears welled up. She grabbed a tissue and pressed it to her eyes, willing herself not to cry.

But she cried anyway.

When she got hold of herself, Cindy left her office and made it to the ladies' room without anyone seeing her. She washed her face and put on fresh makeup. Then she went back to her desk with a newborn and promising idea.

She hit the reply key and typed a return e-mail to Morales.

Subject heading: "Mackie's back in town."

Hi, Mackie,

I wasn't sure where you were, so thanks for letting me know. Let's meet. No tricks. I have a big idea to discuss with you.

Cindy

Before she could change her mind, Cindy hit the send key.

There. Done. She hoped she would hear back from Mackie very soon. If Mackie would meet with her, she might get her interview, and Mackie might get the kind of notoriety she might actually crave.

Her computer pinged.

There was mail in her inbox marked undeliverable. It was the message that she had just sent to Morales. Morales must have written to her from public internet access or a boost phone, so Cindy's sketchy connection to her no longer existed.

Cindy exhaled a breath she hadn't known she was holding.

Morales had made her, cut her, dropped her, and every bit of that hurt like a hot poker had been thrust through her heart.

What are you going to do now, Cindy?

What are you going to do?

Chapter 54

YUKI HAD BEEN huddling against a bulkhead on the Pool Deck for a long time, terrified for Brady, having no sense of what these terrorists wanted in exchange for releasing the passengers of the *FinStar*.

And if they didn't get what they wanted, what then?

Start shooting?

Blow up the ship?

She was very aware that she was wearing a see-through nightgown under the short ship-provided terry-cloth robe. She tucked the hem of the robe under and around her, then interlaced her fingers in front of her life preserver as if it could actually save her life.

These were the questions going around and around in her head on an endless loop: *Where was Brady? Had they done something to him?*

About six hours before, Yuki had been savagely woken by an unimaginably loud air-cracking boom. Her bed had pitched sideways, throwing her to the floor.

She had grabbed the floor as the ship rolled in the other direction, and she had fallen head-first hard against the bed frame. She'd screamed, "Brady! What's happening?"

Glass crashed and doors swung open and slammed closed while the echo of the concussion rumbled long and low below her and the ship rolled again. Light flashed where light should not be—outside the windows, below their balcony.

Yuki got to her knees, grabbed the side of the bed, and pulled herself to her feet. Although the bed had been tumbled, Brady's side of it was still neatly made.

She turned to the bathroom and screamed "Brady!" expecting him to come out, saying, "What the hell?" or "Get *down!*"

But he hadn't been there.

Just then, there had been another loud

boom—a bomb going off, for sure. This boom was more muffled than the first, coming from across the hall or maybe the other side of the ship.

Sirens sounded in the hallway, and then a man's voice came over the public address system, saying, "Crew to emergency stations." It was repeated several times.

Yuki's mother would say, "Find your *husband*, Yuki-eh. Go to your *husband*."

No kidding. *Where was he?*

Yuki had pulled on a robe and gone to the windows. She'd spotted a number of small boats, visible in the still-light night sky of Alaska. The boats were motoring at high speed toward the ship.

Yuki remembered feeling pure gratitude.

Thank God. Help was coming.

Help was on the way.

Chapter 55

AS YUKI SAT on the Pool Deck with hundreds of other passengers, shivering in her thin night-clothes, and not just from the cold night air, she remembered how right after she had seen the boats through her window, the public-address system had come to life again, this time squealing as if it were in pain.

Then she'd heard the uninflected voice of the captain.

"Dear guests, this is Captain Berlinghoff. As you have noticed, there has been a disturbance, but there is nothing to worry about, I assure you we are getting everything under control. We will be escorting you to public rooms. Please cooperate with your cabin stewards and stay calm. We are safe, absolutely safe. I repeat . . ."

What *kind* of disturbance?

The small boats had been closing on the flank of the ship. From her windows, forty feet above the waterline, she hadn't seen any faces. But then she'd seen guns.

Was the Navy coming to investigate the explosions? A sharp pang of fear had shot through her mind like a bullet. *Pirates!* Maybe those men were pirates!

But that couldn't be. There were no pirates in this part of the world. This was the United States.

About then, smoke had begun curling through the air-conditioning vents.

Was the ship on fire? Was it even safe to leave?

Oh, God, what was happening? Where was Brady?

She had looked for her cell phone and finally found it wedged under the night stand, but before she could turn it on, there had been a loud knock at the door.

"Mr. and Mrs. Brady. It's Lyle."

Yuki had looked through the peephole and seen their cabin steward, his eyes so round that there was a circle of white all the way around his irises. She'd opened the door.

"Mrs. Brady. You have to go to the Veranda Lounge."

She had asked, "Have you seen my husband?"

"No ma'am. When did you see him last?"

She'd had a lot to drink last night, and Brady had tucked her in early.

Behind Lyle, people wearing life vests filled the corridor, streaming toward the stairs, their faces wrinkled with sleep and naked with fear.

"What's happening?" she'd asked. "Is the ship on fire? Are we under attack?"

"I don't know anything, Mrs. Brady. Put on your life vest," said Lyle, "and hurry to the Veranda Deck. Take the stairs."

"No, *wait*."

Lyle had snapped at her, "Put on your vest and go upstairs, Mrs. Brady. *Go now*."

Yuki had dialed Brady's number, and when his outgoing message came on, she had left a message of her own.

"I'm going to the Veranda Deck," she said. "Look for me."

Panting, her hands shaking uncontrollably,

Yuki had found her deck shoes on the floor of the closet. Her life vest was under the bed—and so was Brady's.

She had put the vest around her and then had taken a last look around the cabin. Opening the drawer of the night stand, she had found her new coral necklace, her wedding gift from Brady. Clutching it, she joined the throng heading for the stairs.

Chapter 56

THERE HAD BEEN four armed men at the top of the stairs. They wore camouflage and ski masks, black with slits for the eyes and mouth. They had held serious assault weapons, and that was when Yuki understood that the captain had nothing under control. He had lied trying to keep order.

Her blood had rushed to her feet.

Lightheaded, close to fainting, she'd grasped the banister and begun to climb. Terror had squeezed out any hope in her mind that this evacuation was about engine failure.

This was an attack.

Where was Brady? Was he even alive?

The men—pirates, as she thought of them— had directed the passengers at the top landing, sending the elderly and the women and children to the left. Men were sent to the right. Anyone who hesitated was shoved or poked with a gun.

Yuki and the rest of those sent to the left were herded into the Veranda Lounge, the pirates deliberately terrorizing the passengers who were as vulnerable as baby birds on a high window ledge. Then all the lights had gone out and Yuki had heard muffled gunfire.

What was happening?

A woman in a red kimono-like robe, her hair in a topknot, leapt up from the floor and shouted at the closest gunman.

"I need my medication. I need water. I need to use the toilet. I'm sixty-seven years old. Let me go back to my cabin. I'm not a flight risk."

The gunman told her to shut up and sit down and then gave her a shove.

There was shrieking, and people shrank from the armed men, but another woman shouted, "You can't keep us here like this. We are human beings."

A gunman raised the muzzle of his gun and fired into the air, sending a shower of glass and plaster down on their heads.

The screaming that followed was cold, sheer horror transmuted into sound. It had been a building panic with nowhere to go.

Yuki had taken her phone out of her robe and pushed the button to record. She had narrated her video in a whisper but a gunman had seen what she was doing. As he was coming toward her, Yuki had quickly sent the video to Lindsay.

The gunman had grabbed her phone, dropped it, and crushed it under his boot.

"You're crazy sending pictures," he had shouted into her face. "And crazy has to pay."

He had backhanded her across the face. Yuki staggered back, but due to the sheer density of people surrounding her, she didn't fall. She'd never in her life been struck in the face. The pain was excruciating, and she'd heard herself moan.

She wished she could take that moan back.

She wished she hadn't shown that she was afraid. Another big man appeared in the doorway, at least six feet and maybe two hundred pounds, also wearing fatigues and mask.

He had shouted, "Everyone shut up! Sorry to be blunt, but everyone just shut the fuck up, okay?"

A restive quiet came over the lounge as the passengers muffled their fear and waited to hear what was coming.

Chapter 57

YUKI DIDN'T REMEMBER every word but close to it.

She had a very good memory for the spoken word and was known around the DA's Office for being able to recall depositions and court testimony verbatim.

The big man in the mask and fatigues, who had told all of the passengers crammed into the Veranda Lounge to shut up, had stepped up onto a chair.

"My name is . . . well, you can call me Jackhammer. And this is your orientation session. In a few minutes you'll know everything you need to know in order to survive. We are in charge.

" 'We' is me and my squad, and I mean we are

completely in charge. The ship's crew can't help you. They are locked up, in chains, under guard. And their lives depend on—you. More on this later.

"To continue, the engine room and the communications deck have also been disabled, but if anyone feels like taking a swim, you're welcome to try. No one will stop jumpers. We are twenty-five miles from land. You will suffer shock the moment you hit the water. It will take about ten to twenty minutes for hypothermia to set in, and even if you make it to shore, which no one can, there's nothing out there.

"So, here's the business end. We've made a demand of the Finlandia Line and assured them that we will shoot a passenger every hour until our money has been wired to our bank account in Zurich. We're caught up now for the first three hours in advance. A few passengers made bad decisions. So.

"So if Finlandia gets moving, if everyone behaves, you can go back to your vacation and we will get out of your lives. And your cooperation will ensure that the crew will also survive.

"Now we are moving you upstairs to the Pool Deck. As you go through the door, drop your cell phone into the box provided. Keep cool. That's my advice. Oh. We are looking for a volunteer. Who is the one who took pictures?" Jackhammer asked.

"This one," said the gunman standing so close to Yuki that she could smell his sweat. He grabbed her arm roughly and shoved her forward. She had lost her footing and fallen to Jackhammer's feet, her robe swinging open and her nightgown hiking up to her hips.

Yuki had experienced fear before. But this was an order of horror beyond her nightmares. She expected a gun in her face, a bullet to her head.

Jackhammer glared at her through slits in his mask. "Thank you for volunteering. You are the next to be shot," he said.

Yuki struggled to her feet and backed into the crowd. And she turned her back on Jackhammer, closing her eyes as the tears sheeted down her cheeks.

If nothing else, she was going to stand up for herself as she always had.

Where was Brady?

Was he one of the passengers who had made a bad decision?

Yuki found it hard to even breathe.

Chapter 58

COLD SALT AIR blew the smell of sweat across the several hundred passengers who were packed on the Pool Deck. Yuki shivered as she sat with her back against a bulkhead. She was jammed against that wall, jammed tight.

Yuki scanned the terror-stricken faces of the passengers, who, like her, had been ripped from their sleep and told that they could be murdered at random at any time, pirate's choice.

And although she'd been told she was the next to be shot, two other people had already been dragged to a railing and, while screaming for help and pleading "no, no, no," shot in the back of the head, and their bodies had been hoisted over the side.

As far as Yuki could tell, the murdered passengers hadn't made a break or hit out or started a fight. They'd been sitting on the deck. Whereas she had taken *pictures*. There was a death penalty for *that*.

Possibly she'd been forgotten or her location in the middle of the crowd was inconvenient for Jackhammer's thugs. If they came for her, could she save herself?

She took a visual tour of the Pool Deck, mapping the structures, the doors, and staircases.

At the bow of the boat was the Luna Grill restaurant, with a bandstand outside it, a raised platform for live entertainment outside the pool.

The middle of the deck was all about the swimming pool, with decking between the edges of the pool and the railings. At the back end of the Pool Deck, the ship's stern, was the Wave Spa, with a wet bar that had been overturned by the terrorists.

Metal stairs began at the base of both the Grill and the Spa, and those outside staircases ran up one flight to the Sun Deck and running track above the pool. The track was open above the Pool Deck, and the terrorists were using the track as a spy's nest, a shooting platform.

Right now one of the terrorists was standing above her on the metal stairs near the Grill, only ten feet away. He wasn't tall, but he was muscular and alert and he carried a massive assault rifle with ammo clips on his belt. His mask hid anything that might be human in him. How could she appeal to a man in a mask?

The male passengers had been moved from wherever they had been sequestered to the part of the deck that was opposite the women, at the far end of the unlit swimming pool. Their backs were to the closed doors of the Water Spa.

Yuki searched the silhouetted grouping of men. Some men stood, but more squatted or sat on the deck behind a ragged line of gunmen. She counted about six of them.

A bright flash in the unrelenting dark caught her eye. It was Brady's hair. She was sure of it.

He was standing toward the back of the crowd, and she wanted to screw everything and just *run* to him. But she knew that was irrational. She didn't even dare to draw his attention. She couldn't put him in danger. Her tears welled up as she thought about how close he was while so far away.

Just then, as if she had summoned him with her fear, Jackhammer walked onto the track above the Pool Deck, that long, hollow rectangle, with its gun's-eye view of the passengers.

Chapter 59

JACKHAMMER CAME DOWN the metal stairs, and when he reached the Pool Deck, he stepped through the shadows and began to cut through the crowd.

He walked to the long side of the pool and raked the passengers left and right with his eyes. His sickening gaze seemed to stop on her and then, having touched her, move on.

Jackhammer cleared his throat and said, "I'm so sorry for the inconvenience, everyone. I know this stinks, but, you know, if it were up to me, you would be back to your vacation. Eating good food. Enjoying the good life.

"But your captain can't get anywhere with your cruise line. Apparently there is an obstacle, which means more of you will die. If only the cruise line would wire the money we have asked for. Well for now, be happy that unlike the captain and crew you have fresh air, and perhaps by morning some of you will have breakfast. Sound good?"

Jackhammer turned as one of his men came toward him. They bent their heads toward each other, conferring. Were they talking about her? Yuki saw movement from the stern: a gray-haired man in bright-green pajama bottoms was running in bare feet, holding a deck chair over his head.

Oh, my God, this passenger had snapped.

He stretched up and hurled the chair at Jackhammer, who saw the chair coming toward him and stepped aside.

A woman cried out, "No, Larry, no!"

Jackhammer had his gun aimed even before the chair crashed to the deck. He fired on the gray-haired man. His wife broke through arms that were holding her in place and ran toward her fallen and dying husband.

Jackhammer fired again and the woman's body jerked before she collapsed on her husband's chest.

The shots and the killings sent the entire deck into motion. Those people near the bleeding bodies fell back, and then panic sent all of the women to the far side of the pool. People slipped on the blood-slicked deck and fell. The strongest trampled the weak. Pirates slammed gun butts into passengers, who made for the doorways and staircases.

Gunmen fired in bursts above the heads of passengers, who were screaming like animals being slaughtered.

It was inside this sheer chaos that Yuki saw her opportunity. Obscuring herself among the hundreds of shifting people, Yuki edged along the length of the deck. By the time the shooting stopped, Yuki had resurfaced beside the man she loved.

Brady drew her into his arms, cloaking her entirely.

"I've got you, sweetheart," he said. "I've got you."

She sobbed into his chest.

She loved him so much.

They had to survive this. They just had to.

Chapter 60

I WAS IN the takeout line at MacBain's, crunching peanut shells underfoot while saying hey to various tipsy Hall of Justice regulars, but my eye was on the muted TV over the bar.

A report was coming in from an ABC affiliate in Alaska. Valerie Ricco, a reporter wearing a big green down coat, was standing on a remote stretch of coastline, trying to keep her footing as the wind whipped her hair and shook her microphone.

The captioning read: "This is day two of the hijackers' takeover of the *FinStar,* a lavish passenger liner . . ."

Behind me were a couple of uniforms, drinking their lunch and talking to each other about Brady and how they heard there had been shootings.

I dropped my eyes from the TV and turning my body, faced the restaurant. I didn't want to be recognized or questioned.

I thought about Brady, a genuine tough guy in the best possible way. Brave. Unflinching. Determined. I'd watched him risk his life to save a child.

I could see him making a move against the commandos on the ship even though he was outnumbered, unarmed, and literally at sea. That made me worry for him, and I worried for Yuki even more. She was a fighter. She had taken on cases that should have gone against her and gotten juries who were predisposed to the defense to dance in the palm of her hand. She'd taken on hardcore criminal defense attorneys, big, big names, and while she hadn't always won, she'd made them sweat for their wins.

But could Yuki's courtroom skills help her now? Could she talk her way out of a sudden-death hostage situation?

I don't pray every day, but I was praying every minute now. *Please God, let them get off that ship alive and well.*

I heard my name, spun around, and grabbed

my bag of sandwiches off the bar. I paid at the cash register, and when I got outside, I phoned Joe.

"Anything new?" I asked him.

"Information coming from the Coast Guard ship is limited, Linds. What I've been able to glean is that these bad guys are kind of a hybrid; like pirates, they're doing this for money, but unlike pirates, they're not in it for a quick score. They're looking for a financial *killing*, and they are trained terrorists.

"No names of possible suspects or groups have been discussed, but from what I'm seeing, they are former military. *Our* former military. They're well aware that no one on the ship is armed, not the passengers and not the crew."

"How can they be sure of that?"

"You can't bring guns onto a cruise ship. No one. Not passengers. Not crew. Not FBI agents on vacation or cops. No guns, because in a case of piracy, insurance companies would rather pay the ransom than pay lawsuits if guns get into the wrong hands and shooting happens."

I was crossing Bryant against the light. I kept the bag of lunch under my left arm, held my phone to my ear, and dodged angry lunchtime traffic.

"So the insurance company is going to pay, right?" I said. "What's the holdup?"

"What's going on, Linds? I can hardly hear you."

I reached the sidewalk and said, "Can you hear me now?"

"Okay. Here's the holdup. And it's not good. *FinStar* has a piracy exclusion in their policy. Because they don't run tours into historically dangerous waters, they took out a cheap policy."

Running up the steps to the Hall, I shouted at the messenger, my poor husband.

"What are you saying? The insurance company isn't liable for the ransom? So what the hell is going to happen? Who's going to pay up? Where's the military? What's the government *doing* about this?"

"A Coast Guard vessel is about a mile away, keeping in contact with the head guy, trying to talk them down. Coast Guards have special ops, but nobody wants to go Waco on this ship. Not now. Too many people would die and—"

I interrupted, grunting my thanks, and said "Sorry for yelling. I love you." Then, churning with furious thoughts about cheapskate cruise ship lines, I went back to work.

Chapter 61

WHEN I GOT back to our desks, Conklin had assembled an array of surveillance DVDs from the six Chuck's Prime restaurants in San Francisco. He'd separated the disks into six stacks, one stack for each restaurant. Each stack was six inches high.

He said, "These were shot with cameras inside and out. There isn't one complete two-week set, but this is everything that could be retrieved, including one from Hayes Valley starting the day before the Jeep bombs."

I said, "The FBI has seen all of these?"

"Yup."

"And they found nothing?"

"There are about a hundred million hours here.

The Feebs are human. They could've missed something," Conklin said. "We could save the day."

"I admire your optimism."

"Yeah?"

He grinned at me. Let's just say that Ashton Kutcher has nothing on Conklin.

I grabbed my phone and put in a call to FBI special agent Jay Beskin in his Golden Gate Avenue office.

He picked right up.

"Jay, am I right that your folks have finished going through Chuck's meat-processing plant?"

"We've pulled core samples from about two tons of chopped meat," he said. "Talk about a needle in a haystack. We're looking for pellets that can fit inside a cold capsule. Anyway, we've examined a lot of prime beef. We scoured the prep kitchens and grilled the workers. No red flags. No flags of any color."

"Any suspects—at all?"

"Seems like only angels work at Chuck's. I'm wide open to ideas, Sergeant."

I updated Beskin on *our* big bag of zeros. I summarized the stakeout at Barney's Wine and Liquor, including the hand-lettered threat left in the briefcase. I told him about my day at the product-development plant and the prospective buyout by Space Dogs that might now be off the table. And I said that my partner and I were about to dive into surveillance footage, again.

Beskin wished me luck, and we exchanged promises to keep each other in the ever-widening, thus-far fruitless loop.

I hung up and looked across our desks to my partner. He said, "Let's each take a disk, press play, and see if something jumps out at us."

I stared at the stacks of surveillance footage, thinking how much I'd love to have a single clean fingerprint or an eye witness or a drop of the bomber's blood. That was the kind of forensic evidence cops had long relied on to point the way, to apply the screws, and nail a case shut.

On the other hand, watching a million hours of surveillance tape was probably the perfect antidote to my upcoming nervous breakdown as I thought about Yuki and Brady under the guns of para-military terrorists off the cold coast of Alaska.

"Lindsay?"

"I heard you," I said to Conklin. "We're looking for something to jump out at us. Preferably someone wearing a sign reading, 'I'm the Bomber.'"

Conklin laughed. "Wouldn't that be nice?"

He brought us coffee from the break room and I unwrapped the BLTs. After our trash had been dumped in the round file, we each cued up a CD from our chosen stack.

My first had been recorded on the day before the original belly bomb explosions.

We were 100 percent sure that the two students who'd been killed by belly bombs a week ago had eaten "hamburger bombs to go" from the Hayes Valley Chuck's.

Somewhere in my stack of disks, there had to be a killer.

Chapter 62

SECURITY SYSTEMS IN fast-food restaurants and parking lots rarely produce footage that's HD, in focus, and Sundance Film Festival worthy. Chuck's Prime's Hayes Valley series was no exception.

I cued up the first disk, the footage that was shot inside Chuck's on the day preceding the double belly bombs. The camera was set back and across from the cash register and trained on the cowpoke behind the counter. The camera angle also gave a partial view of the kitchen behind the counter, a sixty-degree-wedge view of the tables, and the front door.

I watched black-and-white images of people coming into the store for morning coffee, and then I hit fast-forward until I reached the three-hour mark, about the time Chuck's began to fill for lunch.

I scrutinized the customers ordering, those picking up at the takeout line, and others who were dining in. Wait staff were doing their jobs and joking with customers. I didn't see anything remarkable. It seemed to be a good day at Chuck's Hayes Valley.

I studied the cooks and kitchen workers through the letter-box view of the kitchen and tried to imagine how one of them might plant mini-explosives in a hamburger patty.

It didn't look all that hard to do.

Meanwhile, the mood inside our bullpen had changed from a high-functioning homicide squad into some kind of powerless mission control center agonizing over a derelict spacecraft. Throughout the afternoon, the day crew kept stopping by our desks to find out if Conklin and I had heard anything new about Brady. At day's end, Cappy McNeil and his partner, Paul Chi, dragged chairs over and sat down. They had both worked with Brady, had friendships with Yuki, and were feeling frustrated and angry and helpless to the max.

Copy that.

Lacking any shred of good news, we batted around theories of how the hijacking might resolve with pirates dead and passengers safe. We put a hopeful face on it, but in fact none of us tossed confetti.

Before Chi and McNeil clocked out, Chi leaned over my desk and tapped a key that brightened my screen. Cappy gave me a pound cake he'd been intending to take home for dessert and kissed my cheek. A first.

After my old pals said good night, Conklin and I went back to hamburgers on parade.

I watched the relentless march of people on my screen, and after reviewing the entire fast-forwarded twelve hours of Day Minus One inside the restaurant, I changed out the disk and watched parking lot videos.

These were more of the same: slices of gray-and-white cinema verité: a bread truck arrival and departure, ditto a refrigerated delivery truck from Chuck's main kitchen, bringing boxes to the back door. And I watched a few hundred cars park in Chuck's lot and then depart onto Hayes Street.

Had I seen a killer and didn't know it?

How could I know?

I went on to the next day's disk, saw the two doomed college kids pick up their lunch from the takeout line, and noticed some of the same customers I'd seen before.

I made a note of the regulars, marking the time that they appeared on the tape, and I took screen captures for later comparison. Again I watched delivery trucks arrive and guys lugging cartons to the back door of the kitchen.

I watched the Hayes Valley kitchen crew dunk trash into the Dumpster outside the back door and lock up the store when the doors were closed for the day.

I got up and went to the ladies', and when I came back, Conklin said, "I'm thinking Italian."

"Fine idea."

Chapter 63

CONKLIN AND I walked out onto a darkened Bryant Street and headed to Enzo's, a greasy pie pan joint on 7th, where we scarfed down a pizza before returning to surveillance footage hell.

It was my turn to make coffee, and Conklin used a letter opener to cut Cappy's donated pound cake into thick slices.

Four hours later, I had marked and snipped out three images of customers who looked suspiciously like the same person in disguise: a skinny guy with (a) a beard, (b) a knit hat, and (c) a hoodie.

That was the extent of suspicious individual sightings. Still . . .

I showed my snippets to Conklin, who said sweetly, "I think you're reaching, Linds."

I took a fistful of pencils out of the mug on my desk and hurled them, one after the other javelin-style, toward the trash can near Brenda's vacant desk across the room.

I made six baskets out of ten. Which sucked. It was a big trash can.

I said to Conklin, "Maybe I'm reaching. Maybe I'm right on the nose. You don't mind if I send these photos to the lab. Get another opinion?"

"There's a naked woman in my bed," Conklin said, reaching behind his chair for his Windbreaker. "I think I'll go now, catch her while she's still in the mood."

"Go," I said. "This will still be waiting for us tomorrow."

Conklin waved good-bye, and then my phone rang.

It was Joe, and he got right into it.

"This just in on the *FinStar*," he said. "Shots have been heard. Another body has washed up. Crowds are gathering all over Alaska, demanding an end to the hostage crisis. The government of Finland is jumping up and down, but there's absolutely nothing they can do. Communications with the Coast Guard vessel have broken down. That's all I've got. I'm sorry."

"Shit."

"I know," said my husband. "Come home now, Blondie. Your family misses you."

Chapter 64

TOTAL DARKNESS HAD descended over southeastern Alaska. Sitting on the deck behind Brady, Yuki pressed her cheek against his polo shirt and just tried to breathe normally.

Brady said softly, "Sweetie, this will be over soon. They can't keep six hundred people in this situation for very long."

She nodded. "I know."

They'd been fed and watered like animals. They'd been given limited access to stinking buckets for toilets and no privacy. They'd slept on their feet or sitting with their backs against others.

The mood on the ship was getting desperate.

The passengers and even the damned pirates looked and acted like they were running out of patience. They circled above on the running track, dropped burning matches, fired off volleys of bullets, and kept terror alive on the ship.

Yuki had met enough criminals with explosive anger issues to know that any one of these men could go off and start mowing people down. She scooted around until she was sitting next to her husband. She looped her arm around his calf and hugged it hard. He put his arm around her back and held her tight. Her feeling of safety was at complete odds with her knowledge that they could easily be dead before the sun came up.

A woman was sitting next to Yuki on her left. She had told Yuki that her name was Susannah. Susannah was in her fifties and was wearing a robe as Yuki was but with red flannel pajamas underneath and fuzzy socks. She was praying for the lives of all of the people on the ship, and she was asking God to forgive the pirates for what they had done.

Yuki didn't understand how she could pray for the men who had just gunned down innocent people.

Now that it was so quiet on the deck, Yuki could hear the water lapping against the sides of the ship, Brady's breathing, and Susannah talking to God under her breath.

A pirate was standing by the rail, maybe fifteen feet away from them. This is the one Yuki thought of as Bigfoot because of the way he walked, with long, heavy footsteps. He lowered his head and cupped his hands to light a cigarette.

Beside her, Brady was watching Bigfoot, too. Watching him puff on his cigarette, then pull his radio phone out of his shirt pocket and speak into the microphone at his mouth. Yuki saw her husband check his watch, then turn his head to the right.

She followed Brady's gaze and saw him make eye contact with another passenger who also seemed aware of the pirate's movements.

She remembered the man's name. Brett Lazaroff. She and Brady had met him at the breakfast buffet line the first morning, which seemed like forever ago.

Lazaroff had dark hair that was going gray and was about sixty and very fit. He and Brady had gotten into a conversation in front of the scrambled eggs tray.

She'd said hello and taken her plate to the table,

where she learned that Lazaroff was widowed with adult kids and owned an auto supply store in Anacortes. He might have said that he'd been in the military.

Now she saw Lazaroff lift his jaw toward Bigfoot and she saw Brady nod. Yuki thought it might be the almost telepathic communication of two men who had been trained to shoot first.

A little bud of hope blossomed in her mind.

Brady and Lazaroff were working on a plan.

Chapter 65

THE CALL CAME in before 7:00 a.m. as I was snoozing deeply, my head on a new pillow that had been billed correctly as "better than goose down."

I looked at my chirping phone and said, "No way."

But I couldn't ignore the call from Michael Jansing.

"Boxer," I harrumphed into the mouthpiece.

"Sergeant Boxer, sorry to call you this early, but I just got a text from the bomber. I told him I couldn't speak to him in private until I got to the office, that I was surrounded by my family."

"You told him when you'd get to work?"

"I said I'd be there at eight."

"Come to the Hall," I told Jansing. "I'll meet you."

I found FBI special agent Jay Beskin's card in my blazer pocket and called him at once, and thank you, God, he picked up.

"Jay, the belly bomber has reached out to Jansing and is calling him at around eight. Can you meet us at the Hall pronto?"

My next twenty minutes were a flurry of dressing and looking for car keys, punctuated by gulps of scalding coffee and the protests of my screaming baby.

"I'll be home tonight, baby girl. I *will*."

I called Conklin from the road and told his voice mail that the bomber was stirring, and that I'd be in the squad room shortly. I called Jacobi and left the same message.

I reached the Hall and parked with ten minutes to spare and met Beskin on the steps to the main entrance. Up to a point, he was central casting's idea of an FBI agent: six-one, square-shouldered and square-jawed, with a government-issue haircut and a good gray suit. And then there were his bright-red-and-silver running shoes.

He saw me looking at them.

"What?" he said. "The fastest way to get here was to *run*."

Agent Beskin and I exchanged nervous chitchat as we waited for Jansing to arrive. Pulling up minutes later, he parked his Beemer illegally but he was on time.

I asked Chuck's sandy-haired CEO, "Did he call?"

"Not yet."

We entered the Hall through the heavy steel-and-glass front doors. I badged Jansing and Beskin through security and we arrived upstairs before the clock struck eight.

Our electronics tech from the radio room, Kelli Pearson, was waiting in Brady's empty office with her bag of tricks open and ready. I knew her to be smart and thorough, and I introduced her as such to Jansing and Beskin. Then we all took seats in the glass-walled hundred square feet that felt almost roomy without Brady's bulk behind the desk.

Jansing said, "The bomber keeps saying no police. And yet, here we are."

I said, "It was either come here and trace the call or go to your office and miss an opportunity to catch this guy."

The call came to Jansing's phone at ten after the hour. Pearson got the number and tapped it from the phone plugged into her laptop. The software chased the number to the cell phone tower that routed the bomber's call but didn't ring the bomber's phone.

On my signal, Jansing said into his phone, "This is Jansing."

I leaned in so that Jansing's ear and mine bracketed his cell phone. I heard the chilling electronically modulated voice say, "Listen up. Five million is the price. If you don't have it ready for drop-off by tomorrow morning at eight on the nose, bombs will go off. Multiple."

"Wait," Jansing said.

Pearson turned the laptop so we could see the blinking dot that represented the bomber's car moving east on Carroll Avenue. This was an industrial area, dense with warehouses, trucking companies, heavy-equipment lots, and commercial truck traffic.

"No waiting," said the robo-bomber. His voice was so freaking mechanical, I wondered if there was really a person speaking into a phone.

"Money for lives, Jansing," said the hollow

voice. "I don't mind blowing up people. Why should I?"

"How can you go from asking a hundred thousand to demanding five million? I can't get that much—"

"Once I have the money, I'll stop. Otherwise . . ."

The phone went dead.

Pearson tapped her keyboard—but there was no blinking dot on the map of the Bayview area of San Francisco.

"That shitbird took the battery out of his phone," Agent Beskin said. "For God's sake! I keep waiting for him to do something stupid."

I called Dispatch from Brady's desk phone.

"I need all cars in the vicinity of Carroll and Third Street in the Bayview neighborhood to report any suspicious vehicular activity."

"What type of vehicle, Sergeant?"

"Damned if I know," I snapped. "Sorry. Anything suspicious, that's all."

Once again, our belly bomber was driving the action. We wouldn't have time to set up a trap because we wouldn't know the drop point until he made his next call to Jansing.

Beskin said to Jansing, "We'll stick with you,

Mr. Jansing, as many agents as it takes to keep you safe and to get this guy when he calls again. We'll be ready for him. He won't get away from us the next time."

I couldn't think of a reason in the world for Jansing to believe him.

Chapter 66

AT JUST BEFORE noon, a refrigerated transport van with the distinctive checked aqua trim and Chuck's Prime logo of a snorting bull on a hill pulled into the loading area behind a Chuck's Prime in Larkspur.

Chuck's was one of many shops and restaurants in a busy outdoor mall called Marin Country Mart. With a yoga studio, a French bakery, a sushi joint, and a brewing company, the whole area was designed to look like a quaint country-style town offering views of Mount Tamalpais and the terminal for the ferry that took people from Marin to San Francisco.

The driver, a wiry, well-built man with dark hair and a two-day-old beard, stepped down from the van and closed the door.

He squinted at the sun, then walked around stacks of pallets and a Dumpster and rounded the corner to the front of the store, where the buff college boys and cute cowgirls were setting up tables under an olive tree. They were busy, earnestly unfurling market umbrellas, spraying Windex on the front window, polishing the chrome trim.

He shouted, "Howdy y'all."

"Oh, hey, Walt," one of the boys said. "I'll get the door."

"Thanks, Tony. I'll be there in a minute."

Walt unzipped his leather jacket, pulled up his hood, and went inside and ordered a Coco-Primo shake to go.

The counter guy, Arturo, turned down his offer to pay, saying, "C'mon, man, it's on the house."

The two men exchanged sad commentary about the fumble at the goal line last night, and then Walt took his shake out the front door. He sucked on his sweet, thick shake for a minute, taking in the sun on the water, and then continued around the stucco wall of the restaurant to the back.

He opened the cab of the van, placed his drink in the cup holder, and then walked toward the cargo doors. He set his hand truck down on the asphalt and began loading twenty-pound cartons of frozen beef patties onto the dolly.

"Let me give you a hand," Tony called out. He was a big kid who probably played football in high school, Walt thought.

"Sure," Walt said. "I'm running late. I've got a few more stops to make before I hit rush hour."

The big kid used a brick to wedge open the back door and went to help Walt.

"You came just in time," Tony said. "I didn't know if we were going to have enough patties to get through lunch."

"I'll tell management to boost your weekly order."

"Good. Thanks," said Tony. "Hey, you know that girl I told you I liked? Gita?"

"Sure. In your drama class."

"That's her," said Tony. "We're hanging out now."

"That's fine," said Walt. "Good luck with that."

Tony grinned and said, "See you next week."

Walt passed gas as he climbed into his van. He

settled in, picked up his cup, and sucked up a long pull of chilly Coco-Primo before putting the van into gear.

He was whistling through his teeth as he pulled the truck out onto Sir Francis Drake Boulevard and headed west to his next stop.

Man, he was like riding the moon.

In the back of the freezer compartment was a box of frozen patties packed lovingly with a little extra bang.

Every way he looked, it was win/win.

Money or *ka-boom*.

Or possibly both.

Why not? Life was good. And he didn't owe anyone a damned thing.

Chapter 67

CONKLIN AND I were in Jacobi's corner office on the fifth floor. Traffic was flowing, and the sun was bright.

I took in my old friend's office, which had been furnished for him in wide, comfy couches and chairs, an expansive desk, and a pretty nice-looking Persian carpet—all of which he deserved after his hard years in Homicide and recompense for his shot-up hip and other permanent injuries he'd taken on the Job.

The three of us were grumbling about the lack of progress on the *FinStar*. As we waited for the new mayor to arrive, Jacobi was saying that Yuki, who weighed barely a hundred pounds, could be broken like a twig.

"But she's got a quick mind," I said. "She's thought her way around killers a few dozen times, you know."

At that the mayor came through the doorway.

His Honor Robert Morley was a serious man of thirty-six, a lawyer and former car-dealership owner, married and the father of four, a pillar of the community. He was charismatic and handsome, and he was building his public service career with no ceiling on his ambitions.

I knew he didn't want to make any mistakes.

He shook hands all around, put his coat over the back of the couch, and took a seat, saying, "Sorry. The traffic was against me. I mean, it fought me like hell."

Jacobi got up and closed the door and gave the mayor a bottle of spring water from the fridge. Then we all took seats in the soft leather furniture. Jacobi led the discussion by saying that he'd been partnered with Conklin and me and added, "These two are the best of the best, Your Honor. None better. Boxer, tell the mayor what we have on the belly bomber."

The mayor leaned forward, clasped his hands between his taupe pinstriped knees, and said, "I've been thinking about this case since I saw those bodies in the Jeep. One of the worst things I've ever seen."

I brought him up to date on the failed stakeout on San Leandro Street and the note the bomber had left behind after he emptied the cash from the briefcase.

When I'd answered the mayor's questions, I ran through the ticktock on the day's events. I told him that I'd called in the FBI and that we'd lost the belly bomber a nanosecond after he made his demand.

"Mr. Mayor, the bomber threatened multiple bombs," I said. "Chuck's may not pay the ransom, and even if they do, this psycho is enjoying himself. I'll bet he wants to kill people more than he wants a payoff. He likes the game too damned much."

The mayor asked me, "What do you suggest?"

"We should shut down Chuck's Primes in San Francisco, which will at least stop people from eating Chuck's burgers immediately. And I think we should ask the governor to close down every Chuck's in California while we and the FBI work on the case."

The mayor, being a lawyer, didn't agree.

"As I understand it, all you have that links Chuck's to the explosive material in the original incident is a lab report of the bomb ingredients. You can't actually place those burger bombs in the actual restaurant, correct?"

I couldn't believe what the mayor was saying.

We had two dead people with Chuck's hamburger wrappings in the backseat of their car. We had explosive material in high-quality chopped steak consistent with Chuck's Prime. We had the bomber holding up Chuck's CEO for ransom to stop further bombings. Surely that was enough to connect the bomber to Chuck's. *Come on.*

The mayor kept talking.

"This anonymous guy who's making the threats could have planted the bombs in that hamburger without being a Chuck's employee, couldn't he?"

I didn't see how.

The mayor went on.

"Or maybe the bombs weren't in the *hamburgers,* but the kids ate them and something else, and the product was in their systems."

He paused, but I didn't know what to say. The guy didn't want to close Chuck's down, and he didn't want me to contradict him.

"Look, Sergeant. I understand you. I don't want more people to die either," Morley said. "But, I can't padlock a company without direct evidence," he said.

The mayor shook hands with us again, told us to keep working—even harder—and to get in touch with him immediately if we had a breakthrough in the case.

He exited Jacobi's office leaving us with absolutely nothing but bomb threats in the wind.

Chapter 68

MORALES HAD BOOSTED another car, a 2004 Subaru Outback, and it was perfect. The sea-foam-green color was boring, the car was dirty, and it had open boxes of old picture frames in the back. There wasn't a person in the state of California who would give this car a second look or even a first.

Not even the cops would be looking for a car worth five grand on a good day.

Randy was humming as she cruised slowly down 7th Street and stopped at the light at Bryant. She took in the whole of the Hall of Justice, the gray granite building where she had gone to work every day last summer.

It gave her a tremendous high to reflect on

those months, going every morning through the lobby, clearing security, working an actual job in Homicide. And she had turned in an award-quality performance that would never be credited by the Academy.

She liked thinking about the killings she'd finessed, no one suspecting her—ever. And she'd gotten Rich Conklin to fall in love with her. Oh, man. He was *so* hooked.

You were dazzling, baby, Randy said.

"I did it for us, lover," she said. "Just for us."

And that was why the outcome was so wrong. She'd scored big-time, and Randy should be alive. And so she was stuck remembering what Lindsay Boxer had caused. She hated that woman so much, her thoughts alone should have been enough to kill Boxer dead.

The stoplight changed and Morales turned onto Bryant and drove slowly past the Hall. A few cops were grouped around a squad car at the curb. She knew them, could remember all of their names. She had an impulse to wave.

Randy said, *Get a move on, sweetheart.*

"I know. No showing off," Morales muttered.

She stepped on the gas and, after clearing the

Hall, turned left onto Harriet. There was a parking lot on her left, right near the ME's Office, and Boxer used to park her car there in the shade of the Interstate.

Morales peered along the rows of parked cars but didn't see Boxer's blue ride. Hell, she had probably gone for the day. No problem. She knew where Boxer lived, had memorized the address months ago. When her lover was still alive. When she still believed in a happily-ever-after life.

The kind of life Boxer had.

Morales took a left on Harrison Street, and headed north toward Lake Street. She hoped the Boxer-Molinaris kept the curtains in their apartment open. She wanted to see the sergeant at home with her husband and child. She wanted to get a feel for their neighborhood.

And then, after she'd seen her mom and little boy, she was going to come back here and destroy everything that Lindsay Boxer loved.

Chapter 69

LAST NIGHT, THINKING about the f-you e-mail she had gotten a couple of days ago from Morales, Cindy had lain awake in bed, trying to figure out if there was a way in the world she could locate that hateful woman.

Cindy didn't remember falling asleep, but then daylight pried her eyes open. She picked up last night's thoughts as though she had never dropped them.

But now she had an idea.

She cleaned up, made coffee, and then called her new pal in Wisconsin, Captain Patrick Lawrence of the Cleveland, Wisconsin, PD.

The captain answered on the first ring and said he was just getting in, to give him a second to take off his jacket. She heard the clunk of the phone on his desk and then he was back.

"I've got time to talk right now, Cindy."

"I need some help, Pat, of the usually off-limits-to-reporters kind."

The captain told Cindy he was happy to help her as long as she kept his name out of it. He couldn't chase Morales himself when she was out of his county, but the fact that she was tied to Randy Fish gave the captain some personal interest in the outcome of the case.

Cindy paced around her small apartment as she told the captain about Morales's e-mail.

"She pegged me when I was watching for her outside her mother's house. I didn't get a look at her car. She had her high beams on, but apparently she saw me. I'm thinking she has to be driving a stolen car."

Lawrence said, "Makes sense she'd be boosting cars of opportunity. I would imagine she'd rotate them out pretty regularly, hoping it would take a while for local PDs to catch up with her ride."

"Pat, here's the favor: Could you access a stolen-car database and give me a list of recently stolen cars in San Francisco?"

"Check your e-mail after lunch," he said.

At the end of the day, Cindy met with Henry Tyler in his office. He looked distracted and intense at the same time. He didn't ask her to sit down. He just said, "Where are you on Morales?"

Cindy said, "She's in town, Henry. She sent me an e-mail telling me that she saw me."

"She wrote to you?" said the publisher. He was standing behind his desk and had been moving stacks of paper, looking for something. A pen. And he found it. Cindy had a hundred and ten percent of Tyler's attention now.

He said again, "She *wrote* to you? What did she say?"

"She told me that she knows I'm looking for her and to get off her tail."

"Cindy. What the hell? You were going to let the police know where she was, get her arrested. Isn't that right?"

"Right. That's still the plan. Get her arrested. Write the story. I'm working with a police captain, trading information, and I think I have an idea why she's in town."

"My instincts are telling me to pull you off this, Cindy. It feels like this could go very bad."

"Henry, this e-mail is huge. I'm being careful—"

"Make sure you understand me. Don't go near Morales unless you're in a cop car, *with cops*. Do you hear me?"

"Yes, sir, I do."

Cindy left Tyler, went down the hall to her own office, and called Lindsay again. This was the third message she'd left for her friend, and now she was worried.

It was just a hunch, but she thought maybe Morales was in town not just to see her child but to go after Lindsay. It was no secret that Randy Fish had been fascinated with Lindsay. He had singled her out as the only cop he would talk to, and Mackie knew that. Did that work on her? Was she jealous of Lindsay? It had to have hurt her deeply that Lindsay had been alone with Fish when he *died*.

That must have almost killed Mackie.

Maybe she was getting this wrong, but psychologically it made sense. She had to let Lindsay know.

She texted Lindsay: Call me.

Then she opened her mail from Captain Lawrence.

He had listed six cars that had been stolen in San Francisco this week, most of them cars that could be profitably chop-shopped for parts or sold in Mexico. She printed out the list, which included a BMW and a Jaguar. The last car on the list was a 2004 Subaru Outback that had been parked two to three blocks down from Candlestick Park. She didn't know if Morales had stolen that car, but it was the kind of car that went unnoticed, and she could see Morales feeling very safe in an ancient station wagon.

Cindy left her office and got her own car out of the lot. She had the Subaru in mind when she drove toward Lindsay's neighborhood.

She called Lindsay again as night came on.

Chapter 70

CINDY NEATLY BACKED her car into an empty spot under the curbside acacia and hawthorn trees in front of Table Asia Gallery. To her left, 12th Street dead-ended a half block to the north, where it butted up against Mountain Lake Park. Across the intersection of Lake and 12th, the blocky five-story apartment building where Lindsay and Joe lived dominated her eastern view.

Evening rush-hour traffic streamed past her with the urgency of people fleeing their offices for the relief of home.

Cindy fixed her eyes on the flow of cars, putting her mind on "search" for the recently stolen vehicles on Captain Lawrence's short list. Once she'd locked in, the pissed-off voice in her head was free to carp about the frustrating and demeaning meeting she'd just had with Henry Tyler.

Principally, his order to "go in a cop car *with* cops" was insulting and lame. How was it possible that Henry Tyler, publisher of the *Chronicle,* didn't know that tracking a subject, digging up news to trade with cops in exchange for access, was standard operating procedure for investigative reporters?

She, in particular, had a long history of working with cops and bringing home big stories. Henry knew this full well, and his slap across the face only fueled her determination to nail this god-damned story she'd turned from a stale report of a sighting into a story in three dimensions. Now she needed to bring it home. Collect her prize.

Cindy took mental inventory of the Morales situation. She knew that Morales was in San Francisco, which was a jump on every other reporter in the world and also the FBI. She'd met Morales and knew enough about her to push her buttons. Admittedly, the button-pushing was a two-way street. The inflammatory and scary e-mailed threat from Morales was proof of that.

But, most important, this e-mail had been direct contact between the two of them. I MADE YOU CINDY.

If that wasn't the first sentence in the lede paragraph of her upcoming career story, she didn't know squat about journalism.

Cindy heard the buzz of her cell phone with an incoming text message. She grabbed it. Lindsay.

I'm in a meeting. Later.

She was about to reply when an old greenish Subaru wagon drove past her, heading north on Lake Street. It was almost as if she'd conjured up one of the cars she was looking for—and it was real and right in front of her.

The dusty-green Subaru Outback cruised through the intersection of Lake and 12th and seemed to slow as it passed Lindsay's building. Then it continued on, its taillights receding up ahead, already too far away for Cindy to read the plate number.

She tossed her phone onto the passenger seat, strapped in, jerked the car into gear, pulled out into the lane, and jammed on the gas. Thirty seconds later, she was flying east, past blocks of multicolored Victorian houses, tailing the green all-wheel-drive vehicle that was heading toward the Presidio.

She could make out the silhouette of the driver through the Subaru's rear window three cars ahead, but she wasn't close enough to tell if the driver was male or female.

Was Mackie Morales driving that car?

Actually, Cindy had no idea.

Chapter 71

CONKLIN AND I were taking up space in the tech bullpen at Clapper's forensics lab, peering over the bony shoulders and fuchsia hair of Bo Kellner, a sharp young criminalist who specialized in digital forensics.

The three frames I'd snipped from several days of surveillance footage shot at the Hayes Valley Chuck's Prime restaurant were getting this kid all excited. Well, the frames were exciting, but Kellner was already highly enthused about his new facial-recognition program called Hunting Wolf.

He'd just installed it yesterday, and he was already being given a real-life opportunity to run Hunting Wolf through its paces. He was as excited as if he'd won the Instant Scratch-off Lotto.

I only half listened to Kellner talk about his program because I was juggling anxiety on two fronts: the upcoming ransom deadline from our friendly mechanical belly bomber and my constant thrumming, live-wire fear for the lives of Yuki and Brady.

Conklin, however, appeared to be in the present, and he wanted to get to know Bo Kellner's new baby.

"What do you know about facial recognition?" Kellner asked Conklin.

"Pretty much what's been produced in this lab and what I've seen on cop TV."

Kellner laughed. "Okay, then. So let's start with this."

He inputted one of the faces from the grainy footage I'd sent to the lab twenty-four hours ago. It was a three-quarter view of a thin white man with a full beard who'd been caught on camera ordering from the menu hanging over the counter.

Kellner was saying, "If this was actual footage, Hunting Wolf could read his lips and tell you what he ordered," when my phone chirped. I fished it out of my jacket pocket and glanced at the caller ID.

It was Cindy.

I texted her that I couldn't talk but I'd call her later. Thinking, yes, after I had the belly bomber in my theoretical crosshairs.

Right now Belly Bomber was job one.

Kellner was saying, "So now Hunting Wolf is scanning this gray-and-white image, using algorithms that look for light and shadow and specific features, relaying that information as a face print—a unique numerical code."

"I'm more or less following you," Conklin said.

"Look," Kellner said. "See the flickering at the top of the frame? The program is scanning pretty fast, but when it reaches the center of the face, the rapid movement will slow down as it tracks the features."

Kellner rotated the face from three-quarters to a frontal view. He said, "Now I'm going to mess with the picture a little. I'm going to delete the beard and fill in the lower half of the face with what we call male physiological norms."

Kellner moved the cursor around, twiddled with the image, and within seconds the guy with the beard was clean-shaven with a nice jawline.

Kellner said, "So now, I enter this clean face

into the database and give him a name: Kellner1SFPD. We've gone from facial tracking to facial recognition."

The software jiggled, locked in, and then flashed through millions of faces already stored in the database, ranging beyond the known criminal database to any matching image that had ever been downloaded onto the Internet, at the fantastic speed of thirty-six million faces a second.

But for all the cutting-edge pizzazz, there was no match.

I said, "So he's not a known criminal, and he's not known, period."

"That's right," said Kellner. "If his image was on Facebook or any database, Hunting Wolf would send up a flare. This guy has a very low, almost nonexistent profile."

I leaned in and said, "If you input the second face, it could match to the first. It's still just a cold hit, but maybe we'd get a better image of this guy, right?"

"Correct," said Kellner. "Exactly right."

The second photo from my series was of a skinny guy wearing a dark leather jacket, knit hat, a brushy moustache, and a small soul patch.

Kellner imported it, and technological wizardry recommenced. Images flashed on the screen, stopped on the first skinny guy, now known as Kellner1SFPD, and flashed "100% MATCH."

Kellner said, "Let's go for a triple play."

Skinny man number three wore a hoodie that threw a shadow over his eyes.

The mouth on number three looked different from the first two, and he had a bulge in his cheek that looked like he had food in his mouth. Kellner explained, "Could be chewing gum. That's a time-tested method of fooling ID software. Even smiling can throw off the search function. That's why you don't smile for a passport ID. But don't worry. Hunting Wolf is smarter than the guy chewing gum and wearing a hoodie.

"Watch Hunting Wolf *hunt*."

Chapter 72

AS I WATCHED the computer screen, the software digested the new input at some unimaginable speed, and when it stopped, I was looking at a composite of our three skinny guys without any facial fur.

Kellner's program then did a global recognition search, and when no lights blinked and no bells rang, he pushed back his chair and looked up at us.

"I don't know who he is, but this is a pretty good representation of what your man looks like."

I asked Kellner to get up and let me sit close to the monitor, which he did. I stared into the eyes of the composite image, and I swore that face looked familiar to me.

Was that because I recognized him from watching the facial recognition process? Or did I recognize the actual guy?

I knew my brain was fried from viewing too many miles of gray-and-white surveillance footage, but still, pieces and parts of the man's face matched a man I'd *seen* but didn't *know*. Then I pictured him in *action*.

I recalled a barely registered image of a guy like this one stepping down from a Chuck's refrigerated transport van. He'd been wearing a dark leather jacket and a dark scarf around his neck. No, not a scarf. It was a gray hoodie. He had opened the cargo doors, his back to the camera, then, head lowered, he'd carried a stack of white cartons to the back door at Chuck's Hayes Valley location.

My mind saw it now, more vividly than when I'd watched the unending surveillance footage.

The skinny guy had delivered food to Chuck's.

Then, having handed off a half dozen white cartons to the kitchen, he'd pulled up his hood and gone into the restaurant. I was staring at his composite image right now.

But even if my sketchy memory was dead-on,

this might mean only that the delivery truck driver liked to buy lunch after he made a delivery.

But why hide his face?

If he was a deadbeat dad, or if there was a warrant out for him, and he wasn't the stupidest person on earth, he might have fooled around with his facial hair to avoid detection by the security cameras.

Or else this guy, who had the means and the opportunity to deliver preformed frozen hamburger patties to Chuck's restaurants, was no dead-beat dad.

He was Mr. Ka-boom.

"He works for Chuck's," I said to Conklin. "I'm sure of it. Richie? I think we have a suspect."

Chapter 73

BO KELLNER FORWARDED the composite image of our suspected belly bomber to my phone. I thanked him, said, "Great job, Bo," and handed my car keys to Conklin.

Once Conklin and I were inside the elevator, I checked the time again and saw that, as if I didn't already know it, we were edging up on the bomber's deadline. We had about twelve hours to name, locate, and arrest the man I'd tentatively identified as Mr. Ka-boom. The sun was down and offices were closed. Catching this guy without a name was a lot to hope for.

We piled into my Explorer and burned rubber in the forensic lab's lot, then headed out to Emeryville at high speed.

I texted and then called Michael Jansing's cell.

The phone rang three times and then rolled my call over to Jansing's voice mail. So I called him at home.

This time a woman answered and identified herself as Emily Jansing. When I said I had to speak with her husband, she complained that he was at dinner and said that he'd call me later.

"Mrs. Jansing. I'll come to your front door and kick it in if you don't put your husband on the phone. Now!"

I guess she knew I meant that.

The phone clattered onto a hard surface. I heard raised voices in the background, then footsteps on hardwood floors, and finally Jansing came on the line.

"We have a suspect," I said. "I'm sending a photo to your phone."

"You think I know him?"

"Let's hope and pray to God that you do," I said.

I sent the image of a possible Chuck's delivery man as Conklin took a hard right onto the US 101 North on-ramp. I could see the bridge up ahead, but we were still twenty minutes away from Chuck's Prime's headquarters.

Jansing said, "I don't know him. He doesn't look familiar to me at all."

"He may be one of your truckers. Does that help?"

"I don't know our truckers," said Chuck's CEO. "None of them."

Traffic slowed as we approached the Powell Street exit, and after an interminable sixty seconds of stop-and-go along Hollis, Richie said, "Hang on."

He flipped on the lights and the siren, and while that didn't exactly blow vehicles out of the road, the noise meant that I had to shout to communicate with Jansing. "We have to get into your personnel records."

A volley of yelling back and forth concluded with Jansing's offer to have his assistant, Caroline Henley, let us into the office so that we could examine the company's personnel files. "Caroline lives two blocks from the office," said Jansing.

Which was a relief.

At half past six and there was no fast way to get a warrant.

By the time Conklin pulled my screaming, flashing car up to Chuck's cream-colored corporate headquarters, my heart was pounding hard against my rib cage—like it was trying to crash out of jail.

Was I right that the skinny delivery man was the belly bomber?

If so, could we stop him before he bombed again?

Conklin set the brakes and asked, "You okay?"

"There's Caroline," I said, pointing to a brown-haired woman wearing tight jeans and a short tan coat, who was lowering her head against the wind as she came toward us.

We got out of the car and exchanged greetings, then climbed the steps to the Emery Tech Building's front door. Henley swiped her access card in the reader, and the locks thunked open. Once we were inside the lobby, I showed her the composite of our one lone suspect.

"Do you know him?" I asked her.

She took my phone in hand and said, "Yeah. I think that's Walt."

My hopped-up adrenal glands squirted a little more juice into my bloodstream. *Jansing's assistant knew the guy.*

"What's Walt's last name?" Conklin asked as the elevator doors slid open.

"Brenner. Or something like that," Caroline said. "I only met him once, but I think he's a very popular guy in our delivery fleet. He's not in any trouble, is he?"

"How fast can you get into the files?" I asked her.

Chapter 74

IN HER OWN humble opinion, Cindy was a good driver. She kept to the speed limit, slowed at yellow lights, and let moms pushing baby strollers cross the street in their own good time.

So it was against her own rules of the road that Cindy sped up Lake Street at sixty-five, cutting in front of slower cars as she shot through the residential neighborhood.

If only she could be sure that the taillights up ahead belonged to the green Subaru. She pulled out of line to pass the vehicle in front of her, but she was forced to return to her own lane as an oncoming van leaned furiously on the horn.

It was frightening and embarrassing, and Cindy hunched reflexively, worried that if Mackie was up ahead and looked into her rearview mirror, she might once again make Cindy.

Still, Cindy pressed on.

At the moment, she was riding the tailgate of a Ford Escape, flying past the fenced-in, well-cropped lawns of St. Anne's Home of the Poor. The Subaru was two cars ahead of the Escape, and although Cindy couldn't identify the driver as Mackie Morales, she thought that the back of the driver's head definitely looked to be that of a young adult female with short dark hair.

The driver turned her head to check her mirror, and Cindy saw her face.

That was her. That was Mackie Morales. For sure.

Cindy reached for her phone in the seat beside her and hit number three on her speed dial.

Lindsay's voice came through the earpiece: "You have reached Sergeant Lindsay Boxer. Leave your name and time that you called—"

Damn it.

Cindy needed both hands on the wheel. She clicked off without leaving a message and tossed her phone back onto the passenger seat. Up ahead, Lake Street terminated at a T intersection. Cindy saw the Subaru take the left onto Arguello

Boulevard toward the Presidio, and she followed the Outback into the turn too fast. Centrifugal force sent her handbag and cell phone off the passenger seat and onto the floor.

Cindy kept going, past the gate to Presidio Terrace and onward toward the Presidio, a former army post for more than two hundred years and now a National Park.

Where was Morales going?

It didn't really matter. All Cindy had to do was follow her to her destination, then park inconspicuously, and call Lindsay, text Lindsay to death, wait for Lindsay.

As Cindy passed Inspiration Point on her right, she saw the Subaru gather speed around the next curve. Traffic had thinned so that now there was very little cover on the two-lane road between her Honda and Morales.

Whatcha going to do now, Cindy?

Cindy eased up on the gas. That was really her only option. She let a gray Lexus pass her and then a line of three motorcycles, and now the road split at a fork; it continued as Arguello on the right and was Washington Boulevard on the left. And there, up ahead, was a stop sign and there was no running it. This was a damned three-way stop. Cindy swore as she braked, and traffic filled in from Washington, crossing in front of her, blocking her view. And when she could move forward again, she didn't see the Subaru anymore.

Had Morales stayed on Arguello, the main route to the lower part of the Presidio? Or had she taken the left onto Washington? Cindy stayed on Arguello, but a short distance later, as she passed Infantry Terrace, she knew that she had lost Morales and maybe given herself away.

She drove on at a steady fifty, her eyes going everywhere looking for a station wagon that would no longer look green in the dark.

She wanted to call Richie. She wanted to hear him say, "What is it, Cin? What's wrong? Okay, I'll put in a BOLO for that Outback. We'll find her. You sit tight."

It was a compulsion the size of a long-haul truck, but her phone was somewhere on the floor and there was no place to stop. Cindy was actually glad she could wait out the urge to call Richie.

Just then, somewhere near the gas pedal, her cell phone started to ring. Cindy had a horrible feeling it was Mackie Morales calling to tell her that she was an asshole and a loser.

She wished she could take that call. She wanted to tell her, "Grow up, Mackie. Meet with me. I want to talk with you and I'm not giving up. Not now. Not ever."

Chapter 75

CINDY BACKTRACKED ON Arguello, still looking for Morales, knowing that for tonight at least, there was no fucking way.

She slowed as she neared Infantry Terrace. She turned into the entrance between tall stone gates, backed around so that she was facing traffic, and braked her car.

Her hands were shaking, but don't tell that to her boss.

Shit. She hadn't eaten anything in eleven hours.

Cindy shut off the engine and the headlights. She felt around on the floor, picked up her handbag and located her phone under the seat. She checked her missed calls and was relieved that her last call hadn't been from Morales.

Seriously, she wanted to talk to that bitch, but she wanted to talk to her from a position of strength. And she wasn't there yet.

Her last caller had been Lindsay, returning her calls.

"Sorry, Cindy. I couldn't call until now. Call me back."

Cindy stabbed redial and listened to the ringtone.

Lindsay's voice came through her earpiece and Cindy said, "Linds—" before realizing that once again she'd gotten Lindsay's voice mail.

She pounded the wheel with her palm, and at the beep, she said, "Linds. This is urgent. Mackie is in town. She coasted past your apartment about an hour ago. She could be looking for you. Understand. She could be looking—"

The beep cut her off.

She pressed redial, and after Lindsay's tiresome outgoing message finished, Cindy said, "Linds. She wrote to me, so believe me, I'm not hallucinating. I ID'd her. I followed her and then I lost her somewhere in the Presidio. She's driving a stolen green Subaru Outback, so watch—"

She had about one bar left of battery life on her

phone and figured she'd better save it. In case Mackie was waiting in front of her apartment house for *her*. She opened her purse and took out her gun. She considered it. It was one thing to shoot at targets, but could she actually shoot a person?

She put it back in her bag, picked up her phone again, and hit speed dial number 5.

The phone rang three times and then Claire's voice came through: "You've reached Dr. Claire Washburn. My office hours are from eight a.m.—"

Cindy clicked off, dropped her phone into her bag, and started up her car. Totally disgusted, she headed toward her dark and empty home.

Chapter 76

YUKI FOLDED HERSELF under Brady's arm, her nightgown cold and wet with sweat in the aftermath of the killing moments ago.

The woman's name had been Kara. She had thick red hair and taught special education in Ann Arbor. She was young, in her twenties. Kara's parents had given her this cruise as a gift. Kara had been standing right next to her only a few days ago when the whales had dazzled and amazed the passengers by swimming so close to the ship.

That girl. The one who had jumped up and down on her toes, and hugged Yuki squealing, "This is one of the best things, isn't it?" She had been sitting in the thick of the crowd when she was plucked like a kitten by the scruff of her robe and dragged through the scattering passengers across the width of the Pool Deck to the rail.

Yuki heard her plead, "No, no, *nooooo*. Not *meee*. I didn't do *anything*. I was *good*. *Please, don't. Let me talk.*"

The terrorist said, "Nice knowing ya. Good-bye."

And that's when Yuki had screamed wordlessly, high and long, her voice sharp with terror, cut off by the crack of gunfire.

Instantly, she dropped flat to the deck, horrified at what she had done. She had been *forgotten* by those killers, and now she had called attention to herself—and to Brady—and for what? She was beyond stupid. She was crazy, delirious, insane.

Over by the railing, another pirate joined the first and they picked up Kara by her arms and legs.

"And a one, and a two, and a *three*."

They swung her overboard and walked away before her body hit the cold water.

How could they have done this?

These were Americans.

Moans and long keening cries seeped from other passengers. Yuki knew they were all

327

thinking, "Am I next?" Praying to God, "Please, not me, not my wife, not us."

Why didn't Finlandia *pay? Why didn't they pay?*

Yuki bit the back of her hand and tried to fight her nausea.

Only last night she had gone to bed feeling so lucky. She was married to Brady. A good, funny, sexy man she loved so much. They were on their honeymoon, the opening act to their beautiful wide open future.

And now this *sick* unrelenting dread and terror.

Yuki said to Brady, "That scream. I'm sorry—"

"Shhh, sweetie. You couldn't help it. Stay right here. I'll be just there."

Brady got onto his stomach and wriggled ten feet over to Lazaroff. They talked quietly for less than a minute, then Brady slid back to her side.

She wanted to ask what they were discussing, when she heard the clank of combat boots on metal. Jackhammer came down the stairs from the track deck above and stalked to the long side of the pool, directly opposite where Yuki and Brady sat together.

Yuki was shaking again.

The sight of the man, the way he walked, his

hardy-har attitude, and the random murders were so crazy-making, she felt this close to going bug-fuck. Like the man who'd thrown the chair, she was seized with a need to pick up something, or throw something, or find an insult so humiliating . . . but she couldn't think of anything that would achieve anything but her own certain death.

Brady shifted his position so that Yuki was hidden behind him. She heard him say, "Okay, honey, shhhhh."

She'd been whispering. Or maybe whimpering.

Jackhammer struck a pose, legs apart, hands on his hips, mocking them all.

He said, "I have good news."

Chapter 77

YUKI SHIVERED BEHIND her husband's broad back, remembering other times when Jackhammer had said he had good news.

About an hour ago he had said, "Good news, everyone. The execution is over and we have sent proof of death to your hosts back in Finland. You can all relax for a little while. Uh, for fifty-nine minutes to be exact. Maybe we'll be lucky enough to see the northern lights."

What news would Jackhammer deliver *now*?

Buffet dinner in the Luna Grill? Aerobics on the sports deck?

Yuki reached around her husband and gripped his chest.

He patted her hand and said beneath the sound

of the water lapping the hull, "We're going to be okay. I mean it."

Brady would protect them if he could, but what chance would he have? Jackhammer's crew had already shot six people she knew about, and maybe dozens of crew had been gunned down when he and his gang had first boarded the ship.

If he didn't get his money, he might have himself a real party and shoot every passenger on board. A bloodbath. A massacre.

Jackhammer spoke from across the pool. "Guess what, everyone? We got an e-mail from your cruise line. They say they're going to be transferring money soon. Won't that be great? We're standing by for our bank's confirmation of the wire transfer from Finlandia. Okay? Didn't I tell you I had good news?"

There was a sprinkling of applause from the captives who were bunched, crouched, sick with fear.

Jackhammer said, "Hey. Let's hear it for money coming, all right?"

The faint applause increased. Whatever it took to mollify the monster.

Jackhammer said in his most mocking ringmaster voice, "And now, let's have some music."

Chapter 78

AFTER THE HIGH-PITCHED feedback squeal from the sound system just about uncorked the top of Brady's head, salsa music jumped out of the speakers on the Pool Deck bar. The dance-y Latin music was incongruous, crazy, and from Brady's perspective a good thing.

The music seemed to change the mood of the terrorists. He hoped it might make them a touch complacent. Dance fever covered low conversation.

Brady said to Yuki, "What a mindfucker that guy is. He could write a book on it. Don't believe a word he said."

Brady knew that crowd control was one of the terrorists' biggest problems. The nineteen shooters were overwhelmingly outnumbered by the combined thousand passengers and crew. But Jackhammer's brutal, successive, random killings had created paranoia, enforced compliance, and put thoughts of rebellion down cold. He'd overwhelmed their ability to fight back. He'd undermined their sanity.

Brady wrapped both his arms around his wife and held her tightly. Yuki was a strong person, but the direct threat to her life had shaken her hard and he wasn't sure how much more mind control and terror she could take.

A lot of pictures came into his mind, and not the kind of thoughts he usually had. He thought about grabbing one of those AK-47s and just going Rambo.

Yuki squeezed his hand.

"I'm okay," he said.

No, he wasn't. He was a cop. He couldn't let these guys keep shooting people while he just hoped that the accountants and bankers would come through for a bunch of people they didn't know.

Brady had to do something about this. He was fatter now. Years of smoking had cut his wind. But he still had a strategic mind and the will to kill. He *would* protect Yuki.

What he had to do was stay focused, look for an opportunity, have a workable plan ready to go. And pray for the physical strength and the reflexes to carry it out.

Chapter 79

BRADY WAS TRYING on ideas about how to take back the *FinStar* when there was a light tug on his sleeve. He started, almost lashing out with the edge of his hand, but he paused long enough to see the face of the man who had crawled over to him on his elbows.

It was Lyle, their cabin steward, and he was wearing a blue spa robe over his whites.

Lyle was overheated, breathing through his mouth. He dropped to his stomach, turned his head so that his cheek was flat on the deck, and spoke through the raucous Latin beat.

"Mr. Brady. You're military?"

"No. I'm a homicide cop. What do you know, Lyle?"

"There's a citadel amidships. Somewhere near the officers' quarters."

"A citadel. You mean there are guns?"

"I heard there were guns and maybe a radio."

"And the officers? They're alive?"

With one of the gunmen close by, Lyle didn't reply. He dropped his head and wept into the inside elbow of his robed arm. Yuki also cried softly, but none of the pirates noticed. So many people were crying.

Yuki hugged Brady from behind and he patted her little hand. The first time she'd taken his big rough hand in both of hers, her touch had gone all the way through him. He'd felt sure of her. He'd known that he was in the presence of good.

It had been *his* idea to take this cruise. He'd never been much of a romantic, but this trip had seemed like a really good idea—the sea, magnificent scenery, a luxury liner taking care of everything so they could start their marriage in a beautiful way.

Now fucking *this*.

Brady waited until the masked goon with the running shoes had finished padding between and around the passengers and run up the metal stairs to the track.

When Brady was sure the gunman was out of earshot, he said, "Lyle, what about the officers?"

Eventually Lyle said, "These guys killed everyone on the bridge when they boarded. That's what I heard. It wasn't the captain's watch. He was sleeping in his quarters. He made an announcement after that, so he could still be alive.

"And the third mate. He was asleep in the officers' quarters across from the captain. He's probably alive. Chief Engineer. Master of the hotel. They're also alive as far as I know. So a few of the senior men are in their quarters. Probably. I can't speak for the hundreds of waiters and cabin boys and laundry crew, guys like that. I think they're locked in the hold."

Brady said, "But the citadel is near the officers' quarters. You could take me there."

"There are guys with guns in front of the door, don't you get it? I'm not a fighter," Lyle said. He plucked at his robe. "I put this on so they wouldn't know I was crew."

"You found a way to survive," said Brady. "We need the officers and we have to get weapons. You have to want that, too, right? You've heard the expression 'like shooting fish in a barrel'? Christ! That's what *this* is. That's what *we* are. You like being a *fish,* Lyle?"

The cabin steward shook his head madly, desperately.

"How old are you?"

"Nineteen. I'm going to be nineteen. Maybe."

"Do you want to be a nineteen-year-old who helped put down a stinking paramilitary platoon of fucking crazy killers?"

"I don't know. I don't think so."

Brady grinned.

"You're going to like it better than you think."

PART FOUR

WHERE'S THE BEEF?

Chapter 80

CONKLIN AND I were in Michael Jansing's office with his dogged assistant, Caroline, who was plumbing Jansing's computer for Chuck's Prime's personnel records. After a global search, the computer flagged a Walter Brenner, thirty-nine, truck driver, living in El Cerrito, just north of West Berkeley and Albany.

He'd been working at Chuck's for about three years. He had gotten a two-dollar raise each year. There were no comments in the spaces provided for them, just check marks to show that he'd had satisfactory performance evaluations.

"Is there anything you can tell us about him?" I asked Caroline. "Anything at all?"

She shrugged. "I'm still pretty new here." She

printed out Brenner's contact info, including his address, and also sent the file to my phone.

I thanked Caroline and bid her a fond adieu, and Conklin and I left the building. We boarded my antique Explorer and, setting out at warp speed, arrived at Belmont Avenue, a quiet street at the foot of Albany Hill Park, at just about 7:45 p.m.

The 1920s Craftsman-style homes in this residential street were garnished with a fringe of trees out front and had good-size backyards with gardens and swing sets and occasional shade trees. Although the homes were cute and folksy, the freeway provided a persistent industrial undertone.

Walt Brenner lived in a small, yellow house trimmed in white and squarely placed on a corner of the block. It had a slab-porch entry, a fruit tree in the front yard, and a stockade fence shielding the backyard from the roadway.

We didn't stop at the house, but instead rounded the corner and stopped a block away. Stepping out and opening the hatch, I took out two vests and handed one to Conklin. I put mine on and zipped my Windbreaker over it.

We got back into the vehicle, crawled along

Belmont Avenue, and returned to Brenner's tidy little home.

Conklin pulled the Explorer into the driveway next to a newish black SUV, which seemed a little above a truck driver's pay grade.

Conklin said, "I'm thinking softball approach. Walter makes a weekly drop-off to all the Chuck's in this area. We ask him what are your thoughts on anyone who might be angry at the bosses, blah-blah-blah."

I said, "I like it."

I raised my fist to knock. But my knuckles never touched wood. The door opened, and to my utter amazement, Donna Timko was standing right there.

It was Donna, all right. She was wearing a flowered tent dress and slippers and had a quizzical look on her face.

I wondered what kind of expression she saw on *mine*.

Donna said, "Sergeant Boxer and, uh, Inspector Conklin. This is a surprise."

Conklin said, "We didn't realize you live here, Donna. This is Walter Brenner's address, right?"

She nodded. Conklin went on.

"He lives here? And you're expecting him home?"

Donna nodded, again, looking from my partner's face to mine, then back to his.

Conklin said, "Well, if you have a couple of minutes, maybe we could come in and talk while we wait for Walter."

"Certainly. Come in. Go right on through to the dining room," she said.

I had a lot of questions for Donna, starting with "Who are you to our belly bomb suspect?"

But that could wait until I was looking into her big brown eyes.

Chapter 81

WALTER BRENNER'S HOUSE smelled like a bakery.

"My new recipe for Baby Cakes," Timko said, as Conklin and I preceded her into a small white-painted living room furnished with country upholstery and bookshelves bracketing a fireplace. Half-folded laundry was in a pile on the furniture. Stairs to the second floor were in a hallway to our right.

We continued on through an arched pass-through to the dining room. Donna said, "Have a seat at the table. I was just making coffee."

I looked at Conklin, shrugged, and he shrugged back.

Then we pulled out a couple of ladder-back

chairs at the round, four-person dining table and sat down. The dining room was small, maybe a hundred fifty square feet, with a view of the kitchen just ahead and, through the windows to our left, the charming houses across the street.

In a couple of minutes, Donna Timko returned with a tray of coffee cups and individual-size cakes and some details about the recipe.

I was watching Donna's expression as she busied herself at the table. She was talkative but definitely preoccupied.

I had my hand around a gold-rimmed coffee cup when I asked, "Donna, what is your relationship to Walter Brenner?"

"Oh, you didn't know? Walt is my half brother. We own this place together."

"Terrific house," said Conklin. "Very homey. How long have you been living here?"

"About three years. What's wrong? Is Walter okay?"

Conklin said, "He's fine, just fine. You know we're talking to all of Chuck's employees. We noticed that Walter pretty much goes to every store once a week. We hoped he might have some thoughts on anyone with an attitude, a grudge against the company, something like that."

"Walt loves his job, if that's what you want to know. He's the poster boy for happy employee of the year. Gee," said Donna, "talk about timing. Here he comes. You can ask him whatever you like."

I followed Donna's gaze to the windows and saw a white van with a Chuck's logo on the side pulling up to the garage doors. I hadn't planned on the complication of Donna Timko, so the next few minutes were going to require finesse.

I thought of several scenarios, including the one where Timko shouts at Walt to run—and he does it.

Timko said, "Walt's a very funny guy. Everyone thinks he ought to do stand-up. Sit, sit," she said to us. "He's coming through the back door."

Timko placed her napkin next to her plate, got up from the table, and went into the kitchen. I heard the kitchen door open to the garage and then I heard the voices of a man and Donna talking low.

I took out my gun and put it on my lap and was looking to Richie to do the same, when Donna returned to the dining room with her brother.

There he was in the flesh, Walter Brenner, the skinny man I'd seen in several different guises on security tape. But this time he was life-size, in color, and clean-shaven, and he had dimples that hadn't shown up in the Hunting Wolf run-through. He was also holding a .38.

I jumped to my feet, raised my gun, and shouted, *"Drop the gun. Do it now."*

I was aware of Conklin getting to his feet at the same time, but my eyes went to Donna as she lifted her hand from behind her voluminous house dress and pointed a small gun at me.

She said, "Take it easy, Sergeant. Sit back down. Put your gun on the table and slide it over to me. Take your partner's gun and give me that, too.

"Let's *go*," she snapped. "Or I'm going to shoot the two of you where you stand."

Chapter 82

I SAT DOWN, took my gun up out of my lap, and put it on the table as Donna had told me to do. But I didn't release it from my grip. I moved slowly, using whatever few seconds I could gain to assess our situation.

The dining room was a twelve-by-twelve-foot open-ended box with two arched entranceways, one from the living room to the dining room, the other from the dining room to the kitchen.

There was a squat lowboy on the wall to my right, and past Conklin, on the opposite wall, were a pair of windows.

The table and chairs were too big for the room and took up the center of it, leaving very little margin around the sides.

Donna was standing six feet across the table from me, aiming her ladylike Colt with steady hands. If I leapt for her, she'd shoot. No doubt about it. The only way she could miss was if her gun jammed or she had a heart attack.

I couldn't count on either of those possibilities. Accordingly, I didn't see how we were all going to get out of this room alive.

I put the safety on my gun and slid it across the table. Conklin was also sitting down. He's a quick draw and good shot, but his gun was in its holster on his hip.

He showed Timko that he wasn't holding a gun and said in a very reasonable tone of voice, "Donna, no. Put that away. You, too, Mr. Brenner. We're just here to talk. No need to get bent out of shape. You don't want to accidentally shoot a cop. You really don't.

"And just so you know, I called for backup before we entered the house. So there are going to be cruisers in your driveway any minute."

Had Richie called for backup?

That would have been prudent, but I'd been busy getting out our Kevlar vests and hadn't noticed what my partner had done.

Time had slowed to one solitary frame per second. I was alert to the facial expressions of the two people holding the guns, watching the tension in their hands at the same time.

Donna Timko was focused and tightly coiled.

Walt was relaxed. He handled his weapon casually, like he was familiar with it and welcomed an opportunity to let 'er rip.

"Right," Walt said to Conklin. "Cops are on the way."

Conklin said, "Pulling a gun on a cop is plenty bad enough, Walter. But, if you *shoot* a cop, no one can help you. Understand what I'm saying? Put the guns away and we'll forget this happened. Right, Sergeant? Or, you have a running head start. See how far you go."

Donna sat down and braced her elbows on the table. She held her Colt with both hands, the muzzle pointed at my face.

I was still desperately trying on scenarios, looking for something that would get the fewest number of us killed.

Sweat beaded on my scalp. I thought of Julie and Joe. That I might not see them again. Had I even kissed them on the way out the door this morning? I couldn't remember.

I knew that I wouldn't survive a head shot.

Donna Timko was showing visible signs of stress. She was red-faced, and the muscle in her left jaw was twitching. It looked to me like she could go off any moment.

She said, "Walt, take Mr. Conklin's weapon, why don't you? And then we've got to figure out what to do with these crumbs."

Chapter 83

I HAD NO problem believing that Donna Timko was a loose cannon. She was adrenalized. Her gun was braced four feet directly across the table from me. Her finger was on the trigger and she'd aimed her gun *just so*.

If she sneezed, she'd shoot me between the eyes.

Two feet to my left, Conklin sat in the chair with his hands in the air at shoulder height.

Walter Brenner stood to the right of his sister, training his gun on Conklin, grinning and bouncing on his feet like a four-year-old waiting for a pony ride.

Forget ponies. Make that a *crazy* four-year-old with a *gun*.

Some wave of serenity came over Timko's face, which I read as her having made up her mind. To her we were dead cops walking, and now she was thinking ahead to how to get rid of our bodies.

She said to her brother, "Walt, here's an idea. We can get into the processing plant. You can work the grinder, right?"

"You're thinking cop burgers?"

"Exactly. Cop Prime. With bacon. Well done."

They both had a good laugh.

I couldn't help it. I pictured my body going through an industrial-grade meat grinder and heard the whirr of the blades cutting through muscle and bone. It gave me the horrors.

Why didn't Walter and Donna just shoot us now?

Simple answer. It would be easier for *them* if we went into the transport van on the hoof.

I wanted to look at Conklin but didn't dare take my eyes off the sweetheart of Chuck's executive board, a woman who had sympathized with the bomb victims and the little people who worked at Chuck's and was now transformed into a grinning, bloodthirsty *ghoul*.

Timko was not only thinking ahead, she wanted my opinion.

She said, "That'll work, right, Sergeant? Take you out through the garage, and we all get into the van. Who knows, we might drop you off somewhere and make a run for Canada."

"That's a better idea than the meat processor," I said. "We go missing, the FBI will be all over that plant, and you know human blood and remains will spell it all out, PDQ."

"Good point. Well, I'm loaded with ideas. That's my best one so far. Walt, get his gun. Come on. I can't do everything."

Walt was a lefty.

He walked over to Conklin and pressed the gun muzzle to his temple. Sweat rolled down my sides, but my partner was cool, give him credit. Give him all the credit in the world.

Walt said, "Take out your gun with the tips of your fingers and pass it to me. No sudden moves. My metabolism is high, *normally*. Now? I could shoot you out of pure freaking jitters. So do what I say. Okay?"

If Conklin didn't hand over his gun, Brenner might reach for it. That would give my partner an opportunity to head-butt him, elbow him in the groin, any number of moves that might work—or get us both killed.

Timko flicked her eyes toward Conklin, who was gauging the situation, looking to see what her brother was going to do.

I knew what *I* had to do, and that I had to get it right the first time.

It might be the only chance Conklin and I had to get out of El Cerrito alive.

Chapter 84

MY HANDS WERE flat on the table, but I hooked my thumbs under the edge of it. I took a breath, gathered my strength, and exhaled. Rising out of my chair, I flipped the dining table away from me and toward Donna Timko.

Donna yelped as the tabletop went vertical. She bolted out of her chair before the hundred pounds of tiger maple came down on her thighs, but she lost her footing and fell backward to the floor along with her chair and the fancy bone china crashing around her.

At the moment I flipped the table, Walt reflexively turned his gun on me.

Conklin went into action. Using both hands, he slammed Walt's forearm away from his head to the left, and using the power of his legs, drove Walt into the wall. He followed that body slam up with a knee to Walt's groin, then moved to get the gun out of his grip. He wrenched Walt's gun backward. The angle of the trigger guard snapped Walt's finger.

I heard it break.

Brenner's scream was part shock, part fury, and then there was the pain. And Conklin wasn't through with him yet.

As Conklin forced Walt's arm behind him and brought him to the floor, I went for Timko.

I'm fit and she was a loose pile of what-the-fuck happened crammed into the corner behind an upended chair and dining table. I threw the chair out of my way, got around the table, and found the big woman lying on her shooting arm.

Her gun hand was flat to the ground and I stomped on it, hard. Timko shrieked, releasing her Colt, and I kicked it under the lowboy and out of the way.

My Glock had also fallen to the floor during the table flip, and I picked it up. Then, gun in hand, I squatted down to Donna's eye level. I was blowing hard and my heart was still galloping. I was pumping so much adrenaline, I might have been able to fly. But I kept my wheels on the ground and spoke in measured tones to the helpless criminal staring at me defiantly with hard, furious eyes.

"Donna, you don't have much time. I'll bet that the belly bombs were Walt's idea. Tell me the whole story before this house fills with cops and I'll work with you."

"Neither of us is guilty of anything."

I kept going, giving her another chance to give me the confession I wanted.

"Right after the cops, there's going to be a wave of pumped-up FBI and ATF agents who are going to see belly bombs as a career maker. Feds trump local. So I hope you understand, Donna. When the Feds show up, this deal goes out of my hands for good. Feds will seek the death penalty."

"I want a lawyer. That's all I have to say."

"Sure thing, Donna. No problem. You can call your lawyer after you're booked. In the years to come, I hope you'll remember that I told you that your best chance to get a break was right now, with me."

Chapter 85

DONNA LAUGHED MANIACALLY. I was pretty sure that losing control of this shooting match was making her hysterical, but still. She was laughing.

I shrugged and said, "Well, I tried."

"Am I under arrest?" Brenner asked from where he was cuffed and facedown on the scatter rug.

"Not yet," said Conklin. "But when I hear sirens, I'm reading you your rights. That gives you, I don't know, two minutes to play ball. Confess or don't, I don't really give a shit."

I said to my partner, "I think I can still get home in time for a late dinner with my husband. That'll be a nice change."

"So what are you actually saying?" Timko said,

squirming and pushing against the wall in an effort to sit upright in her corner. "You're making us a real offer?"

"No promises," I said. "You tell me who did what in these bombings. And I need to know if there are any more bombs in play. Talk to me. Get me on your side and I'll help you with the powers that be."

She said, "Huh. What are you, Sergeant? Size eight?"

I said, "Uh, ten. Why?"

This was prelude to girl talk, I guessed. My cue to get Timko to think I liked her. I pulled over a chair, sat so that I was looking down at the woman who couldn't do a thing but look back.

"Fast food is *all* about hooking the consumer," she said. "Making food addictive. That's what we do. What *I* do. It's like dealing drugs. We work like crazy to get the fat-salt-sugar 'bliss point' to a T. It's a science. And I've got the degrees in chemistry to prove it. And of course, there's *this*."

She grabbed folds of belly fat through her house dress with both hands and jiggled them. Where was she going with this?

"I'm not sure I follow you, Donna. You're not

saying you set off *bombs* because you're addicted to fast food?"

"Hell, no. I had nothing to do with any bombs. I'm just saying I don't feel *bad* that someone's holding Chuck's up for a fortune. Corporations like Chuck's are corrupt. Unconscionable."

I said, "I thought you might tell me that you were getting screwed on the potential merger. That Walter was going to lose his job. Because that I might understand."

"Well, that's true, Sergeant. You think I was going to get a fair share in Chuck's merger with Space Dogs? I was the *fat* girl, supposed to take whatever I was offered. How do they *dare* treat me that way? How do they *dare* after all I've put into *Chuck's* and the *zillions* they've made off my brains and talent and my hard work?"

Conklin answered his ringing cell phone and said, "How long? Okay. We've got the situation under control."

He ended the call and said to me, "The cavalry is on the way. They're just entering El Cerrito."

Chapter 86

SIRENS WAILED IN the near distance, closing in on the cozy yellow Craftsman-style house on Belmont Avenue.

I took out my phone and called Jacobi.

When he answered, I said, "Warren, we need a search warrant for a refrigerated transport van and for the house belonging to Donna Timko and Walter Brenner. We're bringing them in as soon as you convince the Feds that they belong to us. We caught them and we want them."

I gave Jacobi the particulars as the sirens got loud enough for him to hear them over my phone, and then I hung up. I looked through the window at the neat suburban houses across the street, lights and TVs on in the front rooms.

The neighbors were going to be shocked.

Walter and Donna are such nice people. I just can't believe that they'd put bombs—No wayyy. Really?

"See that?" I said as squad cars drove up on the lawn and the flashing red-and-blue lights lit the dining room up like Christmas Eve in an alternative universe.

I said, "This is Walt and Donna saying goodbye to their best chance to get a break."

"You're too funny," Timko said, laughing again. "You've got nothing on us. No evidence. No witnesses. No confession. No nothing. We'll be home in the morning."

"Take your toothbrush with you just in case. We've got you on threatening a police officer, resisting arrest, unlawful restraint, and of course, suspicion of murder. That's before CSI goes through the van and this house."

"Be my guest. There's nothing to find," Timko said.

"Really?" My turn to grin. "Not a trace of explosives? Not a print matching one on a ransom note? You're sure?"

The look on Timko's face said she was terrified. Out of her tiny freaking mind.

Conklin moved the dining table out of the way, and we each took one of Donna's arms and hauled her to her feet. I cuffed her. The pleasure was all mine.

"Donna Timko, you're under arrest on quite a few charges," I said, "most of them felonies." And then I listed them.

She shouted, "I have *diabetes*. You can't lock me up. I'll *die*."

"I'm pretty sure they can scrounge up some insulin at the Women's Jail. Meanwhile, you have the right to remain silent. If you can't afford an attorney, you'll be provided with one, courtesy of the City of San Francisco. Anything you say can and will be used against you. Do you understand everything I just said?"

Conklin read Walt Brenner his rights as car radios squawked right outside the house. The doorbell rang and knuckles rapped hard on the front door.

"This is the police. We're coming in."

Guess what? The killer with the large brown eyes started to cry.

Chapter 87

YUKI HEARD THE gun go off. She didn't know who'd been executed, but she knew how the victim had felt. First the shocked terror of being pulled out of the crowd. Then disbelief. Then not-not-not ready to leave her friends, her family, her *life* because it wasn't her *time*. Then the pleading, followed by . . . maybe relief in the sharp report of the gun. That she couldn't know.

She kept her eyes down as she stepped around clumps of passengers huddled on the deck. She edged along the narrow path between the pool and the railing, keeping tabs on her new best friend, Becky, who was whimpering behind her, "Don't let it be Carl or Luke. Please God. Not them."

Yuki and Becky had been to the stinking waste bucket, each of them acting as a privacy curtain for the other, while a gunman in fatigues and mask watched over them with an assault rifle and hurried them along.

Taking along a buddy to use the bucket was more for company and support than for protection from men's eyes. This late in the game, Yuki didn't care who saw her squatting over a bucket. She just didn't care anymore.

This ship was a prison camp.

And soon another hour would pass. Another one of them would be murdered.

Becky touched her arm and whispered, "This will be over soon. They'll pay."

"I know," said Yuki.

Becky dropped down beside her husband and son, and Yuki headed toward the spot where Brady waited for her. He raised his hand and she went to him and placed her hand on his shoulder. He helped her down beside him.

"Are you okay?" he asked.

"Freakin' fabulous," she said.

She handed him the bottle of water the gunman had given her. Brady twisted off the cap. He returned the bottle to Yuki, who took a few gulps and then passed it back to Brady.

Twenty yards away, on the other side of the pool, three guards leaned against railings. One smoked, one paced, and one talked on his radio, speaking to someone in their militia, checking in as they did every half hour.

Another goon was on the track above them. He swept the mass of prisoners with his torchlight, three or four times before shutting the light off.

Brady put his hand to the back of Yuki's head and, drawing her close, kissed her temple. She hugged her knees in the chilly dark, glad for the comforting weight of Brady's arm around her shoulders.

The guard who had been pacing went to the rail on their side of the pool. He flicked his cigarette into the water, then, still with his back to them, lit a match and bent his head. Brady was on his feet fast, like a panther.

The match was still burning when Brady reached his left hand around the man's face and hooked his mouth with his fingers, getting a grip on his skull with his right.

It took less than the count of three.

Before the gunman even got his hands up, Brady had twisted his head with a powerful jerk.

The gunman went slack and Brady lowered him soundlessly to the deck.

Yuki put her hand over her mouth to muffle a scream as Lazaroff got up to help Brady. The two worked as one in the dark, wordlessly stripping off the dead pirate's clothes and mask, then sliding his body under one of the lounge chairs piled nearby.

As soon as that was done, Lazaroff melted into the amorphous blackness of the crowd and Brady sat down beside her.

He lifted his shirt, took her hand, and placed it on the terrorist's fatigues and mask. Then he put her hand to the waistband of his jeans, before wrapping his arm around her again.

My God. My God.

Brady had on pirate gear, and more than that, he had a *gun*.

Chapter 88

ONE OF THE masked thugs had put a seventies rock track on the bar's sound system. As "You Make Loving Fun" blasted overhead, Brady and Lazaroff lay next to each other on the deck, talking mouth to ear in the dark.

When Brady worked narcotics for the Miami PD, he'd worked with undercover cops, run stings with them, and led raids against drug traffickers. Cops got almost no training in hand-to-hand combat, but Brady had taken some training in mixed martial arts on his own. As for guns, he knew and could operate almost any weapon in current use.

His new friend aboard the *FinStar*, Brett Lazaroff, had been a Navy corpsman in the early days of Vietnam. He had been involved in search-and-destroy missions and worked with the Marines as well as local irregulars, going into villages and finding and killing guerrillas.

Lazaroff was in his midsixties and had arthritis all through his joints, but the two of them would make a good team.

And then there was Lyle.

Lyle was a nice kid, but that was all he had in his kit. He'd told Brady that he had held a variety of odd jobs over the past three years: washing cars and mowing lawns before moving to Alaska and getting a dishwashing job in a one-star hotel. He gave that up when he heard of an opening as a cabin steward on the *FinStar*.

Lyle's no-forethought series of pickup dead-end jobs had accidentally positioned him to be a part of a life-and-death operation he could never have imagined.

After Brady and Lazaroff blocked it all out, Brady filled Lyle in.

"Lyle, you have to take us to the crew quarters. Lazaroff and I are going to keep you out of the way when the shooting starts."

"My mom's name is Leora Findlay. Hoboken,

New Jersey. If I don't make it, Mr. Brady."

Lazaroff said in a husky whisper, "Lyle? It's okay to be afraid. In fact, we're counting on it. You won't have to *act* scared and that's good."

Brady knew that there were three gunmen on the Sun Deck above them, a half dozen patrolling the Pool Deck, and others inside the body of the ship.

Their "pattern of life" was to make radio contact every half hour. Each gunman identified himself by position, not by name: Pool deck 4 to base. Veranda 2 to base. Roving patrol 1 to Sun Deck.

Brady watched for the pale-green light of the radio on the track to go out. Then he glanced at his watch. It had been five minutes since the start of the pirates' last check-in. A pale gray line on the horizon in the east signaled morning getting ready to bust through some cloud cover.

It was now or never.

Over a period of ten minutes, Brady pulled the dead pirate's lightweight, waterproof camouflage pants over his jeans, buttoned the shirt over his sweater, switched out his deck shoes for lace-up combat boots, and cinched the ammo belt around his waist.

Last, he put the dead guy's walkie-talkie radio back in his shirt pocket and hung the rifle strap across his shoulder.

He covered Yuki's cheek with his hand and kissed her. She held his hand against her face and trembled.

"I love you so much," he said.

"Come back to me," she said. "We have to make a life."

Doubts saturated Brady's mind. He was out of shape. He didn't know the ship very well. There were hundreds of moving parts that could go so far out of control that people would die. And that would be on him.

"There's no way I'm not coming back," he said to Yuki. "Have you got that?"

He pulled on the black knitted mask that smelled of cigarette smoke, then signaled to Lazaroff and Lyle to stand.

When they were all on their feet, he said loudly, "Let's go, assholes."

He waved the rifle and Lazaroff and Lyle raised their hands. With Brady bringing up the rear, the three men stepped around the weeping, cringing clumps of humanity on the deck and made their way toward the Luna Grill doors and the interior of the ship.

Chapter 89

BRADY LED HIS group from behind, the three of them leaving the open Pool Deck and entering the Luna Grill, which was like a furniture warehouse now, piled with café tables and chairs from the deck outside. A gas lamp that had been placed on top of the piano threw a dim light over the formerly elegant room, which now looked debased, like a used-up exotic dancer turning tricks on the street.

Brady's three-man resistance force walked around overturned furniture and garbage heaped on the plush carpets past curved windows reflecting the sputtering gas light.

At the far side of the lounge, an open doorway led into the public corridor. Lyle, in the lead, took them to one of the hand-painted murals lining the corridor walls.

He said, "This is how you get to the crew's stairs."

He pushed on a panel and a door opened into a wide metal stairwell that ran the entire height of the ship, from the Sun Deck down to the hold. Caged emergency lights on the walls lit the stairs with a flickering low-wattage light.

The three were on the stairs, the hidden door closed behind them, when a voice called out, "Yo. Wassup?"

Brady snapped around, flashed his light up, and saw a man in fatigues sitting on the landing one flight above them. The gunman was fully armed, but he'd taken off his mask, revealing him to be a young white guy in his early twenties with short blond hair.

Brady said, "Chief wants me to take these two to the hold. Cabin steward. And the old dude is an engineer."

"Why bother locking them up? Why not just—*pyewww?*"

He put a finger gun to his head and pretended to fire.

"You want to ask Jackhammer?" Brady said. "Go ahead."

Brady wanted to stop talking and start moving. He didn't know how tight this unit was, whether they were a band of brothers or mercenaries recruited individually for this mission.

If the kid on the stairs challenged him further, Brady would have to shoot him. That would bring other gunmen rushing into the stairwell and that would be bad.

The young gunman scoffed at the idea of calling Jackhammer, saying, "Yeah, right. Go ahead. God, I was really hoping you were my relief."

"Sorry, man," said Brady. "Hey. Put on your mask."

"Yeah. Sure."

Brady waited while the gunman masked up, then said to Lyle and Lazaroff, "Okay, you two. Down we go."

Brady prodded Lazaroff and Lyle with the barrel of his AK, and they started down the stairs, one ringing metal flight after another times three sets of footsteps. They passed signs to various decks and public rooms: the Casino, the Spa, and so on, until they saw the arrow marked OFFICERS' QUARTERS.

The arrow indicated a forty-five-degree turn to the right.

Brady knew that the crew slept in narrow, windowless cabins no wider than four feet across, with single bunks hung on the walls. He wondered how many crewmen were still alive in those slim, airless cells.

He and his team turned the corner and saw a brighter light at the end of this spur off the main corridor. The light came from a gas lantern on the floor next to a man in fatigues who was sitting in a folding chair, guarding the hatch door to the crew quarters.

The guard got to his feet. He was holding his radio phone, and Brady thought the guy upstairs had probably given this one a heads-up.

The guard said to Brady, "What's up, brother? Who've you got there?"

He pocketed his radio and held his AK-47 with both hands.

Chapter 90

BRADY KNEW WITH dead certainty that the guard positioned in front of the crew quarters would shoot without provocation. Shooting would be very, very bad. Gunfire inside this metal staircase would be like setting off a fire alarm.

Jackhammer's entire crew would be on them in about a second and he would be dead.

Along with the AK-47 and the combat clothes, Brady had taken the dead gunman's knife and belt, which he was wearing.

As he and his two wingmen closed in on the guard at the door, Brady still had hope that he could talk the guy into opening the crew door. If not, he would be bringing a knife to a gun fight. And he'd have one chance to pull it off.

Using Lazaroff and Lyle to shield him from the gunman's view, Brady reached across his body, and gripped the knife handle in his fist so that the blade faced up.

Ten feet from the guy, Brady said, "Jackhammer told you I was coming plus two, right? I was there when he called you."

This guard had a huskier voice and build and was older than the kid on the stairs. Brady thought he might be an actual soldier.

He said, "Jackhammer called *me*? Because I don't know nothing about *this*."

"Let's not talk in front of these mutts," said Brady as he closed in on the guard. "Do you mind? After I stow them, we can talk about it all you want."

The gunman hesitated.

Then he said, "No fucking way. I'm calling the chief."

Brady said to the guard, "I'll save you the call. Jackhammer is on the line with me right now."

The guard said, "Yeah?"

Coming toward Brady to take the radio, he stretched out his hand. Brady grabbed his wrist with his left hand, jerked him forward, and slashed his throat, slicing through his carotid artery, larynx, and jugular.

The gunman reached up but never got his hand to his neck before he dropped, blood pumping out of him, adrenaline speeding up the flow. He breathed in blood, coughed up more blood, and gurgled his last words as he tried to speak.

Lazaroff got behind the dying man as the blood gushed and held him down until he no longer moved. Then he took the AK away from the dead man while Brady told Lyle to sit on the chair and put his head between his knees.

Lazaroff got up, checked the corridor, and reported back, "All clear. Great job, Brady. They teach you how to do that in the police department?"

"I picked up a few moves along the way."

He and Lazaroff each took one of the gunman's arms and dragged him through the blood pool to the side of the corridor. Then Brady took off his mask and turned the wheel on the hatch door.

The hinges squealed as the door to the officers' quarters swung wide open.

Chapter 91

A GROUP OF officers stood in the narrow aisle between two rows of cabins. They were unshaven and rumpled and pale. They stood shifting on their feet and angry, what you'd expect of men who'd been imprisoned in their cabins belowdeck while their ship was under siege.

Brady saw knives and lengths of wood or pipe in their hands. He put out his hands to show that he wasn't armed, then put his finger to his mouth in the universal signal to be quiet.

He said, "I'm Jackson Brady. I'm a passenger, also a cop. We're getting you guys out of here."

Men exhaled, sheathed their knives, and broke into tears. Some rushed forward to shake his hand.

Brady told Lyle to get the lantern and then waved him and Lazaroff through the hatch door. He followed them in and introduced them to the ship's officers.

One of the officers, a balding older guy in his sixties, had on glasses and grubby whites with captain's stripes on the shoulders. He held a pistol loosely in one hand and shook Brady's hand with the other.

"I'm Captain Berlinghoff," he said. "George. Thanks very much . . .," he said, choking back tears. "Mr. Brady. We haven't seen light. We haven't spoken with anyone. What's happening to the ship?"

Brady said, "The terrorists are in charge and executing passengers on the hour."

He briefed the captain on the terrorists' demand for payment.

"They've killed a lot of people," Brady said. "I don't see that they've got a viable exit plan whether they're paid or not. At some point, they might realize that. There's no telling what they'll do."

"What are your thoughts?" the captain asked Brady.

"Got to get control away from them. And that

means arming as many people as possible. Are your guys trained on the weapons in your citadel?"

"Who said we had a citadel?" the captain asked.

"I did, sir," Lyle said.

"And who are you?"

Brady put his arm around Lyle's shoulders.

"Lyle Davis. Our cabin steward and a very brave young man."

The captain said, "I don't know what you've heard, Mr. Davis, but there's no citadel. There's a lockbox on the Sun Deck marked OPEN IN CASE OF FIRE.

"We have a few handguns in there, some flares, and fire extinguishers. That's it for our weaponry except for *this* thing," he said, lifting his revolver by the trigger guard with a finger. It looked like a souvenir from the Korean War.

"There's one bullet in it. I'm saving it for Jackhammer. I've been waiting by this door since he took over my ship."

Brady nodded his head, then asked, "These stairs go to the Sun Deck?"

He was thinking of the lockbox with some make-do weapons, the blond kid with the assault rifle sitting on the top landing, and then the pirates up on the track.

They'd have to go past all of them.

Berlinghoff said, "Mr. Brady. Tell us your plan."

Chapter 92

BRADY CLIMBED THE crew's stairs alone, catching his breath between flights. When he reached the veranda level, he called up to the gunman at the top landing.

"Hey. Buddy. I need you to take a look at something for me."

Distract. Disarm.

The ploy had worked before. Would it work again?

He heard Kid Commando getting to his feet, the scraping of boots on metal stairs echoing up and down the dimly lit stairwell.

The kid called down, "What's the matter? What happened?"

"The dude I relieved told me to pass something

on to you," Brady shouted back. "He didn't want it going over the radio."

Brady was almost panting from walking up five flights. Too much desk duty had layered some fat over his frame. He shouldn't have missed all those workouts.

This was not good. Not good at all.

Walking up the last flight, he got his breathing under control. He was going to need everything he had to neutralize this kid.

"He wanted to keep something from Jackhammer?" the young man asked.

Brady had the two-way radio in his hand. The time was counting down on the screen, telling him that in about three and a half minutes, Jackhammer was going to be looking for his eighteen guys to check in.

Brady wasn't sure of the answer code. The password. Or whatever the fuck these guys always said to let him know that they were at their posts and that all was well.

He stood three steps down from the kid and said, "Can you just read this? Will you fucking just look at it?"

The kid adjusted the eyeholes in his mask and

walked down two steps and bent his head to look at the radio.

He said, "I don't see what the prob—"

Brady stepped up, putting his weight on his left leg, and reached his left hand around the kid's neck and pulled down hard. The kid yelled, "Hey," striking out and wind-milling with his arms, but he couldn't regain his balance.

The kid's feet shot out from under him, and as he slid down the steps on his ass, Brady got behind him and got his neck in the vise he made with his right biceps and forearm.

The kid cried out and Brady tightened his neck hold, his forearm pressing against the kid's carotid.

The kid tried to reach behind him, and Brady applied pressure, not enough for the kid to black out but enough for things to start to go fuzzy.

Then he let up just a bit.

The kid said, "What the fuck are you doing? What the fuck is wrong with you, man?"

Brady asked himself the same question. Thinking that over the past half hour, he had crossed some defining line. Was this really the person he had become? Or would any man if pushed this far do the same damned things?

Brady said, "You want to breathe? Lie still. What's your name?"

"Brian."

"What's Jackhammer's name, Brian?"

The kid got it now. He was going to die.

He said, "Don't do it, man. Please don't hurt me."

Brady applied some pressure and the kid grabbed futilely at his bulked-up arms. This kid was either a murderer or he was complicit in the many murders aboard this ship. But there would be no by-the-book interrogation for Brian. No Miranda rights.

Brady relaxed the hold and gave the kid a little blood to his brain, a little air.

He asked again, "What's Jackhammer's name?"

"I don't know. I don't know *anyone*. None of us do."

"So why did you do this? Why did you take this job? You wanted to kill people? Ruin people's lives? Why?"

The kid was exasperated as well as frightened.

"I don't even understand your question. Look. Let me up. You've got the wrong guy."

There was no way around this kid. None. Brady

said, "I'm sorry, Brian. There's no other way."

He squeezed the kid's neck in the V of his arm, pressing his left hand to his right wrist to double the pressure. The kid passed out a few seconds later, but Brady held on until a couple of minutes passed and the kid stopped twitching.

He could think about this later. But not now. There was no time to do it now.

Chapter 93

BRADY DRAGGED BRIAN'S body off to the side of
the landing and turned his mind to the Sun Deck
layout, where more shit was waiting for him and
there was less than a fifty-fifty chance that he'd
survive the next ten minutes.

He'd been up to the Sun Deck a couple of times.

Before it had turned into a shooting platform.

There was teakwood decking fore and aft, lined
out with lounge chairs. At the middle of the deck
was an eight-foot-wide running track, rectangular
in shape, a hundred yards long by fifty wide and
hollow at the center so that the sun could shine
through to the Pool Deck below.

A railing ran around the inside perimeter of the
track, making it a perfect catwalk and doubling

with a first-class gun rest for sighting the captives directly below. Like prison guards looking down from the walls over inmates in a prison yard.

And now footsteps clanged against metal as the ship's officers climbed toward him on the inside stairs. When they reached him, Brady, said, "I'm going out there first. After that, you all know what to do, regardless."

The captain said, "Good luck to you, Mr. Brady."

"And to you, sir. Everyone."

Brady's assault rifle hung from the strap over his right shoulder, and he had a loaded pistol on his hip. He said a quick prayer and pulled the knitted mask down over his face. Then he turned the wheel that opened the lock and pushed open the door to the Sun Deck. He closed it behind him.

Squinting through the mask, Brady tried to see everything at once.

The rising sun was streaking the horizon with pink bands, backlighting mountains in the distance and glinting on the railings at the bow.

There were three men on the track, two on the far, short side of the rectangle, the third guy standing by himself on a long side, fifty feet away.

Brady called out to that one, "Bro. Got a second?"

Without waiting for an answer, he set out along the composite rubber track toward the guard.

"I hope you brought me the beef taco," the man said. "I already had the chicken. Beef is better if there's any left."

Brady had considered using the knife, but he wasn't that good or that fast. So he pulled the gun.

"I don't know anything about the chow," Brady said.

Continuing to walk toward the guard, he said, "There's been a slight change in the rotation."

The man was only a few feet away.

He said, "Don't tell me I've got to go another watch. I'm dead on my feet, already."

The guard sensed something wrong in Brady's posture or demeanor, or maybe he was close enough to see the gun.

He backed up, saying, "Let me see your hands, man," while shouldering his rifle.

Brady aimed, squeezed the trigger, and fired twice, hitting the guard in the throat and chest.

Immediately shouts came from the men on the far side of the track.

Brady dropped his handgun, gripped the automatic rifle, and fired across the open track. The bullets made the gun's signature *pop-br-br-br-br-br* report, hitting the gunmen who were running toward him like cartoon commandos in a video game.

The men flailed and then dropped.

Brady heard the tinny voice of a radio in the shirt pocket of the man lying near his feet.

"Pool deck four to track one."

Brady picked up the radio and, what the hell, said into the dangling mouthpiece, "Yeah, track one. All secure." Then he went to the hatch door and tapped on it.

The door swung in, and Brett Lazaroff, George Berlinghoff, and three of his officers, including the hotel manager, dashed out onto the track.

Berlinghoff went directly to the locker with the small lot of weapons. He shot off the lock and his officers emptied the box, then pocketed what they could as others collected guns from the dead gunmen before returning, as planned, to the crew staircase.

Brady was standing with Brett Lazaroff on the track when gunfire exploded upward through the center of it. They propped their AKs on the railing, aimed at the muzzle flare, and returned fire. Then there was a break in the shooting.

Brady said, "Lazaroff. You ready to roll?"

Chapter 94

YUKI WAS SCRUNCHED up against the over-turned wet bar outside the Spa when gunfire opened up from the track deck. There had been shooting before, sporadic blasts of automatic-weapon fire meant to scare the prisoners who had already become zombies from unrelenting, paralyzing fear.

The spate of gunfire was worse now, more sustained. Purposeful. There was a spray of gunfire and a gunman near the pool grabbed at his neck and went down, toppling half into the pool.

What was happening?

Were they being rescued? Where was Brady?

Music was blasting from the speakers across the deck.

Bullets rained down from the track. Passengers screamed, scattered, and tried to hide under lounge chairs. Gunmen took cover and fired back.

Yuki moved aside as three passengers converged on the wet bar, looking for protection from the gunfire.

"We're going to storm the Spa," one of the passengers said to her. He grabbed her hand, briefly and said, "Good luck."

Then he was gone.

There were shouts and the sound of breaking glass. Everything was happening fast.

Automatic weapons fired from the bow sent people running toward the stern, where Yuki was crouched near the barricade. Then a movement on the staircase over the Spa caught her eye.

A guard jogged down the steps from the Sun Deck. He stopped outside the Spa's shattered doors and pulled off his mask. White-blond hair spilled onto his shoulders.

Brady. Oh, my God, it was Brady.

He'd been shot. Blood ran down the side of his face and the shirt he was wearing was dripping red. He didn't see her.

Brady shouted, "Passengers. I'm a passenger,

too. The crew is now *armed*. Lie flat. Keep your head down."

The double doors opened out from the Spa and the Luna Grill at the same time.

Men in whites ran out and took positions where they could find them. They were ordinary men, pot-bellied, gray-haired, and some of them were holding rifles, others handguns. Yuki recognized them as ships' officers.

Looking around, she saw six men in fatigues, all of them finding cover. There was shooting, and people yelled and cursed. Glass shattered. Bottles flew through the air. Yuki squatted behind the bar, hands over her ears when Becky grabbed her arm.

"Yuki. Come with us. *Run!*"

Yuki said, "That's Brady. My husband."

But Becky was already heading for the Luna Grill, her arm around her ten-year-old son, her husband corralling them from behind. A blast of gunfire came from a gunman kneeling beside the bandstand outside the Grill, and Becky's husband went down.

Becky's screams were lost in the commotion on the deck, but even in the gray dawn, Yuki saw that the passengers were fighting back with guns, knives, and glass shards—whatever they could throw, swing, or stab with.

Yuki looked for something she could use to arm herself. There was a bottle of champagne deep in the back of the bar and she grabbed it by the neck. She found a paring knife in a drawer, and slipped it into her pocket.

She looked for Brady. He'd been right there! Suddenly, a hand in her hair pulled her from behind the bar. She kicked out, dropped the bottle, and punched air, and then she was dragged to her feet.

It was Brady who yelled, *"Put her down!"*

The voice belonging to the man who held her asked, "Is this your wife?"

Yuki recognized the voice: It was Jackhammer's.

The realization rose in her from her feet to her throat, as if her body had filled with frigid water. She wasn't going to be saved. This was her last moment on earth. She looked at the pink line of sun rising over the railing. She thought of her dead mother, Keiko, holding out her arms to her.

She looked at Brady for the last time.

She focused on her husband's eyes and heard Jackhammer say into her ears, "Here's my little volunteer. Just in time."

Chapter 95

CAPTAIN GEORGE BERLINGHOFF ran out onto the deck from the Luna Grill at the bow, four of his officers behind him, men who'd never been in battle, men with wives and children and aspirations.

Maybe they thought of the ones they loved as they stared out at the chaos and the bloodshed, the downed passengers crawling, trailing blood, the nearly dead and the clearly dead, innocent people in pajamas, many of them fighting back with fists and bottles and whatever they could find.

As the captain of a tourist ship, he was going by Brady's plan and a lot of old war movies he'd seen from his couch. He waded into a battlefield, armed with one of the dead commandos' assault rifles.

He did what Brady had said to do.

He assessed the situation and he looked for opportunities. And then he saw Brady, frozen in place right at the foot of the stairs.

Incongruous music from the speakers in the bar wafted across the deck.

As Berlinghoff tried to put the scene together, he saw that Brady was advancing on the overturned bar. Actually, he was coming toward one of the terrorists, who was holding a woman in front of him, using her as a *shield*.

He heard the gunman shout at Brady, "Is this your wife?"

Berlinghoff slung the AK and pulled his handgun from his belt—the old revolver with one round in the chamber.

Jackhammer was occupied with Brady and didn't see or hear Berlinghoff come up from behind. Berlinghoff looked over the gun sight to the back of the commando's neck. He was too close to miss.

He had his finger on the trigger—when suddenly shots rang out and his gun spun from his hand. Blood spurted from his wrist, and he shouted, "Damn!"

He gripped his wrist but blood pumped out between his fingers. More bullets punched into him.

Mother of God. He was hit.

Chapter 96

BULLETS CHATTERED ACROSS the Pool Deck. Pop music blasted out of the bar speakers. But despite the terrifying and discordant sights and sounds, Brady's focus was on Yuki in Jackhammer's headlock, staring at him as though she was already a ghost.

Jackhammer had pulled Yuki tight to his body and he leaned over her shoulder. Brady thought he was talking to her.

Like he was telling her that she was going to die.

Brady saw that his only way to save Yuki was to shoot her himself. He would aim for her shoulder or her hip and hope that she would drop and Jackhammer would lose his grip on her.

Could he fucking shoot straight?

Please, God, help me.

As he was taking aim at Yuki's shoulder, Brady saw George Berlinghoff come up behind Jackhammer, unseen. He was holding his one-shot revolver pointed at the pirate's neck.

Brady saw what would happen. Berlinghoff would kill Jackhammer. He could not miss. And then Brady would come in quickly and swoop Yuki up before Jackhammer hit the ground.

But, it didn't happen.

In the split second before Berlinghoff pulled the trigger, there were shots from Berlinghoff's right-hand side and the revolver spun out of his hand.

The captain yelled, "Damn!" and Brady saw him grab his wrist. More shots hit him, sending blood spurting across the captain's white uniform as he fell.

Jackhammer was distracted by Berlinghoff's shout. He swung his head to see Berlinghoff's falling body, and in that instant, Brady yelled at Yuki, *"NOW!"*

Yuki seemed to come back to herself. She twisted in Jackhammer's grip and kicked him in the knee. Then she pulled something from her bathrobe pocket and punched out at Jackhammer's gut.

Jackhammer grunted and relaxed his hold enough for Yuki to wrench herself free.

As she ran to Brady, Jackhammer aimed at them. Brady saw that he was steady enough to stand, and he knew that the bullets would cut both of them down.

But, no. Jackhammer was switching out his empty magazine.

Brady shoved Yuki away from him. He dropped to his knee and fired the last rounds in his AK's magazine at Jackhammer's legs.

The terrorist-in-chief dropped his weapon and went down screaming.

Chapter 97

BRADY SCRAMBLED TO his feet, tossed Jackhammer's weapon away from him, and then bent close to the man's face.

He said, "I'd happily kill you, you son of a bitch. But you have to answer for all of this."

Brady shouted out for help, and passengers brought belts, sashes, and strips of torn clothes. Brady rolled Jackhammer onto his belly, tied his hands and bleeding legs, cinching tourniquets above his wounds.

Yuki stooped beside him.

"The shooting stopped," she said.

Then she pulled up Brady's shirt and saw where the blood was coming from.

"I'm lucky," he said. "That was close."

She touched his right ear, just above where the lobe had been shot away.

"Oh, Brady," Yuki said.

He took his wife in his arms. Bottles were being cracked open. Passengers were drinking, and the stinking sound system was shut down.

"It's not over," Brady said. "Counting Jackhammer, that's thirteen men down. The other six . . . they could be retrenching."

Brady heard Brett Lazaroff call out from the rail.

"Brady, Yuki. Come and look at this."

His broken ribs were killing him, but Brady leaned on Yuki, and they joined Lazaroff at the port side of the Pool Deck.

Following the line of Lazaroff's finger, they saw moving specks coming from the eastern shore of the passage.

"Whales?" Yuki asked. "Is that a pod of Orcas?"

"Boats," said Brady.

A dozen zodiacs were motoring toward the *FinStar*, and within minutes they pulled up to the hull. Grappling hooks were fired. Men in ballistic gear began climbing the ropes.

Lazaroff's voice cracked when he said, "Those are Navy SEALs, my friends. That's the United States Navy."

Chapter 98

IT WAS EVENING, in the thick of rush hour. Joe and I were in his Mercedes, heading out to San Francisco International Airport, as the sky turned a rich cobalt-blue. Two black SUVs with government plates and flashers bracketed us in front and behind, helping to speed our way.

After a news blackout of two full days, word had exploded over all media channels at once: The surviving passengers of the *FinStar* were returning home.

Yuki and Brady, along with about a dozen other San Francisco residents who had been aboard, were arriving by Air Canada at a yet to be disclosed time and I definitely wanted to be there when that plane landed.

Naturally, traffic didn't know or care what I wanted, and I swore at the vehicular knots and snarls, tried to drive from the passenger seat, jamming on the imaginary gas pedal whenever Joe had to take his foot off the real one.

I stared ahead at the highway and thought about the last time I saw Yuki, a pale night-blooming flower in her après-wedding dress as Brady twirled his new bride around the dance floor.

Then another memory pushed the party right out. It was the ten seconds of unfocused autumn colors on my iPhone accompanied by Yuki's frightened whispered voice—"Lindsay. Our ship was *attacked*"—before her phone was snatched and the lights went out.

The car swerved as we took the exit, and Joe said, "Hon. Lock up your gun."

I stowed my Glock in the glove box as we turned up the airport access road and swooped to the curb fronting the magnificent winged entrance to the international terminal's arrival hall.

Homeland Security agents jumped out of their SUVs, opened our doors, and turned us over to a pair of Air Canada's security officers. We were taken through the wide-open terminal with its soaring ceilings and oversize spaces, past gangs of press seeking a glimpse of *FinStar* passengers' loved ones for a fresh clip or maybe a quote.

Our security escort led us through metal doors, down a corridor, and into a small elevator, before we finally disembarked in a private buff-colored lounge. There was food and coffee, cushy uphol-stered furnishings, and dense carpeting. I knew that this lounge was generally used by the grieving families of passengers involved in airline fatalities.

As we waited, the lounge filled with babies and grannies and moms and pops, all red-eyed from crying, holding on to toys and blankets and handmade signs, and to one another.

The three TVs were turned to CNN.

Wolf Blitzer was telling his viewers that some of the terrorists were in detention and others were at the Alaska State Medical Examiner's Office in Anchorage.

Next he showed a satellite image of little stars bursting, blooming, and winking out—the big firefight aboard the *FinStar*. Then Blitzer intro-duced a live guest, a former admiral who said, "The SEALs couldn't board until they mapped out where the shooters were. If they'd gone in too soon, there would have been many more casualties. But when the firefight started, they just went in balls to the walls and took the ship back."

A tight-faced man who had been sitting with his large weeping family got up and switched off the television sets one after the other.

"I can't take any more," he said.

No one protested.

I looked around at the friends and families of *FinStar* survivors and at the pain on their faces.

I know my face was radiating the same kind of pain.

How was Yuki holding up emotionally? Was Brady more badly injured than we knew? Would the two of them want to come home with us? Or would they want to be alone? What did my friends need? What could we do for them?

I couldn't know a damned thing until I saw them come through the door.

Chapter 99

IT FELT LIKE ball bearings were rolling around inside my guts. I couldn't sit still. I ate food that I didn't want and paced the floor, texting friends and searching the Web for any tidbits that might be leaking out around the edges of legitimate news.

I was taking a lap around the lounge when I glimpsed the small Air Canada jet with wheels down, rolling toward the gate.

I shouted the completely obvious "They're here," then pressed my hands against the windows as the plane was waved in. Joe joined me, and then everyone in the lounge found a few square inches of glass that they could claim as their own.

People bounced on their toes, shouting, and thanked God.

But then nothing happened. Time crawled on its hands and knees one slow second at a time. Cranky babies were shushed. An elderly man in a yellow Windbreaker began repeating, "God damn it. God damn it."

By now the passengers must be in the building, right?

What was the holdup?

Where were our people?

Joe put his arm around me as we waited, and then finally a door opened. There were a lot of people between me and the door, but I found a gap in the crowd and focused through that.

First in, an Air Canada pilot came through to cheers and mad applause. He was pushing a young woman in a wheelchair. People screamed, "Jenny!" and raced toward the chair.

Other crew came through that narrow doorway pushing wheelchairs, and every time a chair came through, the new arrival was greeted with shouts and tears.

I was tearing up before I saw Yuki and Brady—and then slowly they came through the doorway, and I saw some of what had been done to them.

Brady had been wounded more than once.

His left arm was in a sling, and there was a huge bandage over his left ear. He walked stiffly, and it looked to me like his ribs were taped under his shirt.

Yuki looked like a child who'd been living on the street. Her jeans and sweatshirt hung from her frame. Her face was thin and pale. I yelled her name.

She turned toward my voice, and when she saw me, it was as if a light went on behind her eyes.

She broke away from Brady and I ran toward her, and when I got my arms around her, I hugged her bony little self half to death.

"How are you? Are you okay? Are you hungry?"

She said over my shoulder, "I'm never letting Brady plan another vacation as long as we live."

Brady was right there and he heard her. Grinning painfully and holding on to his rib cage, he said to Yuki, "I want another chance."

Joe was shaking Brady's hand when a woman in a bright red sweater appeared and grabbed Brady's right biceps. She said, "You're in my prayers for life, Mr. Brady. Christmas cards until the end of time. I'll write to you soon."

People flowed around us as Yuki said to me,

"He saved us. I mean, Lindsay, he saved us *all*. I don't know how many passengers. Many, many. Hundreds."

Brady said, "You have no idea what strong stuff my wife is made of. She—"

Brady stopped, putting his hand over his eyes. His shoulders shook, and that great big man, the hero who fought for the passengers of the *FinStar,* started to cry.

Yuki put her arms around him, very gently.

"Okay," she said. "It's okay, dear one."

"I'm not crying," he said. "This is . . ."

It hurt to hear his huge wracking sobs, but I understood that he was feeling overwhelming relief. He was alive. Yuki was alive. He was home.

"Let's get out of here," Yuki said.

"Car's right outside," said Joe.

Chapter 100

EVERY COP IN Homicide, all three shifts, as well as Robbery, Vice, and the brass on the fifth floor, was crowding our squad room, spilling out the gate and into the waiting room and halfway down the hall.

It was an insanely happy crowd and a very tight fit.

Cappy and Samuels were trying to hang a WELCOME BACK BRADY banner over Brady's office door. Really. Watching those two extra-large cops balancing on wheelie chairs, ordering each other around—well, it was hilarious.

I was putting out cookies on Brenda's desk, telling Conklin about last night.

"So Yuki says, 'I want barbecued spare-ribs.

417

No, make that I *neeeeed* barbecued spare-ribs.'
And Brady says, 'Pasta with red sauce. Eggplant
parmigiana. Osso buco.' "

Conklin laughed and popped a chocolate-
walnut cookie.

"And Yuki says, 'Egg rolls. Pork fried rice. Oh,
my *God*. Lobster in black bean sauce. Anything in
black bean sauce.' And Brady tries to hold his
broken ribs, and he says, 'Please darlin', whatever
you want. Just don't make me laugh.' "

Conklin and I both fell apart at that and then a
shadow fell across my desk.

It was Jacobi. There was a bad look on his face.

"There's been another belly bomb explosion,"
he said. "Young guy, just back from Afghanistan.
Supposed to get married next week."

Conklin said, "Not possible, Chief. Not a belly
bomb."

"Tell that to the dead soldier with his guts
blown out. This time, the victim had his burger 'to
stay.' There were assorted nonfatal casualties as
well."

Jacobi took out his phone and showed us the
interior of a Chuck's restaurant after a consumed
belly bomb went off.

"Aw, fuck," my partner said.

Jacobi nodded, then said, "Conklin. You and I are going upstairs to question Walt Brenner. Maybe he'll brag on planting a delayed-action bomb. That's what we're hoping for."

"I'll talk to Timko," I said.

The women's jail is around the corner from the Hall on 7th. Timko was incarcerated there, awaiting trial, and I hoped she was getting a good sense of life without an office, a staff, a new Caddy, a house—nothing but a jumpsuit and a lot of time to catalog her mistakes.

I made a couple of calls as I jogged down the fire stairs and then continued out the lobby onto Bryant. Five minutes later, I ran up the steps to the huge Sheriff's Department Building. I passed through security with no hassle, found my way to the appropriate reception area, and twiddled my thoughts while Timko was located.

An hour later, Officer Bubbleen Waters found me.

She'd gone blond since I'd last seen her, and she'd been working out with weights.

She said, "Lucky you, Sergeant. Ms. Timko will see you now. What a nasty piece of work."

"And her lawyer?"

"She doesn't want him, because she didn't do anything and she's not going to say anything. And that's a verbatim quote."

"Huh."

"She wants to give you the evil eye, she told me."

"Okay. I'm wearing my invisible force field. So."

"Oh, wow. Where can I get one of those?"

"Walmart, where else?"

Officer Waters laughed, and I followed her into an elevator. I stared up at the blinking numbers as the car rose to the seventh floor.

She escorted me past more security checkpoints and through several gates to a gray windowless room with two plastic chairs and a yellow Formica table. This is where I waited to talk with the former head of Chuck's product-development division.

Then I heard Bubbleen's voice in the corridor, saying, "You got fifteen minutes to stare your eyes out, Ms. Donna Timko. Go right in."

Chapter 101

DONNA TIMKO SHUFFLED into the small meeting room. She was dressed in orange, wore no makeup, and had stringy hair. She looked sallow and yet cheerful. Why? She should be hitting the bottom about now, I figured.

With shackles clanking, she edged onto the plastic chair across the table from me and was compliant as Officer Waters linked her cuffs with a chain through the hole in the table to the chain around her waist.

"I'll be baaack," said Officer Waters.

The door closed and Timko and I were alone.

"I'm getting that déjà vu feeling," she said. "Only this time, no coffee, no Baby Cakes."

Okay, good, she wasn't giving me the silent

treatment. I said, "Donna. How're you doing?"

"Not bad. First vacation I've had in years. Nice of you to ask. Why are you here?"

"Well, maybe you could help me out with something."

"I refuse to answer any questions that you'll try to use against me, so, let's talk about what *I* want to talk about."

"Go ahead."

I sat back in my wobbly seat as Donna teed up whatever she had on her twisted mind. She wanted ballgame scores and headlines on "Dancing with the Stars," and she wanted to know if I knew how Walter was doing.

I told her about the 49ers' crushing win over the Packers, said that I didn't watch the other thing, and told her that as far as I knew, Walter was making friends in jail. "I'll get word to him that you were asking after him. I promise.

"My turn," I said after that.

"I'll listen," she said, "but I told you, Sergeant." Then she motioned zipping her lip.

Donna Timko was looking playful, almost cute.

But Bubbleen Waters hadn't exaggerated when she said of Timko, she's a "nasty piece of work."

My mind filled with pictures dominated by the color red. The red Jeep on the bridge, followed a few days later by the bloodied interior of a car in a Chuck's parking lot in LA.

And the latest, Corporal Andy Licht, twenty-three years old, rented tuxedo hanging from a hook in the backseat, St. Christopher hanging from the rearview mirror. This returning soldier was two days from marrying the young woman who'd been waiting for him and praying for his safety. Now Licht was dead, his blood sprayed all over the white tile on the restaurant floor.

Jacobi had said, "Get them to brag. That's what we want."

I looked at Timko and said, "Something just happened. I'd like your thoughts on it, Donna."

"Oh, yeah? What's the magic word?" she said, cocking her head like a predatory bird.

Chapter 102

I DON'T THINK it's a secret in our squad that when we're doing an interrogation, I'm the bad ass and Conklin is the good cop that women can't resist. Well, I had Conklin's role now, and I asked myself, what would Conklin do?

No doubt he would play along with the mean girl in cuffs and tangerine-colored jumpsuit, being attentive and sympathetic and almost for real.

I decided my version of Conklin's style was "Just us girls."

I said, "Between us, I've got a disaster on my hands and I don't know what the hell to do next."

"Oh, yeah?"

"Definitely, yeah," I said. "A belly bomb went off *inside* a Chuck's restaurant in Alameda. Same effect as your bombs, but with a shorter time between ingestion and explosion. So, it's a *better* bomb."

Timko's face crumpled. "Better? How could it be better?"

"That's what I want to know. You've got advanced degrees in chemistry. So how did this copycat improve on your formula? Could someone you know be advancing your work? Give me your thoughts. Please. There. I said the magic word."

Tears came into Timko's eyes, beaded up on her lower lid, and spilled over.

What the hell?

"Someone else died because of Chuck's?" she asked me. "How is that better, Sergeant? What kind of person are you, anyway?"

I guess my face registered surprise, even shock.

This made no sense. Last time I'd seen Timko, she was threatening to run me through a meat grinder.

And then Timko's face lit up. She was beaming at me.

Man, oh, man. She was like a shape-shifter.

And I remembered that the first time I saw Timko, she was on a monitor attending a Chuck's senior staff meeting virtually. And she'd been crying.

Crocodile tears.

Timko said, "I kind of love this, Sergeant. Do you know what it's like to be treated like you're nothing? Like you don't even exist? No. That's *my* life. Well, I don't feel like *nothing* right now. I think I could bend steel bars with my bare hands."

I had wanted Timko to scoff. To say that this latest bomb was all hers and Walter's, that there was no accomplice, no copycat. That one of their bombs had been sitting in a freezer until it was slapped onto the grill and served up to a soldier.

I especially wanted her to tell me if there were other bombs out there lying dormant in Chuck's kitchens, and that she knew where they were and that she'd trade that information for a deal.

But no.

I wasn't playing Timko.

She was playing *me*.

Still, she was telling me her motive for the killings. She did it for the power: over her victims, over the police, over the heads of Chuck's, over the FBI, and over *me*.

She was grinning, and I felt the twist, like a

knife between my ribs. The more bombs that went off while she and her brother were in jail, the better it was for them.

She said, "I had nothing to do with any bombs, Sergeant. And you can't prove anything. In fact, our attorneys are going to call this 'reasonable doubt.'

"Problem solved, right?"

She winked, then called out toward the barred door.

"Bubbleen, get your fat ass in here. Sergeant Boxer and I are done."

My husband is a modest guy, and he's almost always right. He'd said to me after the first bombs, "Sooner or later, the bomber is going to take credit."

Well. Hadn't happened yet.

As soon as I got out onto the street, I called Jacobi.

When he answered, I shouted into my phone, "Jacobi. Timko admitted nothing, but bombs are gonna go off. Call the FBI. Call the mayor. Get Chuck's *closed*! Every last Chuckburger has to be recalled so no one else *dies*."

Jacobi snuck in a few words edgewise.

"Exactly right," I said. "We nail them on hindering prosecution, interfering with a police officer, reckless endangerment, everything else we've got. We buy time. We buy time and find the one forgotten thing. We find the thing that proves that she and Walter made those damned dirty *bombs*."

PART FIVE

HIGH NOON

Chapter 103

JOE CALLED OUT to me from the foyer, "I'll be back in an hour, Blondie. And that's a promise, more or less."

"Godspeed," I called back.

I was in a hurry, closing the snaps on Julie's pastel-striped onesie and looking for her knitted hat with the daisy in front, when the phone rang. I'd ducked her calls too often.

"Cindy—hey."

"Tell me everything," she said.

I was glad to hear her voice. It had been a while.

"Joe's picking up Martha from the vet and I'm using my lunch hour to take Julie to the park."

Cindy laughed, said, "That's fascinating, but I meant, tell me everything about Brady and Yuki."

I only had time to give her the Twitter version, so no need to go off the record. I told her that Brady had made an appearance at the squad this morning and was going to be back on the job as soon as he was able to pull a full day.

"Lost part of his ear," I told her. "An earlobe. Four broken ribs, too, but he's going to be fine."

"Whoaaa. And Yuki?"

"Yuki is down to about two-thirds her fighting weight, which means she couldn't go one round with a chicken. But she seems pretty good, all things considered. She's going to take off work for a couple weeks."

"Sure. She probably needs to sleep with both eyes closed."

"She said the ground is still moving under her feet."

Julie was fussing, gearing up for a tantrum. I picked her up while keeping the phone between my ear and shoulder. I unfolded the stroller with one hand and said to Cindy, "How are you? Just the headlines."

"Everything is good, well, except for." Cindy's voice dropped. "Morales."

I looked at the time. I had a meeting with Jacobi

in forty-eight minutes and I hadn't left the house.

Cindy was saying, "I still worry, you know. That she's got it in for you."

I said, "Please don't worry about me, Cindy. Please? I'm a cop. I carry a gun. And now I've got a playdate with my bossy baby girl."

We said good-bye and I strapped my precious daughter into her stroller.

"Wow, you look amazing with that hat," I said. "Hold it." I got my phone. I took Julie's picture and sent it to Joe.

"Are you ready?" I asked Julie.

And then I said her lines, too.

" '*Ready?* It's about *time* you got off the danged phone. I certainly am ready to go to the park, Mom.'

"All right, baby girl. Let's go."

Chapter 104

THE SUNLIGHT WAS soft and the air was scented with eucalyptus. In fact, I could almost smell the ocean, too, as I walked Julie's stroller through my neighborhood, its diversity reflected in the restaurants and shops.

I wanted to enjoy this unexpected quality time with Julie.

All I had to do was kick Donna Timko out of my head, put my faith in the powers that be to recall every last Chuckburger on earth, and—relax.

"Mommy helped shut down a multimillion-dollar hamburger chain, baby girl," I said. "I hope so, anyway."

I unbuttoned my jacket, took the band out of

my hair, and shook out my pony. Julie babbled happily as we turned west on Lake and took a left onto 12th, heading into the seven-block-long straightaway to the park.

I said, "So, the dog run, right, Julie? Or you want to see the birdies in Stow Lake? I'm pretty sure you got your eyes and your hair from dear old dad, but when it comes to dogs, you take after—"

Julie interrupted me with a long string of baby foolery, beating the air with her hands—*soooo cute*—making me laugh. I stopped to kiss her face and then we pushed along the eclectic residential block to the intersection at California, where I paused for the light.

I tried to imagine having a day like this every day. And the idea held some appeal. Sunshine, baby and me, and if I actually wasn't working, we would go home in a bit, have Gerber mixed veggies and turkey, and then take a nap.

The light changed and we crossed the road and headed toward Clement, entering the business section of the Richmond District. Traffic was congested. Car horns and radios blared and—*holy crap!* I saw something I just didn't like.

Gripping the handlebar of the stroller, I started to run.

I used the crowded sidewalk as a buffer, looking ahead of me and on both sides all at the same time. All I cared about was Julie. Getting her out of sight.

I stepped on a crack in the sidewalk, turning my ankle, but I recovered my balance before I dropped. Julie wasn't aware that I'd almost gone down, because I kept the stroller steady. A clot of teens were taking up the breadth of the sidewalk, smoking cigarettes, texting, and joking around.

I screamed at them to get the fuck out of my way.

They yelled back, but they made way for me, and I kept going, running fast and furious.

Between 12th and 11th, I turned onto Clement and stayed on the south side, which was lined with a wall-to-wall row of shops.

There was an alcove halfway up the block, an entrance to a Chinese restaurant. I shoved the stroller down the stone steps and stumbled behind it, hiding behind the alcove to the shuttered Wing Ho's Happy Eating.

Julie was wailing now, and I stood between her carriage and the street, semi-protected by the wings of the alcove and pretty much out of plain sight.

I watched, and when I felt it was safe, I grabbed my child and held her over my shoulder. I picked up the stroller with my free hand, took the stairs up to the sidewalk, and ducked into the boutique next door, Rosalie's Fanfare.

I found a shopgirl at the back of the store. She was wearing a black tunic, tight pants, and black leather boots to her knees. She froze and stared at me with huge blackringed eyes.

I tucked my baby into the stroller and said, "I'm a cop. On a case."

I opened my jacket, showed her the badge pinned inside and my gun on my hip. Then I touched Julie's head and said, "Honey. I'll be right back."

The shopgirl said, "No, no, you can't leave her here."

I said, "You. Watch. Her."

The baby's cries followed me as I went back toward the front of the store. I bumped hard into a woman coming out of a dressing room. She fell back against a bunch of cartons that tumbled like a stack of blocks.

The sound of the customer's curses mingled with Julie's screams as I made for the shop's front door.

The weight of a human female heart is about nine ounces. Every bit of mine was with my baby, as if that small pounding muscle could protect her.

Chapter 105

I HAD MY gun out before I exited Rosalie's Fanfare.

I stood in the doorway, peering out onto Clement Street. I checked out the pedestrians on both sides and stared into the shadows and the glaring sections of pavement.

I was sure that I'd seen a woman who could pass as a teenage boy—a lean five foot six with an angular face, wearing boyfriend jeans and a hoodie, hands in the pockets and possibly holding a gun.

It was Morales. Wasn't it?

I always said I'd know Mackie Morales in a grizzly bear suit. I'd spent three months with her in her role as a summer intern. She was lethal as a rattlesnake and crazy as a loon.

Yeah, and she was foxy, too.

Had she been staking me out, waiting for a moment when I was alone with Julie, on foot and very vulnerable?

I thought of calling for backup. None would get here in time, and what would I say?

That I'd seen a boylike girl who might be Morales?

No. I needed Conklin. He was my first choice for backup, and not just because he had his own issues with Morales. Also because he would not call me paranoid.

I slapped my right-hand jacket pocket, going for my phone. But my phone wasn't there. It wasn't in any of my pockets. What the hell? I slapped my pockets again.

Damn it. Was my phone in the stroller?

And then I remembered taking the picture of Julie, then putting down the phone as I got her ready to go.

Julie. How long had it been since I left her? One minute? Five?

I trotted a half-block to the corner of 10th, checking out people with such a fierce look that many pulled back as if I were crazy. Meanwhile, a lot of people were dressed in jeans and hoodies. Christ, it was practically a uniform for kids of a certain age.

I crossed Clement and doubled back toward 11th.

After five minutes of searching for Morales, the heartstrings that connected me to my daughter like a bungee cord yanked me back to Rosalie's Fanfare.

I ran like a 49er with the ball, goalposts in sight, in the last seconds of the game.

I dodged and I wove and I sped down the street, homing in on the fashion boutique where my little girl was waiting. I stiff-armed the door—and ran right into Cindy.

She was holding Julie in her arms, staring out the window, waiting for me.

"Cindy. How—?"

"I saw you leaving your place. I called out to you, but you didn't hear me."

I hugged Cindy and the baby together, tears coming.

"I followed you," Cindy said, hanging on to me. "I do that sometimes. Don't be mad, okay?"

"Mad? She's out there, damn it. Did you see her? You were right."

"I didn't want to be right."

"Thank you, Cindy."

We were safe for now—and I had been warned.

Chapter 106

ROSALIE'S FANFARE WAS two blocks from my apartment, and Cindy had parked her Honda just up the street from my front door. No cab and no cruiser would get to us in the five minutes it would take us to trot home.

Cindy stayed with Julie inside the boutique while I looked long and hard at the foot traffic outside. Then, I signaled to my friend and we all started out toward Lake Street at a very quick clip.

Cindy and I were both paranoid, but Julie was enjoying herself. Maybe it was the swiftness of her little stroller and the two of us hovering over her, or maybe her stars had suddenly aligned.

All I knew for sure was that Party Girl Molinari was laughing.

Our little group of three cut through lunch-hour pedestrians on 12th and a block later, when we crossed California, I almost began to breathe normally.

The residential block between California and Lake was humming sweetly. The street was wide and homey, dotted with trees. Ground-level garages had SUVs in the driveways, retirees walked dogs, and a woman in pink sweats was sweeping her walk while talking to her neighbor, who was unloading groceries from her car.

Cindy was saying, "So, what now? You'll get out an all points bulletin?"

"Too bad I can't make a positive ID, but anyway, the FBI is going to want to talk to us."

I was doing my own APB, checking out everything that moved. Dogs barked from a doorway. A man slid out from under his car and got on his phone. He wore a sweatshirt with the sleeves ripped off. He was a man's man, not a slim-hipped psycho killer.

Cindy was saying, "Until Mackie Morales is in jail, I'm not going to be able to think about anything else, or even sleep. Or even eat. You think I'm obsessed?"

I laughed.

Cindy said, "So, that's a yes."

And then we both stopped talking until we arrived safely at the sunny corner of 12th and Lake. My apartment building was directly to my right, and Cindy had parked her car just a few doors to our left. I checked out the moderate two-way traffic, the cars parked on both sides, and the trees between the cars and the storefronts.

Then Cindy and I grabbed each other over the stroller and kissed cheeks.

She said, "I'm calling Yuki. I need to see her."

We blew kisses and waved good-bye, and then I said to Julie, "Ride's over, baby girl. Daddy is probably home already, and I think he's going to put you down for a nap."

I walked toward the front door of our building with my keys in hand, and that's when something I'd half seen, a peripheral flicker, or an instinct, gave me a chill.

I jerked my head toward the mailbox on the corner.

There was a woman there, wearing a long white skirt, a white drapy sweater jacket, and a straw hat with a band around it.

She had been crossing Lake when her image imprinted itself in my mind. Now she had her back to me and was closing the letter slot on the mailbox. It made a dull, metallic clang.

I was on high alert, but I was just scaring myself.

Mackie Morales didn't dress like that.

That couldn't be her.

Chapter 107

THE WOMAN IN the long skirt and crocheted sweater jacket turned to face me. My mind made a psychic leap, feeling a sense of danger, rather than recognition. Cold sweat broke out over my body, especially the palms of my hands, where I was gripping the handle of Julie's stroller.

And then I was sure.

This was Mackie Morales, now dressed like some kind of angel, but with a gun in her hand. I'm so keyed to guns that the sight of one bypasses logical thought and goes straight to my lizard brain: fight or flight.

But I had neither option.

If I ran, she'd shoot me in the back.

If I pulled my gun, Julie could get hit.

I said, "Mackie, I'm putting the baby out of harm's way. Put the gun down. Then we can talk."

"You think we give a damn about your baby?" she said.

I shoved Julie's stroller hard to my right so that it rolled across the sidewalk and wedged itself between two parked cars. Traffic whizzed by as I turned back to Morales.

She was pointing her gun at me with a kind of nonchalance, as if she were in a dream. I understood the situation with crystal clarity. Morales wanted to die, but she wanted to kill me first. And with me standing ten feet away, she wouldn't miss.

I knew that I was going to die.

But in my last mortal moment, my rage was focused. I was determined to put Morales down, right now.

She said, "I've got her, lover. No worries."

She was talking to her dead psycho boyfriend.

I went for my gun, but before I could get it out of the holster, there was a shot. Mackie yelped. Her hat blew off and she grabbed her right shoulder. But she still held on to her gun.

Who fired that shot?

Then I saw something that made no sense.

Cindy was running up 12th Street directly toward us.

She held a gun with one hand straight out in front of her.

Mackie turned, took aim at Cindy, and fired.

I had one chance only, and I took it. My first shot went into Morales's back. She spun to face me and I fired again, center mass. She jerked, staggered back, and sat down hard. She lifted her gun hand, and aimed.

I fired again, got her right between the eyes.

Morales flopped back flat on the sidewalk, as if someone had cut her puppet strings. Her skirts fanned out. Her gun clattered to the sidewalk. Her hat blew into the gutter.

Julie bawled. I had the awful thought, maybe she's been bawling since I sent her stroller off the sidewalk.

I screamed, "Cindy, I'm coming."

I checked to see that Julie wasn't hurt, then went to my dear, sweet friend. Cindy was sitting on the sidewalk with her back up against a parked car. Blood was soaking through her pale-blue sweater.

She looked up and said to me, "I'm hit, Lindsay." She sighed. "Damn it. She shot me."

Chapter 108

MY DEAR HUSBAND had heard the gunshots. He had called 911 and then run downstairs. After I told him that I was okay, he took the baby inside, saying he'd be right back.

I sat next to Cindy on the sidewalk. She was pale, and the blood was still spreading across her sweater from what looked like a shoulder wound. I pressed a diaper against the bloodiest place and held it there, hoping she wasn't bleeding out, that she wouldn't go into shock.

The waiting was awful.

She looked so damned frail. I wanted to hug her, to hold on to her so that she didn't slip away. I could hardly stop myself from jumping up and running out into the street to look for the ambulance.

Cindy tried to tell me what the hell she thought she was doing with a gun. But I truly didn't care.

"You don't have to explain, Cindy. The bullet you took—that thing was meant for me. If you hadn't—look. You probably saved my damned life. So, thank you. Thank you very much."

"Protect my exclusive, okay?"

"Your what? *Oh*. Of course. Interview me all you want, Cin. I'm exclusively yours. Until the end of time."

She gave me a wan smile. "That'll be great."

I squeezed her hand, and two and a half minutes after Joe's call, black-and-whites screamed into the street.

Doors slammed. Cops advanced.

I unclipped my badge and held it up. I identified myself to a uniformed cop from where I sat at Cindy's side.

"Boxer. It's Nardone. Bob Nardone. You okay?"

Sergeant Nardone asked what had happened, and I kept it simple.

"The shooter was Mackenzie Morales. She's a fugitive. Wanted by the FBI. I shot her in self-defense."

I was spelling out Cindy's name and Mackie's

when incoming sirens drowned out my voice and the ambulance wailed to a stop. Paramedics swarmed around us and questioned Cindy as they lifted her onto a board.

I struggled to my feet, then stepped over to where Morales lay in her bloodied white drapery. No one was there anymore. No one home at all. Maybe Mackie was already checking in at the gates to Hell. *"Room key, please. Mr. Randy Fish is expecting me."*

Joe called out to me.

"Julie is with Mrs. Rose," he said of our neighbor across the hall.

I said, "Great. Joe. I'm going to the hospital with Cindy."

He said, "Take this."

He handed me my phone, then put his arms around me. I think I was shaking as I held him tight.

The EMTs were closing the doors to the bus, so I broke away from my husband and told him, "I'll call you."

I never made it into the ambulance because Jacobi was standing between me and the doors.

"Jacobi. You see what happened here? It's

Morales. She's the one who shot Cindy. I have to go with her," I said.

"You can't leave, Boxer. We've got a fatality here. You know that."

I had no fight left and it wouldn't have helped if I had. I said, "I need a minute."

I climbed up into the back of the bus and said to Cindy, "I'll see you later. You're my hero. And I love you. And Cindy? You're going to be fine."

I stepped back down to the street. I gave my gun to Jacobi and walked with him to his car.

Chapter 109

MY ARMS WERE full of flowers when I burst into Cindy's room at UCSF Medical Center.

Cindy shouted out, "Thank God the flowers have arrived."

I looked around. There were flowers everywhere, lining the window sill and on the various dinky tables, with some potted things on the floor.

"Who died?" I asked.

Cindy laughed. "Not me."

She was in the bed that was cranked up to sitting position, wearing a little pink robe. Right beside her in the bed, wearing oversize denims and a navy-blue SFDA sweatshirt, was Yuki Castellano Brady.

"Hey—hey," I said.

And, yep, Claire Washburn, MD, was hovering

over the two of my girls with a plastic cup of neon-green Jell-O and a spoon.

They all looked very merry.

"You think this is lime Jell-O, don't you?" said Claire. "Well, you'd be wrong. This is my own brew. Made with Margarita mix."

I laughed. "That explains everything."

Since all the vases and vaselike objects were in use, I went to the bathroom, took the lid off the toilet tank and dropped the flowers in, stems down.

When I returned, Yuki said, "There's a no-crying rule. Okay, Linds?"

I nodded. I was too choked up to speak, really.

Cindy was fine. Yuki was fine.

I went around the room and kissed each of my friends and they kissed me. There were hugs, too, long ones, no one wanting to let go. Speaking for myself, I was thinking how life could end without warning and how freakin' wonderful it was to have moments like this.

When we were exhausted from the hugging, I pulled over a chair for myself and sat down hard, next to the bed.

I said, "I want what you're having."

There were peals of laughter, one distinctive peal coming from Yuki.

She said, "Was that me laughing? I haven't done that in a while."

She was a little drunk, but that was appropriate. She had told me and Joe most of the horrific story, including that she'd shivved the bad guy.

"You told everyone?" I asked her.

"Yep. The Women's Murder Club kicked ass this week."

"I've got Ms. Mackie's three-eyed corpse in my cooler," said Claire. "So I'll drink to that."

Claire raised her cup of Jell-O, and just then there was a knock on the doorjamb.

The unsung hero of the hour, the man who'd taught Cindy to shoot, was standing there. I said, "Well, I've gotta go now, Cindy. I hear my baby calling me."

Claire added, "I've got a baby, too, and I'm driving Yuki home. I need to get a look at Brady."

There was a little rustle as we gathered our things. More kisses for Cindy and then we each said hi, as we edged past my good-looking, good-doing partner, who was standing in the doorway.

I hoped to God Cindy was well enough to handle *this*.

Chapter 110

CINDY SAID, "HEY, where's everyone *going?*"

The girls waved good-bye, blew kisses, and let themselves out the door, letting Richie in. Her pulse shot up. She touched her throat as he came into the room, looking great, wearing a jacket, his tie loose at the collar, fresh blue shirt, and khakis. His hair was falling over one eye.

"Richie. Hi."

He looked around the room at the garden on the window sill and said, "Cindy, I would have brought flowers but a birdie told me that you have plenty."

He turned his eyes on her, smiled, and shook a white paper bag with a gold-foil seal holding down the flap.

"I brought this instead."

"Come *onnn*. Chocolate orange peel? Let me see."

"Some grapefruit peel, too. Thought I'd mix it up a little for you."

Rich approached the bed, put his left hand on the rail at the far side and rested his weight on it. He leaned over, pressed his cheek to hers, then gave her a soft cheek kiss.

Cindy breathed him in.

He stood up and handed her the bag of candy, which she held in her lap. Then he pulled up the chair Lindsay had been sitting in.

"Thanks, Richie."

He sat down and said, "Welcome. How are you doing?"

"Pretty good. The shot missed the bone, missed the artery. I think it's what they call in cowboy movies, 'just a flesh wound.'" She grinned. She had rarely felt better.

"You been drinking?"

She kept grinning, nodded her head. "Dr. Washburn's orders."

Richie laughed.

"So, are you in a lot of pain?"

"Not too much. I can take it. They're checking

me out in a couple of days or maybe tomorrow. Made me promise to take Cindy's Flower Shop with me."

Cindy wanted him to touch her again. She could still feel his whiskers against her cheek.

He said, "Well, anyway, did you get your story, at least?"

"Hell, no. Lindsay killed it."

"Uh-huh." He laughed, like it wasn't right to laugh but he couldn't help it.

"There's a story there, anyway," she said. "It's not the one I had planned, but Mackie, Lindsay, and me, intersecting in that way at that place and with that result. I can do a lot with that. I could do a lot with *half* of that."

Richie sighed. Leaned back in the chair. Ran his hands through his hair.

"What is it, Rich?"

She knew what. There had been guns and shooting and death. And she wasn't a cop. And as they both knew full well, she'd never shot a gun off the range.

"That deal could have gone so wrong, Cindy, in so many ways. I don't like to think about it, but I do."

"Me, too."

He sighed, giving her a long, steady look. Cindy thought he was trying to convey to her what exactly she'd done, what she'd been through. And that she'd been lucky.

"I'm glad you're okay," he said at last.

She felt that. Her eyes watered just a little. She kept it together by gripping that white bag of candied citrus peel.

"Thanks, Richie."

He said, "I'm glad Lindsay is okay."

"I know. Me, too."

"I love you both."

Cindy watched his cheeks color. He cleared his throat. Then he looked at his watch. Oh, no. He just got here.

Richie said, "Hey, the game is on in a little while. Uh. You want me to keep you company and we'll watch the Niners kill the Seahawks?"

Cindy laughed. "That's the best offer I've had since I got here."

"I'll go out and get a pizza. Okay?"

"Excellent."

"Mushrooms and sausage."

"Perfect."

Richie stood up, pointed to the chair, and said, "Keep my seat warm. I'll be right back."

When Richie was gone, Cindy opened the bag of candy and bit into a chocolate-covered orange peel. Delicious.

She rolled down the top of the bag and held it for a while, thinking about Lake Street. About Richie. About how she was very much alive.

Hey. It would be really fun to do something with Richie again.

Cindy put the white paper bag on the table by the bed, grabbed the clicker, and turned on the TV.

ACKNOWLEDGMENTS

Our thanks and gratitude to these top professionals who were so generous with their time and expertise: Captain Richard Conklin, Stamford Connecticut Police Department; Dr. Humphrey Germaniuk, medical examiner and coroner, Trumbull County, Ohio; attorneys Philip R. Hoffman and Steven A. Rabinowitz, New York City; Chuck Hanni, IAAI-CFI, and forensic science consultant Elaine M. Pagliaro, MS, JD. And special thanks to Donna Nincic, Director, ABS School of Maritime Policy and Management, Professor, California Maritime Academy.

We are grateful to our researchers, Ingrid Taylar and Lynn Colomello, and to Mary Jordan, who keeps it all together.

THE MOST TERRIFYING THREAT IS THE ONE THAT IS...

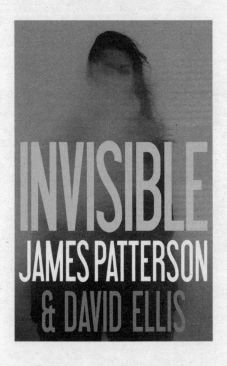

FOR AN EXCERPT, TURN THE PAGE.

THIS TIME I know it, I know it with a certainty that chokes my throat with panic, that grips and twists my heart until it's ripped from its mooring. This time, I'm too late.

This time, it's too hot. This time, it's too bright, there's too much smoke.

The house alarm is screaming out, not the early-warning beep but the piercing, *you're-totally-screwed-if-you-don't-move-now* squeal. I don't know how long it's been going off but it's too late for me now. The searing, oven-blast heat within the four corners of my bedroom. The putrid black smoke that singes my nostril hairs and pollutes my lungs. The orange flames rippling across the ceiling above me, dancing around my bed, almost in rhythm, a taunting staccato, popping and crackling, like it's not a fire but a collection of flames working in collusion, collectively they want me to know, as they bob up and down and spit and cackle, as they slowly advance, *This time it's too late, Emmy—*

The window. Still a chance to jump off the bed to the left and run for the window, the only part of the bedroom still available, like the enemy is cornering me, like they're daring me, *Go ahead, Emmy, Go for the window, Emmy —*

This is my last chance, and I know but don't want to think about what happens if I fail—that I have to start preparing myself for the pain. It will just hurt for a few minutes, it will be teeth-gnashing, gut-twisting agony but then the heat will shrivel off my nerve endings and I'll feel nothing, or better yet I'll pass out from carbon monoxide poisoning.

Nothing to lose. No time to waste.

The flames hit my flannel comforter as my legs kick over to the floor, as I bounce up off the bed cushion and race the one-two-three-four steps to the window. A girlish, panicky squeal escapes my throat, like when daddy and I used to play chase in the back yard and he was closing in.

Invisible

I lower my shoulder and lunge against the window, a window that was specifically built to *not* shatter, and ringing out over the alarm's squeal and the lapping of the flames is a hideous roar, a hungry growl, as I bounce off the window and fall backward into the raging heat. I tell myself, *Breathe, Emmy, suck in the toxic pollution, don't let the flames kill you, BREATHE—*

Breathe. Take a breath.

"Damn," I say to nobody in my dark, fire-free room. My eyes sting from sweat and I wipe them with my T-shirt. I know better than to move right away; I remain still until my pulse returns to human levels, until my breathing evens out. I look over at the clock radio, where red fluorescent square numbers tell me it's half past two.

Dreams suck. You think you've conquered something, you work on it over and over and tell yourself you're getting better, you *will* yourself to get better, you congratulate yourself on getting better. And then you close your eyes at night, you drift off into a netherworld, and suddenly your own brain is tapping you on the shoulder and saying, *Guess what? You're NOT better!*

I let out one, conclusive exhale and reach for

my bedroom light. When I turn it on, the fire is everywhere. It's my wallpaper now, the various photographs and case summaries and inspectors' reports adorning the walls of my bedroom, fires involving deaths in cities throughout the U.S.: Hawthorne, Florida. Skokie, Illinois. Cedar Rapids, Iowa. Plano, Texas. Piedmont, California.

And of course, Peoria, Arizona.

Fifty-three of them, in all.

I move along the wall and quickly review each one. Then I head to my computer and start opening e-mails.

Fifty-three that I know of. There are undoubtedly more.

This guy isn't going to stop.

I'M HERE FOR the Dick. That's not what I actually say, but that's what I mean.

"Emmy Dockery for Mr. Dickinson, please."

The woman parked at a wedge of a desk outside Dickinson's office is someone I've never met. Her name plate says "Lydia" and she looks like a *Lydia,* cropped brown hair and black horn-rimmed glasses and a prim silk blouse. She probably writes sonnets in her spare time. She probably has three cats and likes Indian food, only she would call it *cuisine.*

I shouldn't be so catty, but it annoys me that there's someone new, that something has changed since I left, so I feel like a stranger in an office where I faithfully labored for almost nine years.

"Did you have an appointment with the director, Ms. . . . . Dockery?"

Lydia looks up at me with a satisfied smirk. She knows I don't have an appointment. She knows because they called up from the lobby to see if I was authorized to enter. She's just reminding me that I've only gotten this far as some kind of courtesy.

"The *director*?" I ask with faux confusion. "You mean the *Executive Assistant Director* for the Criminal, Cyber, Response and Services Branches?"

Okay, I can be a bitch. But she started it.

I wait Lydia out, because I wouldn't be standing here if The Dick hadn't agreed to see me.

He makes me wait, which is so like him, but twenty minutes later I'm in the office of The Dick. Dark wood walls and trophy photographs on the walls, diplomas, ego stuff. The Dick has a tremendous and entirely undeserved opinion of himself.

Julius Dickinson, he of the ever-present tan and combover, the extra ten pounds, the smarmy smile, gestures to a seat for me. "Emmy," he says, thick with false pity in his voice but his eyes alight. Already, he's trying to get a rise out of me.

"You haven't returned any of my e-mails," I say, taking a seat.

"That's right, I haven't," he says, making no attempt to justify the stiff-arm he's given me. He doesn't have to. He's the boss. I'm just an employee. Hell, I'm not even that at the moment; I'm an employee on unpaid leave whose career is hanging by a string, and whose career could be destroyed by the man sitting across from me.

"Have you at least read them?" I ask.

Dickinson removes a silk cloth from his drawer and cleans his eyeglasses. "I got far enough to see that you're talking about a series of fires," he says. "Fires that *you* think are the work of a criminal genius who has managed to make them appear unrelated."

Basically, yes.

"What I *did* read in its entirety," he adds with a sour note, "was an article just last week from the *Peoria Times,* the local newspaper in a small Arizona town." He lifts up a print-out of the article and reads from it. " 'Eight months after her sister's death in a house fire, Emmy Dockery is still on a crusade to convince the Peoria Police Department that Marta Dockery's death was not an accident, but murder.' Oh, and this part: 'Doctor Martin

Lazerby, a deputy medical examiner with the Maricopa County Medical Examiner's Office, insists that all forensic evidence points to death by an accidental fire.' And this is my favorite, a quote from their police chief: 'She works for the FBI,' he said. 'If she's so sure it's murder, why doesn't she get her own agency to investigate it?' "

I don't respond. The article was crap; they took the police's side and didn't even give a fair airing of my evidence.

"It makes me wonder about you, Emmy." He puts his hands together and collects his thoughts, like he's about to lecture a child. "Have you been getting therapy, Emmy? You badly need help. We'd love to have you return, of course, but only after we've seen some progress in your treatment."

He can hardly suppress a smile as he says this. He and I have history; he was the one who had me brought up on disciplinary charges for *inappropriate conduct* that got me suspended—I'm sorry, in bureaucratic-legal lingo, placed on *unpaid administrative leave*. I've still got seven weeks before I return, and even then, it will be a sixty-day probationary period. If I hadn't had a recent death in the family, I probably would have been canned.

He knows the real reason why I was brought up on charges. We both do. So he's taunting me here. I can't let him get under my skin. That's what he wants. He wants me to blow up, so he can tell the brass that I'm not ready to return.

"Somebody's running around the country killing people," I say. "That should concern you whether I'm in therapy or not."

His eyes narrow. He doesn't have to do anything here; I'm the one who wants something. So this is his idea of torture, sitting there tight-lipped and stubborn.

"Concentrate on your rehabilitation, Emmy. Leave the law enforcement to us."

He keeps repeating my name as if I'm a child. I'd rather he spit on me and called me names. And he knows that. This is the passive-aggressive version of waterboarding. I wasn't sure he'd see me today, unannounced. Now, I realize, he probably couldn't wait to see me, to shut me down, to laugh directly in my face.

He and I have a history, like I said. Here's the short version: He's a pig.

"This isn't about me," I insist. "It's about a guy who—"

"Are you feeling angry right now, Emmy? Do you feel like you're in control of your emotions?" He looks me over with mock concern. "Because your face is getting red. Your hands are balled up in fists. I'm concerned you still can't contain your emotions. We have counselors on staff, Emmy, if you need someone to talk to."

He sounds like a late-night commercial for chemical dependency. *We have counselors waiting to talk to you. Call now!*

There's no point in proceeding further, I realize. It was dumb of me to come. Dumb of me to expect he'd listen to me in person. But I was screwed before I got here.

"Good luck with your therapy," he calls out. "We're all rooting for you."

I stop at the door and turn back to him.

"This man is killing people all over the country," I say, one hand on his office door. "And it's not that we're chasing him and can't catch him. It's that we don't even know there's someone to catch. It's like he doesn't even exist to us."

Nothing from The Dick but his cupped hand, a tiny wave good-bye. I slam the door behind me.

I WAIT UNTIL I leave the building before I blow off any steam. I won't give Dickinson the satisfaction of seeing me angry, and I won't give him fodder to use against me when I try to return to my job in seven weeks. (The truth is I probably already have; he can point to my e-mails, and however he chooses to paint the conversation we just had, as proof that I'm "obsessive" and also committing the greatest sin of a research analyst—"acting like an agent," forgetting my place in the hierarchy.)

When I settle into the return drive on I-95, I give my steering wheel a couple of good hard smacks, which doesn't make me feel any better and, if I'm not careful, could leave me with broken fingers. "Asshole!" I yell. That makes me feel better; the only thing I might hurt is my vocal cords. "Asshole! Asshole!"

Dickinson owns me now, after the disciplinary hearing; I'll be on probation and if I make one false step—or if The Dick even *claims* I misstepped—I'm done. Oh, watching him smirk at me back there, pretending that I'm in need of therapy. We both know my only *disciplinary problem* was that I pushed his hand off my knee every time he put it there, I said no to late dinners and even laughed at the idea of a weekend getaway, just the two of us. It was the laugh, I think, that finally did it. By the next morning, he had concocted some story to the upper brass that *I* was harassing *him,* and becoming more and more aggressive. Add in words like *erratic* and *volatile*—words that are easy to say and hard to disprove—and *voila,* you are a discipline problem.

Asshole.

But really, Emmy, get a grip. Solve the problem. I have to do something. I can't give up on this. I know these cases are connected. But I'm stuck. I can't go outside the chain of command, and The Dick is shutting me down, not on merit but out of spite. I'm stuck. What can I do? What else can I possibly—

Wait.

I let my foot off the pedal, for no particular reason, other than pissing off the SUV driver behind me—he *is* following me a little close—while I think it over. No. No. It's the last thing I should do.

But yes, it might be my only way in. So I have to try it.

Because if I'm right about this guy, he's getting better and better at killing. And nobody even knows he exists.

WITCH & WIZARD SERIES
Witch & Wizard (*with Gabrielle Charbonnet*) • The Gift (*with Ned Rust*) • The Fire (*with Jill Dembowski*) • The Kiss (*with Jill Dembowski*) • The Lost (*with Emily Raymond*)

DANIEL X SERIES
The Dangerous Days of Daniel X (*with Michael Ledwidge*) • Watch the Skies (*with Ned Rust*) • Demons and Druids (*with Adam Sadler*) • Game Over (*with Ned Rust*) • Armageddon (*with Chris Grabenstein*)

GRAPHIC NOVELS
Daniel X: Alien Hunter (*with Leopoldo Gout*) • Maximum Ride: Manga Vol. 1–8 (*with NaRae Lee*)

For more information about James Patterson's novels, visit www.jamespatterson.co.uk

Or become a fan on Facebook

MEET THE WOMEN'S MURDER CLUB

Four women sit at their usual table in Susie's bar, and the conversation, as always, is murder…

LINDSAY BOXER

A homicide detective in the San Francisco Police Department, juggling the worst murder cases with the challenges of being a first-time mother. Her loving husband Joe, baby daughter Julie and loyal border-collie Martha give her a reason to protect the city. She's not had the easiest start in life, with an absent father and an ill mother, and she doesn't shy away from a difficult career. Keeping control of her head and her heart can be tough, but with the help of her friends, Lindsay makes it her mission to solve the toughest cases.

CLAIRE WASHBURN

Chief Medical Examiner for San Francisco and one of Lindsay's oldest friends. Wise, confident and viciously funny, she can be relied on to help, whatever the problem. She virtually runs the Office of the Coroner for her overbearing, credit-stealing boss, but rarely complains. You may hear her called 'Butterfly' thanks to a tattoo just below her waist. Happily married with children, her personal life is relatively calm in comparison to her time in the Women's Murder Club.

CINDY THOMAS

An up-and-coming journalist who's always looking for the next big story. She'll go the extra mile, risking life and limb to get her scoop. Sometimes she prefers to grill her friends over cocktails for a juicy secret, but, luckily for them, she's totally trustworthy – most of the time ... She's just published a book, somehow finding the time to write between solving cases, writing articles for the *San Francisco Chronicle* and keeping her on–off relationship with Lindsay's partner, Rich Conklin, together. Other than reading, she loves yoga and jazz music.

YUKI CASTELLANO

One of the best lawyers in the city, and desperate to make her mark. Ambitious, intelligent and passionate, she'll fight for what's right, defending the underdog even if it means standing in the way of those she loves. Often this includes her husband – who is also Lindsay's boss – Lt. Jackson Brady. Her friends can barely get a word in edgeways when she's around, unless she's got a Germain-Robin sidecar in her hand!

WHEN YOUR JOB IS MURDER, YOU NEED FRIENDS YOU CAN COUNT ON.